Antonio Scotto di ⸺

BULLETS
FROM THE
PAST

Youcanprint Self-Publishing

Title | Bullets From The Past
Author | Antonio Scotto di Carlo
Translator | April Pini
ISBN | 978-88-93327-24-4

© All rights reserved to the Author
No part of this book can be reproduced without the author's preventive Consent

Youcanprint Self-Publishing
Via Roma, 73 - 73039 Tricase (LE) - Italy
www.youcanprint.it
info@youcanprint.it
Facebook: facebook.com/youcanprint.it
Twitter: twitter.com/youcanprintit

Bibliography: English

Hearts Under Fire – Romantic Suspense

Jenny is a beautiful young businesswoman. She lives in an Italian tourist town where she owns a shop. Her need for independence is her strength, but her innate distrust sometimes creates problems with others.

One day she encounters love. More than an encounter, it's a collision, a head-on collision. Her heart isn't Eros's only target, and everything changes …

Police begin investigating suspicious events around her, slowing down the construction of a new great hotel in town and rocking her life even more.

Bibliography: Italian

Il dio sordo – Mia Immortale Amata (2012)

Il dio sordo – IX (2012)

2 Mogli, 2 Mariti e 1 Lampadario (2014)

Cuori Sotto Tiro (2014)

2 Geni, Pirandello e la Legge (2015)

Proiettili dal Passato (2015)

for April Pini

You are such a kind, patient and generous person

that you seem unreal.

I probably met you in a fairy tale.

This book would not exist without you.

Thanks from the bottom of my heart.

My special thanks to Jillian

All characters and events appearing in this work are fictitious. Any resemblance to real events and persons, living or dead, is purely coincidental.

Places and Institutions are mentioned only for fictional purposes. They are not related to any character or event of this book.

1 – The Memory

The taste of bourbon, a cry, his uncontrollable urge to fuck her. He did it. Didn't he? Yes, he did. Probably.

Broken thoughts, soaked with remorse and pleasure, were flirting with his conscience. A diabolic sex collage of blurred and disjointed frames covered the walls of his mind.

"*I can feel you're excited,*" she winked at him, laughing, while they danced intertwined.

She laughed, then she was in.

The fuck if she was!

He could still see her naughty lips round out the angularity of her beautiful face. And the way she bit her lower lip …

Man!

There was lust in those fuckin' brown eyes. She wanted it too.

She wanted, she wanted. The little slut.

But the cry? Her *no* kept reverberating in his memory, louder than the deafening and rhythmic bass. That had been real. His mind recorded it.

"*Please, don't do that. Let me go!*"

She sounded tormented and frightened like someone weeping.

Those words had been spoken. Every time he conjured them up, they were always the same. The hiccupping sound of her despair never changed. Why couldn't he imagine it without hiccups?

Maybe his guilt added them.

Who do you think you're fooling? Huh, buddy?

Damn bourbon. That unreliable doctor, instead of relieving his pain, had stunned his mind and released the beast.

The mnemonic video was still chaotic, but the sequence with her black hair tied in a small ponytail swaying after every push of pleasure—a pleasure that still excited him when he remembered it—kept an unbearably high resolution. And the blackmailing gun that he pressed onto her upper back was the vanishing point of all his memories.

2 – Emily

"Oh, c'mon. Please!" Shanaze whimpered again, while the pounding of the shower sizzled like oil in a pan. "It's important to me."

"If I could, I would. But really, Will would be pissed at me," explained Emily, fixing her gaze on the reflection of the light on the white tile walls.

They were the only two left in the locker room.

Emily glanced at Shanaze, who was no longer insisting. The water slip along with the foam on her smooth black skin: she couldn't say if some tears were mixed with them, but her expression was very sad.

"Really, sis. I'm exhausted. I need to get some rest," Emily added, feeling the pressure of Shanaze's silence. "Spin class killed me today. I think my legs are kind of atrophied. How do yours feel?"

The attempt to change the subject shattered against her friend's long face.

"I swear, I must even have lactic acid in my toes," she giggled, using her painted nails to wash up her blonde bob haircut. "Just wait. After twenty-seven years and one pregnancy, you'll see how exhaustion bites you in the ass."

To veer it into a joke wasn't effective either.

"I wonder why the other girls don't just shower here," she tried again, rubbing the soapy sponge down her legs. "You think they're embarrassed? I could never go out wearing sweaty, sticky clothes."

She kept babbling while glancing at Shanaze, who was impassive and pouting while rinsing her long black hair.

"What's that, apricot?" she tried again, sniffing the conditioner that Shanaze had just used. "It smells so good."

No way. She had to go back to the topic. She hated to disappoint her—even though they had only met her recently, Shanaze had unconsciously granted her wish to be an older sister: her parents had let her down and she'd never happened to meet a girl who stimulated that instinct in the way Shanaze did.

"Don't you have anybody else you can ask?"

"I've only been living in Austin for a month. It's not like friends grow on trees," said Shanaze, turning off the shower. "I only have a coworker. And you, of course."

Emily was listening, when a sudden burning blinded her. Some shampoo must have dripped into her eyes.

"Well, why don't you ask her?" she suggested, rinsing her face and strongly rubbing her eyelids.

"Her father passed away last week. I don't think she'd be in the mood."

"There are so many other girls in your office, though."

"You know how it is between colleagues," Shanaze said, wrapping her go-go dancer body in a broad towel as white as Emily's skin. "A clerk who dreams of becoming an actress ... Maybe some would encourage me up front, but behind my back? They'd make fun of me at any given chance."

Her eyes were a little better now. Just a light flickering. She shut off the water too, stepping out of the shower.

"What about that hunk you're dating?"

"Isaiah?" laughed Shanaze, sitting on the bench next to her gym bag. "How'd you think it'd end up if I let him come to my place to help me with the script?"

"If you gotta practice a love scene, he'd be a better fit than me," Emily joked, joining her by the lockers.

"It's not a love scene. It's dramatic. I'm the heroine's sister, and I gotta tell her that her boyfriend's been diagnosed with leukemia. It's a poignant scene. I really need to be able to let myself go."

Emily frowned because she was missing the point. So she wrapped herself in her pink bathrobe and sat down beside Shanaze, while her own golden hair was dripping on her lap.

"Let yourself go, how?"

"I feel comfortable with you, sis," Shanaze said, turning another towel into a turban for her own hair. "It's your gift with people, I don't know, but I could act relaxed with you."

"Thanks, sis. That really means a lot to me."

"It's true. With you, I wouldn't feel judged while I'm acting, 'cause that's how they treat you if it isn't a real job."

"What do you mean?" Emily asked, rubbing her eyes again.

"If you're in a company or you've got an agent, okay, those who help you practice do it with some respect. But if you're just someone who's auditioning for the first time, you can read *She thinks she's Halle Berry* on their faces ... which is quite frustrating when you're doing your best."

"Oh, I see."

"C'mon, sis. I've practiced on my own so far, and I think I'm almost there. Now I'm gonna meet the director. I'm just scared I'll screw it up 'cause I'm not used to acting in front of people."

"And you just realized this the day before the audition ..."

"Who the hell was expecting they'd call me?! It all happened so fast."

"If you'd told me before, I'd have told Will. But this way ..."

"Before ... when? You haven't shown up at the gym lately."

"Matthew got the flu because he's teething. I'm not leaving him with a babysitter just to come here."

"Course not. I was just explaining why I didn't tell you earlier," Shanaze saddened again.

"I don't know," murmured Emily—seeing how important it was to Shanaze was helping to change her mind. "Will complains I'm never at home, and he's got a point. He'd kill me if I told him to make dinner for both himself and Matthew 'cause I'm hanging out with my friend."

Shanaze's eyes became pitiful. Emily smiled because Shrek's Puss in Boots came to mind.

"Is that a yes?"

By Shanaze's sudden enthusiasm, Emily realized she had put on a compliant expression.

"But I won't stay longer than an hour. Deal?"

"Yeah! Thank you, thank you, thank you, sis. You're my savior," Shanaze hugged her. "By the way, your eyes are so red. You freak me out, hahaha."

"Yeah, freakin' shampoo."

Emily got up and walked to the mirror. In fact, she looked like a hot evil spirit or vampire princess.

"Let's do it like this," she sighed, grabbing the wall-mounted hairdryer but not turning it on yet. "I'll go home and make dinner for them. Then I can be at your place around nine."

"Awesome," Shanaze exclaimed, pulling out a joyful smile and giving two thumbs up.

"Remember this when you become a Hollywood star," Emily blinked, glad for making her *sis* so happy.

3 – Excuse Me

Wrapped in her wool coat, Emily walked through the gym parking lot heading toward her car. She wasn't walking at her usual quick pace, since her weary legs made her gym bag feel even heavier.

It was already dark outside, being the end of February, but the lampposts allowed her to see well. The only noises were the wind and her footsteps.

Usually she waited for Shanaze to fix her fabulous hair and they left together; but it was already late, and considering that she had to stop by Kroger for groceries, she headed out alone.

She was thinking about how to face Will. Her promise—always kept—of a "porno night" was a tested anti-fight strategy, but she had been using it a lot lately; so it was wise to find another option.

Opening the trunk of her metallic blue Ford Focus, she threw her sports bag inside. She shut it and stepped to the door. As she opened it, a male voice from behind startled her.

"Excuse me, Miss."

She turned around.

"Would you please hand me the keys?" smiled a handsome man in his thirties, light complexion, curly hair as black as his mustache.

He was a step away from her. A shock of fear ran through her spine when, lowering her gaze, she realized he was pointing a gun at her.

"Don't worry, I don't mean to hurt you," continued the man in his Bordeaux puffer jacket, friendly as if he were asking for directions. "Gimme the keys, and it's gonna be fine."

Handing them to him, a grip of anxiety squeezed her stomach.

She checked the part of the parking lot that her peripheral vision allowed her.

"What rotten luck! It seems there's nobody around," he mocked at her.

"Can I go now?" she mumbled, on the verge of tears.

"Get in the car," he said, resolute, suddenly losing his boldness.

He had probably changed his attitude because of the car that just entered the parking lot.

She felt the gun barrel pressed hard against her stomach.

The open Focus door was hiding the threat: the newcomer would assume that they were just talking. But she stood, not allowing him to push her inside.

"You know what's gonna happen if you call for help?" he resumed, now calm again. "I'll be taken in for shooting you, and your child will grow up without his mom."

The ice in his voice and the unpredictable evil of his words cut her soul with a butcher's coldness.

"Look here," he continued, while the car was slowly passing right behind him as if in search of a spot to park. "My finger is on the trigger. Keep staring at me and the last face you're gonna see is mine instead of your kid's."

She was panting, strangled by Fear's sadistic hand. The evil shone in his gaze like the moon reflecting on a bloody dagger. Her heart said that to obey him would be her end, but her mind paused on his statement *I don't mean to hurt you*.

"They'll call for help and you'll be dead. I have nothing left to lose."

Not a hint of hesitation or impatience on that mustachioed gray-eyed devil's face. He acted as if he had already planned the epilogue.

"I didn't do anything," she panted through her tears. "I have money, credit cards. Take everything," she said handing him her purse. "It's all yours. Take the car too. I won't say anything to anyone. I promise. But ..."

"Very generous," he interrupted her, turning to the other car which had just parked. "Now the guy will come this way. Noticing something strange, he's gonna ask you if everything is all right. I already told you the rest of the story. But I may shoot him as well, so I'd get time to sneak away. How about that?"

"What do you want from me?" she sniffled, while seeing Matthew, frightened, holding out his small arms to her ...

"I want you to put your ass on that fuckin' seat. Now!"

The bang of the car door thirty yards away and the change of his tone helped her make up her mind.

"Bravo. It wasn't that hard, was it?" he added as she was sitting.

"Don't hurt me, please."

"Throw the purse to the back seat."

She did, also because some male voices coming had given her hope.

"Don't even try to get smart," he threatened her, watchful and in a low voice, pointing to the bulge on his puffer jacket pocket where he hid his armed hand. "Because nothing would save your head from a bullet," and he kept those voices out by slamming the door with his free hand.

She thought to reopen it and escape. It was dangerous, but that man smelled like death. As he walked around the car, she could hear the painful pounding of her heart rate. Her hands trembled, and she couldn't stop them. She tried with a sigh, but her breath was out of control.

"Here we go," said the man, satisfied, sitting beside her. "For you."

He handed her the keys and crossed his arms on his chest. The gun was sticking out from under his armpit, pointing to her side.

When two guys—presumably those from the car that just arrived—passed so close to her, the temptation to honk spawned a violent rush of adrenaline inside her. However, the awareness of being under fire stopped her. She looked at them getting farther away with her last hope.

"Go," he said, as the two guys disappeared under the gym entrance. "Get out of the parking lot and take the left."

"I didn't do anything," she said in a desperate gasp.

"I disagree."

"What do you want from me?"

"What do I want? You'll find out soon. But, don't worry. I give you my word that I won't harm a hair on your head, as long as you follow my instructions."

He had spoken staring into her eyes. She felt he was sincere. Too upset to analyze her impression, she decided to stop thinking and do as he said. She fastened the belt in a mechanic gesture and started the engine.

4 – Colorado River

Emily had been driving for ten minutes. They were now on Lake Austin Blvd. She kept the speed under 50, constantly getting passed by other vehicles.

The man was quiet, except to tell her when to turn. His silence was distressing, but not as much as his voice. It was, in fact, his icy, inhuman tone that made her weep in fear.

He didn't care about money. She was almost sure that he would rape her, *almost* because he had given her his word.

Maybe he lied to keep me quiet.

This thought terrified her, but her motherly instinct won out. She needed to be rational. She must do it for Matthew. He was only four. She couldn't risk abandoning him to destiny at such a young age.

If I do what he wants, then he'll let me go, she persuaded herself, eyes on the road, her mind asphyxiated by thoughts and the monotonous rumbling of the engine.

Besides, she had no chance against an armed man. A man who was crazy enough to risk an abduction at a public place, and so clever—and lucky—to get away with it.

"Slow down. Take the next road on the left," he said, impassive, sleeking his mustache.

The sudden sound of his voice grinded her insides.

She remembered the pepper spray she kept in the pocket of her coat, cursing herself not to have thought of it before. She was carrying it for this exact kind of situation! Perhaps, however, no one is ever really prepared when things only heard in the news happen to them.

Too late. I couldn't make it now, she despaired, afraid to be shot or that the fight would cause an accident.

Realizing they were driving along a desolate road that she didn't recognize, she wondered where he was taking her. The lawns that lined it made her think they were somewhere near the Colorado River.

"At the end of this road there's a dirt track on the right."

For a reason that she couldn't explain, his voice was no longer as traumatizing as before.

"Tell me what you want from me."

He was quiet. She turned to him. A wry grin shaped his face.

"How do you know I have a child?"

"The same way I caught you tonight."

That answer supported the hypothesis that she wanted to ignore so far, as a premeditated kidnapping highly raised the level of danger. That this psycho had been stalking her for God knows how many days, that he knew where she lived, where she took Matthew to school, or where Will worked, made her hands tremble and eyes water again.

"There. Turn," he ordered.

The headlights were the only source of light.

This natural road—while proceeding slowly, bounced them as if the tires ran over stones—was leading them to a small wood in the dark.

She felt like an astronaut adrift in space without anything she could grab hold of. Even with her eyes. That a stroke neutralized him seemed the only way out.

"Stop the car," he said as they passed among some trees.

5 – The Request

"So, back to us," he smirked, pushing his seat back as much as possible. "Now it's up to you."

"What's up to me?" she said in a faint voice about to fade out.

"If you wanna go back to your family and forget about all of this or end it all right now."

She tried to remind him of his word, but her voice got lost between her intention and vocal cords. Her teeth chattered like a wasp's wings. She could hear the terror hoarse groan everywhere inside her.

"I gotta go in a few, I have a bigger fish to fry …" he said, sarcastically. "You can stay there and pray, or you can win your prize. Your kid, I mean."

"Wa…go…ho…"

"Wa…go…ho…" he mocked at her. "If you keep stuttering, I can't understand you. Take a deep breath before you speak."

Her nose was dripping, her eyes as well. She turned to him: she hadn't heard signs of pity in his voice, and she didn't find any in his eyes either.

She opened her mouth to answer. A choked cry was all that came out.

"I don't have all night," he crooned.

The barrel of the gun was still aimed at her. She looked through the windshield, then turned to the window: there could be no worse ally than darkness for that monster.

"What, are you worried about your pussy? If that's what keeps you from talking, relax. I don't want that."

A sudden relief collided against an equally unexpected anxiety. She took a deep breath and tried to stop the trembling of her lips.

"I want to go home."

"I knew you had become a wise woman," he said, pulling out a folded handkerchief from his pocket. "Go ahead, wipe your face."

She felt something strange in his words, but she had no time to think because he resumed.

"This is the deal. Kneel down before me and passionately, intensely and unforgettably suck it. Otherwise, you never go back home, unless they find your body."

His demand, as unexpected as absurd, generated a disdain that clouded her fear.

"You're sick," she hissed, spitefully.

"Please, spare me the indignant scene. It's fit for a lady, not a whore like you."

The meaning of his comment and the ease he had uttered it with made her want to slap him. Only two seconds later she realized she'd spat in his face.

"Wow. You're brave," he said, harshly, taking back his handkerchief. "Too bad you don't get it. I was just trying to be nice to make it less unpleasant for you. But now you're making me mad. You really wanna see me mad?" he added, after wiping his face.

Realizing that she had just risked her journey on Earth ending like a song interrupted before the refrain, she became paler than she already was.

"*Mommy!*"

She swallowed her wave of bravery, lowered her head and unbuckled her seat belt. Then she began to unbutton her coat.

"What are you doing?" he became suspicious.

"It's bulky. I couldn't fit," she said, pointing to the space between his seat and the glove compartment.

"That's how I like you."

She slipped off her coat, placing it on the back seat, taking care that the full pocket ended between them, on the hooking of the seat belts. Then she moved toward him.

"Mind what you do," he stopped her, resting the muzzle of the gun in the middle of her forehead.

His warm breath smelled like mint.

While she was kneeling between his legs, she kept her eyes where she was putting her feet, mainly not to see the weapon. Once she was in position, her back pressed to the glove compartment to limit the physical contact as much as possible, he pulled down the zipper of his jacket.

"Come on, get to work and make my day."

"Can you at least point it to the other side?"

"This?" he chuckled. "I can't. You know, your teeth … You may have avenging appetites."

"How can I do it with …"

"You're getting on my nerves now. Between a fuckin' blowjob and to send you back to your Creator, I picked the first one. Don't make me change my mind. Your kid would be upset."

"How can I know that you won't shoot me anyway after I do it?"

"I gave you my word."

"Your word? You are a fuckin' psycho, what can I do with your word?" she roared in a new and uncontrollable outburst.

"Why, did I take it back?"

In fact, he hadn't touched her, even after she had spat at him.

"My word is … If you satisfy my passing fancy, at some point on our way back, I'll ask you to stop the car. I get out and you won't see me again. Unless you go to the police, in which case you'll force me to come back. And if I got arrested before catching you, my friend is gonna take care of your family."

The evil serenity with which he had spoken had gradually reduced her to tears again.

"But what do you have against us?"

"I don't give a shit about your family. I'm only interested in this pretty little mouth of yours," he said, roughly squeezing her chin with his other hand. "To keep my cock warmly inside, not to hear you babbling. So get this done if you don't wanna end up in the bottom of the river."

Emily's vision was all blurry. She passed her wrist on her cheekbones. She pushed herself to think that she'd wake up from this nightmare within a few minutes, finding herself in her bed between Matthew and Will.

She opened the buttons of his jeans one by one.

Gun in hand, he twisted on the seat to make it easier for her, and she pulled them and his underwear down.

His circumcised dick was disgustingly erected. She grabbed him with her right hand.

C'mon, girl. After all, it's not your first time, she said to herself, looking for any way to tame her rage and repugnance.

"I wanna feel your tongue," he said with a satyr look. "And don't you dare turn your face away when I come. That doesn't count."

The stink of sweat coming from his pubic zone was revolting. Everything about his body sickened her, but not as much as his intent.

Assuming that she'd feel worse during the act and fearing to wind up dead anyway, she decided to risk it: she changed hands, casually grabbing it with her left one, letting the right one drop next to her coat pocket. She would get the spray while he'd be dazed with pleasure.

As she moved closer to him, a question came to mind.

"Why me? Why this?"

He gave her a devastating look, full of obscure meanings.

"Because you owe me."

"I owe you?"

"Yes, Emily Wallace. You owe me."

6 – Landon

"What can I get you, detectives?" the waitress asked the two thirty-year old guys who were sitting at a table in a corner of the diner.

Her voice flourished among the chatter and noise of the dishes like jasmine in the weeds.

"Some pancakes, two scrambled eggs with bacon, a blueberry muffin and orange juice, honey," winked Devin, fixing his grey tie.

"Geez, man! Go easy on that," chuckled Landon, in his beloved black leather jacket, with a cobalt blue shirt visible underneath. "Only black coffee for me. Thanks, Mya."

"I'll be right back," smiled the breath-taking redhead.

"God, what a great ass!" whispered Devin, his eyes glued on her generous backside as she walked among the tables, almost all of which were taken, since the restaurant specialized in breakfast. "She should be working at Hooters. She's gonna give these grandpas a heart attack," he joked, referring to the customers who were mostly elderly.

"Keep on eating like that and you only get babes like her in your dreams."

"You think?"

"Yeah, I do."

"Nah," Devin said. "What matters to women is that you make them feel protected. And if you got some moolah in your wallet, they don't even notice your twenty pounds of fat."

"I know a saying… *The eye wants its share.*"

"What the hell does that mean?"

"It means looks matter," Landon winked, scratching his two-day old scruff, part of his look these last few years.

"Bullshit! I have a couch potato's body, but I picked up six girls so far this year. Six! One and a half per month," Devin said, smugly dusting the edge of his jacket with his knuckles.

"I'm talking about hot chicks, man. I don't know about the other four, but the two you introduced to me couldn't hold a candle to Mya, hahaha."

"What about you, Don Juan?" Devin replied. "How many times have you scored with your tanned, alpha male body? I don't know what you're up to, but I ain't been seeing you with a chick for a long time."

"Don't even try to change the subject, slick. We were talking about your fat."

"Have you crossed the river and ended up on the other shore with that fair lady?" Devin teased him, glancing at the effeminate waiter who was serving a middle-aged couple at the table next to theirs.

"And your hair," Landon retorted. "That marine haircut is even worse than your belly."

"Look, if you've suddenly changed your tastes, I have no problem with that. Just tell me, so I can ask for another partner, hahaha."

"Shh!" said Landon, seeing Mya coming with their breakfast.

"Here we go, guys."

"It smells incredible," said Devin.

"Thank you, Mya," Landon smiled at her.

"Black coffee for detective Vitman and the rest for his funny friend."

"When they handed out kindness, I bet you cheated and lined up twice," said Landon, running his hand through his thick black hair.

She smiled, becoming even more attractive when her cheeks turned into two burning embers.

"Anyway, I was referring to your scent, not the eggs'."

She stood stunned staring at Landon, as if Devin's compliment were white noise. Then she returned to the other customers.

"Son of a bitch!" said Devin, excited. "Did you see how she looked at you? She was fucking you with her eyes."

Landon was flattered, but he tried not to show it.

"Oh yeah, Landon," he whispered, grabbing the edges of the table, in an imitation of a woman who's making love. "Harder, harder, break me inside ... Hmm!"

"Stop it, jackass," he laughed, and threw a jelly packet at him.

"Saved it! Hahaha. Seriously, Landon. Why don't you ask her out?"

"Why don't you?"

"I didn't make the cut."

"But she said you're a funny guy."

"Yeah, funny. We both know what *funny* means in a woman's book."

"What?"

"You're very welcome in my house, in each room but the bedroom."

"Hahaha."

"That's off limits to the funny guys," Devin continued cheerfully.

"When she comes back with the check, I'm gonna ask her if that's true."

"C'mon, buddy. Listen to dad-Devin. She can't wait to be banged mercilessly by you."

"Maybe I'm gonna stop by here when I'm off duty. Maybe not. I don't feel like seeing anyone at this time."

"Anyone? Mya ain't *anyone*, for chrissakes. Mya belongs to the superpussy species!"

"You're brutal, but how can I disagree?"

"So?"

"So nothing," said Landon, giving another sip to his coffee.

"Are you living an existential crises or some shit like that?"

"Sometimes I envy you, Devin. Really. I'd like to be carefree like you," he darkened, giving a moment of melancholy.

"Carefree? What the fuck are you talking about?"

"I'm talking about stages of life. Can't always let your dick set the direction. You know what I mean?"

"Blank."

"There are other equally important things. Deep. Personal."

"What's more deep and personal than Mya's pussy? I really don't get it."

Landon smiled and sipped his coffee again.

"I don't fuckin' understand ya, buddy," Devin shook his head, picking up his knife and fork. "But you must be doing right in a way, since it's the third time I've brought you here, and Mya knows your name better than mine."

"The eye wants its share, told ya. If Mya were thirty pounds heavier, would you still drool after her? Ask yourself that."

Devin darkened. He put the cutlery down and stared at his eggs and bacon with a sudden hostility …

7 – The Fasting

Landon was driving his patrol car through Charleston, the second largest city in South Carolina, with Devin beside him.

It was a quiet and sunny morning in mid-spring. The traffic was light.

"I still can't believe you didn't touch your breakfast," laughed Landon.

"I'm fasting from today on. I'm done with food, man."

"You didn't even take a bite of the muffin."

"I get it, you're so fuckin' right," said Devin, chewing some sugar-free gum. "Let's face the truth. The girls I dated were all dogs. Only one was kinda cute, but she didn't give it up. And I even wined and dined her, fuck it."

"Sure thing is that Mya won't forget about you now, even though telling her that your stomach's been in knots 'cause she didn't remember your name …"

"What?" frowned Devin.

"I would've waited for her with a sad face and my phone in hand, and linked my sudden lack of appetite to some bad news I just received."

"You're mean."

"A little white lie doesn't make me mean," laughed Landon. "Look at the practical side. She sold you something, right?"

"Uh-huh."

"Okay. You paid for it, but you sent it back because of her. You embarrassed her."

"You think?" Devin clouded over.

"Her boss is gonna ask her why the breakfast was returned untouched, and she's gonna have to make up a story."

"Dammit, I didn't think about that."

"I bet you're on her shit list now, hahaha."

"Hear me out, Dr. Strangelove," said Devin. "In a month, or two at the most, Mya will be in my bed."

Landon was as surprised as amused by this prediction, even though his laughter was fed by Devin's confidence.

"Watch, buddy. You just see if I don't screw her."

"I've created a monster," said Landon. "Next time we're gonna ta…"

"Attention all units," the radio suddenly crackled. "Robbery committed at Stone's liquors in the commercial area on Connors Road."

Devin took the transceiver.

"Here Car 1. We are on Washington Drive. We're on our way."

"Copy, Car 1."

8 – The Robbery

Ten minutes later, Landon and Devin arrived at the address. Spotting the liquor shop between a minimarket and a Mexican fast-food place, they parked in front of a strip of grass enclosed by cement.

"Let's see what's going on here," murmured Landon, taking off his sunglasses as Devin opened the shop door.

"Are you the police?" cried a surly toned, stout, balding man from behind the counter.

The customers, focused on the shelves close by, turned to them.

"Shit," chuckled Devin. "They recognize us even in plain clothes."

"Did you call 911, sir?" Landon asked the guy.

"Yeah, about … thirty-four minutes ago," he answered, ironically checking his watch.

"Everything is fine, folks. Please, continue with your purchases," Devin said to the customers, who kept looking.

"Detective Vitman," Landon introduced himself once he reached the counter. "Calm down, mister … Stone?"

"Calm down?" hissed a blue in the face and mad as hell man in his late forties. "It's the third time that this has happened. Three times in two fuckin' months!"

"Sir," said Landon patiently, while Devin was taking a look at the place. "We understand your state of mind, but how is you yelling supposed to help us?"

The man stared at him. His anger seemed to crumple in on itself.

"I'm sorry, detective. John Stone," he resumed, holding out his hand.

"So, what happened, Mr. Stone?" intervened Devin.

"Nitya!" Stone called out.

A beautiful woman in her early thirties—by her somatic features, she must be from India—apparently four or five months pregnant, came out from a side door.

"Can you stay here?" Stone asked her, with a kindness that Landon would never have thought him capable of. "The detectives and I are going to the warehouse to talk."

She nodded, addressing them a welcoming smile.

"With your permission, ma'am," Landon said, following Stone toward the door she'd come from.

"I can't see shit in here," Devin muttered, when they were in a dimly lit, small room that looked like an empty pantry of a fishing boat.

"Try takin' off your shades," Landon teased him.

Stone turned on the light.

The air felt heavy in there, not just to the nose but the skin too—for some reason, the air conditioning didn't reach inside the room. There was a small window, high on the wall opposite the door, but it was closed as if meant to keep the cool air out.

Stone walked up to a plastic, white table set where the walls formed an angle. An old PC filled its flat surface.

"Rather than tell you what happened, I'm gonna show you the surveillance video," he said, seating himself down on a white plastic chair, not that solid by how its legs bowed under his weight. "I made a copy of it while waiting for you to get here."

"Okay," agreed Landon, taking off his jacket and placing it on a big box.

Devin imitated him.

The images showed a half masked guy who resolutely came to the counter. He was pointing a gun to Stone's face, who continuously turned to look at the warehouse.

"I was afraid that Nitya would walk in," he said. "I wanted to get rid of that shitty punk as soon as possible."

In fact, they could see Stone open the cash register anxiously, hurriedly put the money into a paper bag, and hand it over to the guy, who grabbed it and ran away. Stone pulled out a revolver from under the counter and aimed the robber. He remained in a shooting position for a few seconds, before turning to the camera and lowering the weapon. Then he disappeared from the screen, as if he chased after the thief.

"It was wise of you not to shoot him," said Landon.

"The only thing that stopped me is I can't afford any legal troubles at this time. Otherwise, I would've gladly gunned that scum down. The city would've thanked me."

"What can you tell us about the robber?" asked Devin.

"He sounded Hispanic, like he was from Puerto Rico," he said, wiping his sweaty forehead with a crumpled tissue that was next to the keyboard. "That son of a bitch couldn't have been older than eighteen."

"Did you see him run away?"

"When I came out of my shop, an old white Honda Civic Coupe screeched away. I didn't have enough time to get a plate number."

"You should put a camera outside too," suggested Devin, while Landon rewound the video, pausing on a still frame with the robber.

"There is one, but it's broken."

"Now you've got a reason to get it fixed," said Devin. "How much did he get away with?"

"About 800 bucks."

"Geez," said Devin, amazed. "It's not even noon and you've already got 800?"

"If that was the trend, I'd have bought a house in Hawaii by now ... fuckin' chair," he added, jumping on *Hawaii* because he'd relaxed and his chair had creaked. "It was the profits from yesterday. I couldn't bring it to the bank because my wi... because I was busy," he got up from that trap, cutting shortly as if he didn't want to talk about his own business.

"Where's our copy?" asked Landon, a scowl on his face.

"Here you go," said Stone, pulling out a disk from the PC.

"It will help us track down the boy."

"Be my guest, I've already said goodbye to my money."

9 – Carlos

At five in the afternoon later that day, Landon knocked at Clarita's door.

Clarita was a good-looking, thirty-four-year-old woman. He'd helped her get out of a prostitution racket after a roundup six months ago. He'd found her a job in a supermarket and put in a good word—through friends of friends—with the landlord of a three-room house in a suburban neighborhood. It wasn't a place where one dreams to settle down, but at least she could live her life without anyone taking advantage of her or hurting her or her son, Carlos.

"Landon!"

"Hey, dude. It's really hot today, huh?" he added, because the seventeen-year-old boy was showing off his athletic body by wearing only shorts.

"It's gotta be mid 80's. What about you? How can you go around with that thing on?"

"You know what? You're right," he said, cheerful, taking his leather jacket off.

"Better, huh?"

"Much better. Anyway, is your mother here?"

"No. She'll be back at seven."

Landon expected to be invited in, but the invitation didn't come. Carlos was smiling, even though his smile, framed in a very thin and well maintained goatee, was unusually tense.

"Do you mind if I wait for her?" he asked. "I need some advice."

"No problema, amigo."

Once inside, Carlos took him to the small kitchen, furnished with the bare minimum: table, cupboard, and a mid-size mini fridge with a microwave above it.

The ceiling fan made the temperature pleasant.

"Since when did you do that?" asked Landon, folding his jacket on the back of the chair between the table and sink.

"Huh?"

"That," and he pointed to Carlos's earrings.

"Oh. It's a trend, amigo," he winked, taking a baseball cap from the knob of a chair and putting it on. "Am I cool or what?"

"With a necklace and tattoo, you'd look like a rapper."

While Landon was sitting at the long side of the table, Carlos laughed and started to bust a move.

"You're pretty good, dude. Sing me a song."

"I don't have time, amigo. I gotta finish my homework. Here, watch some TV," he handed him the remote.

"Homework? What homework? You didn't go to school today," laughed Landon.

"Yes I did!"

Carlos's protest was vehement.

"I saw you this morning around eleven, so you couldn't have been at school."

"Um ... You must have me confused with someone else," Carlos replied, casually—but Landon could tell he was nervous.

"Can't confuse your *new* Honda."

"What? Hahaha, there must be a hundred like that around, amigo."

"Plus I watched the video dozens of times ..." he added, scowling at the bewilderment that suddenly popped up on Carlos's face. "You know, just to make sure that it was you."

"What video?"

Landon wouldn't show it to him: the inability to deny the obvious was not the right motive for the kind of confession he was looking for.

"The liquor store on Connors Road, does that ring a bell?"

"Um ... I'm a minor. Have you forgotten, man? Why would I go to a liquor store?"

"If you're going for believable, son, you gotta be relaxed. But you're just trying to *look* relaxed."

"I am relaxed," he retorted, emphasizing the *am*.

"Um ... I'm a cop. Have you forgotten, boy?"

"And that gives you the right to come to my house and accuse me ... what you're accusing me of? That I ditched school?"

"Son, you know what you did. And I want you to admit it."

"Haha, I dunno what you're talkin' about, *cop*."

Landon looked at him. Carlos's light-hearted expression matched with the friendly tone he'd teased him with.

"Come here."

"I can hear you from here."

"C'mon," he urged, getting up.

Carlos snorted and looked up at the fan. Then he put the cap back on the chair and walked around the table.

When they were face to face, Landon put his forearms on Carlos's shoulders and leaned forward until both their foreheads touched.

"You know that I care about you, right?"

"Sure, Landon. I know what you did for my mom, and we'll never be able to thank you enough."

"Why do you think I did it?"

Carlos's expression said he didn't have an answer.

"I did it for you."

"For me?" Carlos frowned, moving his head back as if he was uncomfortable.

"Every time I look at you, my heart fills up with joy. Something like that has never happened to me," he smiled, happy because that sensation was one of the few things that made him feel good lately. "I look at you, and I see myself when I was a boy. I see you struggling to make it, despite your situation. I know how hard it can be without a father."

"To see you now, I wouldn't say you were a cool guy, hahaha."

"Son, I'm just trying to help you."

"Well … Thank you, *daddy*," he said, placing his forearms on Landon's shoulders too, although he was a four inches shorter. "But I'm okay. School is fine, Mom's got a good job, so …"

"Why did you have to rob the store?"

"What?!" Carlos said dumbfounded, stepping away from him as if he was baffled by his accusation.

In that second, Landon thought he was wrong. But his doubt lasted just that second.

"Listen up, son. A lot of trouble is right around the corner for you. For now, you're lucky that Devin and I are following the case. But we need to sever the stem soon, before the little flower blossoms …"

"Ah, gotcha," Carlos chuckled. "You're taking the piss outta me. You almost got there, man."

"Don't be stupid," Landon flared up, grabbing his wrist when Carlos was about to give him his back. "I'm trying to save you from juvie. I'm risking myself to protect you, but you have to prove that you deserve my help. Show me that I'm right about you, that you are like me and not those armed hooligans roaming our streets."

"Leave me, dammit," he wiggled out of his catch. "I don't do that shit, man. It's gotta be someone who looks like me."

"The fact that the shopkeeper didn't die will only change your charge from first degree murder to attempted murder."

"Murder?" Carlos stammered.

"You went into his store with a firearm. That's premeditation."

"I didn't shoot him!"

"That the man is in the recovery room right now, states the contrary."

Carlos's face had taken on the color of milk.

"You're under age and have a clean record, you'll be out when you're thirty. But you really wanna spend the best years of your life in jail?"

"Believe me, Landon," said Carlos, terrified as if cracks were opening in the walls around him. "It wasn't me that shot him. I just took the money."

Landon shaped his lips in a tender expression, then spread his arms. Carlos, upset, took refuge in there.

"I didn't shoot him. You gotta believe me, Landon. Even if I would, I couldn't. It wasn't me," he repeated, sobbing.

"Why did you steal?"

Carlos didn't answer, but Landon sensed him stiffen before abruptly breaking free from his hug.

"It's not true that the guy was shot, is it?" deduced Carlos, rage seeping into his voice and gaze.

"I just want to help you, son. Today you started down a bad fuckin' path. Explain to me why. So, if I can, I'll get you back on track. But you must want it too. I'm not gonna waste my time with lost causes. Tell me, are you a lost cause?"

Landon had addressed him with a mixture of affection and firmness that, judging by Carlos's emotional breakdown, had appealed to his good sense. A quality that would be lacking in a lost cause.

10 – The Chance

Two hours later, Landon and Carlos entered the liquor store. They had been waiting in the car for about twenty minutes, until there were no customers. Carlos was in jeans and a shirt just like Landon's, minus the earrings, the final effect of the dramatic talk they'd had before Clarita was back home.

Stone was fixing a shelf next to the counter, when he noticed them, presumably alerted by the opening of the door.

"It's him," he snarled, angry and disbelieving, speaking to Landon and pointing his finger at Carlos with the hand he was holding a bottle. "The bastard who robbed me, it's him!"

Carlos bowed his head. Landon put his arm around his shoulders and whispered to him not to be nervous.

"There's no need to yell," Landon said to Stone, when they were a step away from him.

"Hey, cop. You're not coming into my shop and giving me your fuckin' orders. You got that?"

"Look, I'm just trying to settle the matter peacefully for everybody ... If you're not okay with that, keep being an asshole. I'm gonna remember you and your shitty place. Or you could shut the fuck up and open your fuckin' ears."

Stone looked surprised as well as intimidated by Landon's change of tone.

Carlos looked on in awe.

"The boy, here, has something to tell you," added Landon, no longer threatening but still rough.

Stone was silent. He put the bottle onto the shelf and turned to Carlos, who sighed before looking at him.

"Mr. Stone, I'm really sorry for what I did this morning," he began nervously, handing him the paper bag he was holding. "I live with my mother. We bought a second hand car 'cause the clunker we had before is gone. To afford this car we ended up behind on the rent. We haven't been paying for two months. The landlord warned that he'll throw us out if we can't pay him off at the end of the month. My mother was desperate. She was crying. I had to do something, but didn't know what …"

Carlos had spoken with a broken voice and paused at the end of each sentence, but kept his eyes on Stone constantly. Stone, even though he was busy counting his money, more than once had raised his head during the explanation, as if he wanted to read beyond Carlos's tear-filled eyes.

"His mother works hard. They're good people," said Landon, now affable. "Mr. Stone, I don't mean to put pressure on you with my badge. Actually, what I'm doing isn't even legal. If you want to press charges, go ahead. It's your right. I just wanna tell you, man to man, I believe in this boy. I believe in him so much as to risk my career."

Mr. Stone looked perplexed. Or conflicted.

"Here," continued Landon, pulling out a gun from his pocket.

"That's the toy he robbed you with. I know you believed you were in danger, but in fact you were not. Carlos, if anything, was the one …"

Carlos and Stone frowned, but for opposite reasons: if one had no idea what Landon meant, the other one had understood very well.

"Let's be practical," said Landon. "Nothing happened. No one was hurt, you got your money back, and Carlos is experiencing the humiliation he deserves. Now you can send him to jail and turn the bad, but harmless, bullshit he did out of desperation into anger. Because if he goes to jail, Mr. Stone, he'll meet the kind of people he's now struggling to stay away from. And when he's out, he's gonna be an angry misfit. Or you can grant him the chance to stay on the honest side of the fence."

"You mean, just let him go and that's it?"

"No, sir. If you allow him to, he'll help you with the shop for a couple of weeks, after school. Under my guidance and for free."

Carlos fixed Stone with a shy and hopeful smile.

Stone frowned, as if he was thinking.

"Can I ask you a question, detective?"

"Shoot."

"Are you guys related? I'm asking you because I'd like to understand why you want to help him so bad."

"He's just a friend. I want to help him because … because if I'm a cop today, I have to thank somebody who, nine years ago, gave me the same chance that I'm asking you to give to him."

While Carlos was now staring at his own sneakers, Landon's and Stone's gazes were testing each other.

"Maybe I would've come to rob you nine years ago, with a real gun, if I wasn't given a second chance."

"I don't think so," said Stone. "I started this business only three years ago."

A smile followed his joke.

Carlos looked reassured.

Landon patted Carlos's shoulder and went back to Stone.

"So, what do you wanna do with this kid?"

"I was thinking … My wife is no longer able to come here because we're about to have our first baby. I was looking for someone to hire part-time in the evening."

Carlos looked at him in disbelief.

Landon was surprised too.

"Are you interested, Carlos?" Stone asked him, holding out his hand.

"Very, sir," he replied, shaking it, moved. "Thank you. Thank you."

The joy that shone on his face warmed Landon's heart.

"But, detective, let's make one thing clear," continued Stone, sternly. "I take your word as a guarantee for the kid's honesty."

"That's fine. Carlos is studying and he's very good at school. He'll become somebody. One day, I promise you, Mr. Stone, you'll be proud of the decision you made today."

11 – Natalie

"Hey, guys. Your attention, please," Natalie said to her students, going back to the classroom with a pretty girl after the ten-minute break between Period 1 and 2.

Medium height, slender body and blond hair, the two seemed made from the same mold; there was similarity even in their clothing, both of them in high-necked long-sleeved linen shirts—although one was yellowish and the other was white—and skinny jeans; however, the mint green of the girl's jeans avoided any kind of embarrassment because it had nothing to do with the black of Natalie's.

Her nine students ranged in the age from eighteen to forty; they came from South America, Europe and Asia. When Natalie arrived, they were practicing their English about the topic Travel on sight of the Listening & Speaking Period. Understanding the young teacher's request, they returned to their desks, all in the front half of the classroom.

"I'd like to introduce you to a new student joining us today," said Natalie, opening one of the three windows, welcoming May's cool and bright breath into the room. "That's better, isn't it?" she asked, returning to her chair. "Let's give a warm welcome to Janine."

"Hi, Janine," they chorused.

"Hi, everybody," she smiled, embarrassed.

"So, Janine. Tell us about yourself," Natalie said, with her conviviality that always helped newcomers relax.

"Okay, but my English is not very well."

"You're here to improve yourself, just like everybody else. Am I right?"

"Okay, I try it."

"Go, Janine," cheered Saya, a lively Japanese teenager girl.

Natalie headed toward an empty desk on the side of the windows and sat down with the others, curious to get to know her.

"My name is Janine. I have twenty four years and I am French."

"Paris?" said Eloy, an outgoing thirty-year-old Peruvian.

"No. I am of Grenoble. In the South."

"Good, Janine. You're doing fine," said Natalie, moving a rebel curl that invaded her field of vision at times. "Go ahead."

"I have decided to follow a course to improve my English. I have an aunt here in Charleston. I have come to meet her because I have seen her only on Skype until last Thursday. I study medicine at the University of Grenoble, but I have always loved the languages stranger. I have no opportunity to pratice English at Grenoble because I don't know English persons there. So I taken advantage… correct?" she turned to Natalie, doubtful.

"I don't know what you're about to say," she smiled. "Go on and don't worry."

"Okay. I taken advantage of my trip from my aunt for making a full immersion in the English language. This is all," she concluded, sighing as she had just climbed a rock face.

"Bravo, Janine. You were very clear," congratulated Natalie. "And your English is not that bad," she added, mostly to encourage her.

"Thank you, professor."

"Call me Nat. We're all friends here. Plus I'm only three years older than you."

"All right, Nat."

"Are we done?" asked Henke, a thirty-one-year-old German who was apparently annoyed by the cheerfulness spreading in the room.

"Chill out, man," said Stachys, a Greek man in his thirties, sitting at Henke's side.

"Why are you always so unpleasant?" said Saya, looking back at him.

"What's the problem, Henke?" asked Natalie, cordial but tense, meanwhile she went back next to Janine. "You had your opportunity to introduce yourself at the time. Am I right?"

Yes, you are, Nat," said Larisa, a nineteen-year-old, who would be worthy of the title of Miss Russia, if her cheeks and forehead weren't blemished with pimples. "We started level 3 together."

"That's what I'm talking about," snapped Henke, more determined than before. "Why do we call her *Nat*? She's our teacher. Shouldn't her be *Miss Lunn* to us? We pay to improve our English, to learn to quickly understand the Americans when they speak, without bothering them by asking to repeat what they said. Instead, we're here to make friends, as if we were in a school trip. Plus, wouldn't Janine join Pre-Intermediate level instead of High-Intermediate's? She will slow down the class."

"What an asshole," murmured Larisa, from the first row.

"*Ein, Zwei. Heil Hitler!*" Eloy mocked at him, with the Nazi salute.

Natalie was offended, as anyone would be under the accusation of lack of professionalism. Plus she was embarrassed because, considering her English, Janine was in fact supposed to be part of level 3 instead of 5; nevertheless, this was an internal issue that she obviously wouldn't discuss it with him (level 3 and 4 had already reached the limit of twelve students and the only ones with available space were level 5, 7 and 8). While she was thinking about how to answer him, with other students' rumbling in the background, Henke spoke again.

"I have nothing against Miss Lunn," he said, rolling a pen among his fingertips as if it were a screw. "I just want to learn this damn language well. Is that too much to ask?"

12 – Confrontation

Natalie walked through the school parking lot, heading toward her Toyota, one out of the four cars still there. The cicadas, while hidden, were chattering all around her, creating a mesmerizing background to her thoughts.

It had been a long and tiring day for her, not only because of Henke, but also because she stayed at work until seven in the evening to correct her students' essays—*evening* so to speak, as the sun still cleared the sky.

As she opened the car door, a male voice from behind startled her.

"Excuse me, Miss."

She turned around.

"Henke! You scared me," Natalie replied, forcing herself to smile.

She didn't feel toward him the way she felt with Eloy, Larisa and Saya, who made up the core of the group: they were the only ones that had started the level 3 together—the others joined afterwards in the reshuffling of those who failed prior classes and the newcomers. And after what had happened in class today, she politely disliked him.

"I waited for you all day because…"

His evident embarrassment softened her just enough to allow him to talk.

"… because I feel I owe you an apology for my behavior this morning."

The regret in his grey eyes seemed genuine.

"I was rude and insensitive to say those things. I wish I hadn't."

Natalie wasn't a haughty girl, but she couldn't deny she was enjoying the discomfort in his voice as much as his purple cheeks: that's why she didn't make it easy for him by turning his monologue into a dialogue.

"I wanted to tell you that you're a great teacher, and I'm learning a lot by attending your classes. I hope you will accept my apologies, Miss Lunn. I'm going to apologize to Janine tomorrow, in front of the group. Good night."

"Henke," she stopped him. "Let's do this. You cut the Miss Lunn out and call me Nat, and we can bury the hatchet," she suggested, holding out her hand. "How about that?"

He relaxed his features and, under the orange glow of an amazing sunset, wiped the slate clean.

"Okay, Nat."

"By the way, since you reopened the topic, tell me something. Just out of curiosity," she smiled, leaning her back onto the car and crossing her arms over her chest.

"Sure."

"Why did you say those things?"

"Because…" he blushed again, looking down. "Because I'm … I'm a jerk."

"Henke, although it was distasteful of you… because you could've voiced your displeasure in private… your behavior was too spontaneous not to be based on something you really think."

"Nat …"

"In fact, you didn't take back that I lack professionalism even now that you apologized."

"I have nothing to take back because I don't think that about you at all. I think tha…"

"Have a nice evening, Nat," said a clerk of the school office passing by.

"You too, Helen."

Henke was bewildered as if he had lost his train of thoughts.

He kept looking at Helen getting in her car.

"Henke?"

He jumped.

"I just wanna understand," she continued, minding not to mention Janine. "You know, I thought about it the whole afternoon, while correcting your essays. You may not be completely wrong. Maybe I should be a bit more professional. I don't know. Maybe the only way to improve is to learn from other people's criticism. Don't you agree?"

"Yes, but you're doing a fantastic job. You're perfect just as you are, believe me."

"If you really think so, there must be something else. Otherwise I don't think I believe you."

Henke's eyes shifted and came back, as if he was considering whether to continue the discussion. She thought to push him to open up, but she didn't: she wanted him to feel free to talk about it more than the answer itself.

"The story isn't that short…" he said, after hesitating a moment.

"Well, I'm not in a hurry."

"No?"

"Nope. I have nothing waiting for me tonight."

"Okay, Nat. Um… Wanna go to Starbucks?

13 – Starbucks

Natalie and Henke sat at a table inside, an iced coffee with milk for her, a cappuccino and a slice of iced lemon pound cake for him.

They were the only couple in the place. Apart from three free tables, the others were each occupied by a single, young customer—more women than men—equipped with earphones and busy on their laptops or iPads.

"So, are you comfy now?" Natalie joked. "Ready to spill the beans?"

"Ready," smiled Henke, adding some sugar to his cappuccino.

When he smiled, he was cute. She never noticed that, perhaps because she had never seen him smile for the three months since they'd met. And he was also nice when he put aside his German seriousness: the joke he'd told her on the way here had her in stitches.

"Come on, hit me. But don't go below the belt."

"Of course not. I'd be a masochist, given that it's about me and not you."

"Okay, let me hear it," she said, taking a drink from the straw.

"As you know, I'm a programmer for a computer company."

"Uh-huh."

"The German staff of our South Carolina branch was becoming a minority, and our boss wasn't happy about that. So he decided to reorganize the employees. As I learned of this opportunity, I applied. You know, I wanted to move to the US since I was a child. I was one of the five guys selected and here I am."

"Got it. So?"

"I can say that living in this country is better than I imagined."

"Are you planning to settle here for good?" she guessed.

"That would be my plan. But there is a *but*."

"What *but*?"

"I have to go back home in early June because my Visa is gonna expire. The point is that I have a good feeling with my boss here."

"And …?"

"He told me that a programmer is moving to Seattle this November and offered me the job."

"That's wonderful," she said, happy for him. "Your dream is coming true."

"Supposedly."

"These are not the most suitable drinks for a toast, but whatever!" she laughed, raising her iced coffee.

He put his cappuccino close to hers. It wasn't a memorable cheer.

"I'm clearly missing something," she muttered, puzzled—Henke's expression wasn't bursting with joy like she expected.

"My problem is, I don't always understand everything when you guys talk."

"Really?"

He nodded.

"Um… I didn't think you would miss something. I mean, when you and I talk, you get me, am I right?"

"Yes. I can understand you because I'm used to your vocabulary, voice, pronunciation, and the fact that you speak more slowly when you address us … that's a big help."

"I don't speak slowly when I address my students," she said, surprising herself with her flirty tone.

"Maybe you do it unconsciously, but I assure you that when you chat with your colleagues, you speak faster."

"You think?"

Henke smiled, before biting into his cake.

"Well, then thank you for letting me know that," she smiled. "But, still... What does it have to do with your outburst this morning?"

Henke took a moment to swallow.

"Nothing. That's why I said I'm a jerk. It's nothing about you. It's my fear of missing this opportunity that makes me grumpy lately. I become quite irritable and I often mess with those around me."

Natalie thought he was absolutely right when he called himself a jerk; nevertheless, she avoided telling him, not even through irony, because he had the expression of a vases collector who had just dropped a Ming.

"I'm not sure I understand your point, Henke."

"To miss some words in a conversation is frustrating, because if I focus on the word that I didn't get in the first place, I miss the rest of the conversation that goes on in the meantime. Maybe I even know that word, but the pronunciation itself has camouflaged it to my ears. And while I'm thinking of that... phew, I miss my connecting flight and the plane is gone."

"Don't you think you're being too anal?" she said.

"Anal?" he opened wide his eyes.

"Not that kind of anal, Henke. Hahaha. It's just a colloquial way to say *meticulous*."

"Oh. That makes sense," he laughed. "We say it in a longer way, which is that one counts the hair inside the hole of somebody's butt."

"Hahaha, anyway… You miss a few words, so what?"

"I was watching a debate on TV the other day. There was this recurring word, *ethnic*, that I wasn't able to figure it out. I by-passed it and kept listening, but when I got it the day after, I realized that the whole talk was about races. Bottom line, I didn't understand a thing."

"To be honest, I can't follow debates on TV either, and they're in my language…"

"Hahaha, you're funny."

"And you're a foreigner, so?" she winked at him.

"Yeah, but can you imagine if it happened at work? At this time, I'm the internal staff, I don't deal directly with customers and my American colleagues are lenient with me. But it would be different with the new job. I'll have to deal directly with customers. Strangers. Your countrymen. And what am I gonna do when I can't catch up with them in the conversation? Should I ask them to repeat? To be patient because I'm a foreigner? You know how you Americans are. I'm not perfect? Buzz… Supervisor! I'd embarrass the company with customers, and myself with the company."

"Is this how other countries see Americans?"

"Um … Yup."

"Wow!"

In his worry, Natalie recognized the anxiety she herself had experienced her first week at school, when she doubted her ability to teach English to foreigners.

"I wish I had this cake this morning, so instead of talking, I'd have used my mouth in a more clever way. I'm so sorry, Nat," and he bit into it.

"Never mind, Henke. Let's focus on how we can solve your problem."

"What do you mean?" he asked, barely understandable since he was chewing.

"You're gonna be here another thirty days before going back to Germany, am I right?"

This time, he only nodded.

"You could hang out with me and my friends sometime. So when you miss a word, you can tell me and we work on it."

"Would you really do this for me?"

"I'll be your conversation crutch," she winked, before sucking another bit of her coffee. Then she added, "A good teacher cares that her students learn well. And I'm the best."

"You definitely are, Nat. You leave me speechless. That's exactly what I need. You're an angel. I'll thank you for ..."

While he was babbling, she stood up in disbelief, and took a few steps in the direction of the TV in the corner.

It was on the news. The report was about the discovery of a Ford Focus in the Colorado River, in Austin area. There was the corpse of a woman inside. They said she was shot in the head.

"That's horrible," he said, getting close to her.

"Oh my God, Henke. I knew that woman," she turned pale with shock, while a photo of the victim was on the screen with her name superimposed.

14 – Mallory

"Hello?"

"Ray, honey. It's me," said Mallory, in the late afternoon of mid August.

She was sprawled, exhausted, on an armchair in the living room, her long light-brown hair hanging beyond the seatback.

"Hey, baby."

"Hi."

"You okay?"

"Yep, don't worry. I just called 'cause I miss you."

"Or cuz you're gettin' bored?" Ray chuckled.

"Very funny … What are you doing?"

"Watching the Tigers."

"How are they doing?" she asked, although she barely distinguished a baseball ball from a tennis' one.

"Lousy. But the whole game is lousy. Forty-one years of my life, never seen such a poor game. They're in the bottom of the seventh inning and it's still zero-zero. But the worst part is that each team has only made it as far as second. Good thing I didn't waste my day off and money on a ticket by going to the stadium."

"So I'm not bothering you?"

"You serious? I'm watching it just cuz I ain't got shit to do until you come over. When you comin' home?"

"Your baby will be there in two hours. She's going to give you that little pretty thing you love so much, so you can quickly forget that horrible game."

"How the old fogeys doin'?"

"They're having dinner in the kitchen," she said hesitantly.

"What'd you make for 'em?"

"Ray... something wrong?"

"No, baby. Why?"

By his tone, he seemed surprised by her question.

"You changed the subject so ... I don't know."

"C'mon, baby. You know the affect your voice has on me when you play the kitty cat in heat. Then I jerk off and when you get here I'm no longer in the mood."

Mallory smiled. She knew that all her Ray had in common with Romeo was the first letter of their name—also because he was fourteen years older and worked as a handyman in a motel—but she appreciated the easiness and naturalness of his temperament. And, the main thing, he really loved her; not like her last two boyfriends who thought more of having fun than building a future together. Plus he was always nice to her. Never aggressive. Never mind if romance was his kryptonite.

"Then I'm gonna talk to you about Janet and Robert, so it will wilt with depression."

"You always have some snappy comebacks, don't ya?" laughed Ray. "Okay, demolish it."

"I took 'em to breakfast at Denny's this morning. Then we ..."

"Don't they get bored going to the same place every day?"

"At their age, people become methodical," Mallory smiled. "At least I think so, since Robert suffers from Alzhcimer's, hahaha."

"That's my point. How can he always be wanting to go to there, if he don't remember shit? What, his wish is triggered like the first time any time you guys pass by there, or something?"

"Nope. He just follows Janet like a puppy. And you don't wanna take her somewhere else, believe me," she explained in a low voice, glancing at the kitchen door.

60

"And after breakfast?"

"We went to Target and bought some things. After that, we went back home and I placed them in front of the TV while I was doing chores. They took a nap as I was making dinner and finally, I sat for a while, waiting for them to finish eating. Then, I'm gonna clear the table, wash the dishes and put them to bed."

"Come on, baby. Don't lose heart. You'll find something better soon. You're smart as shit!"

Only by his answer, did she realize that her bitterness had leaked into her voice. She liked Robert and Janet. She'd been working for them for six months, and had grown fond of them. The problem was that she hated this kind of a job, and hated the fact that she needed it even more. It diminished her too much in others' eyes, but especially in her own. Not to mention that spending her Sunday like this was really depressing.

"I bet some clinics are gonna call ya for an interview next week," continued Ray, spreading optimism with his tone. "No way they miss an assistant with your resume."

"How much you wanna bet?" she said, aware that some tears started to fall down as she blinked her eyelids.

"I bet ... let's do this. If you don't get a new job by the end of the month, when I take my vacation days, you decide where we're gonna spend them. And we'll spare no expense, even if it takes all of my savings!"

"Really?"

"No joke, baby. But don't start planning anything, since that's a bet I cannot lose."

Mallory was moved by how much he believed in her. And even if it wasn't about believing in her skills, she was still happy because he was thoughtful as only a man in love could be.

"Ray?"
"What, baby?"
"You know I love you so much?"
"Sure I know. Otherwise you think I'd risk my fuckin' savings?"

15 – The Mishap

Mallory was walking, glowing from her conversation with Ray, to her car parked in the driveway of Robert and Janet's house. Her heart shone and warmed more than the afternoon sun.

Throughout the day, she had partnered with Melancholy, but after talking to Ray, she'd got rid of that miserable companion, her mood now wore the flashiest dress she owned, and she couldn't wait to paint the town red with him.

As she opened the car door, a male voice behind startled her.

"Excuse me, Miss,"

She turned around.

"Would you please hand me the keys?" said, tense, a fair-complexioned handsome man in his thirties, black hair and mustache, in a light summer jacket.

When she noticed the gun in his hand, an internal thunder turned light and warmth into darkness and coldness.

"Don't worry. I'm not gonna hurt you," he said, with a nervous expression that didn't match with his polite tone. "Gimme the keys and everything will be fine."

Paralyzed by fear, Mallory did as he said.

"Get in the car," he added, turning from side to side as if he was checking that nobody was around.

She felt the barrel of the gun against her hip push her toward the car. Her thoughts, as frantic as the beating of her heart, mingled in a rhythm of terror.

Gloves in middle August? Uncovered face... No fear to be identified. No fingerprints. He's gonna kill me.

"Take the car, just let me go," she stammered, starting to cry.

"Get in!" he got mad, looking around again. "Nothing bad is gonna happen. I give you my word. Now get in the fuckin' car."

She looked around too, but with the opposite hope. The instability of this man scared her as much as the pressure that the gun made on her.

"Hurry up!" he pushed her.

She lowered her head and sat in the driving seat.

"Throw the bag in the back."

She did.

"Stay there. Don't get any smart ideas. Got it?"

She nodded and he slammed the door.

She watched at him turn around the car, his armed hand hidden under his jacket. She could feel death's coils wrap her limbs, hips, and throat. Maybe she had to wait and hear what he wanted from her, but would she get another chance to run away? His black leather gloves seemed the ones of a professional killer... A surge of panic shook her.

When he was on the passenger side, and she saw his leg get into the car, she quickly opened the door and dropped herself on the asphalt. She rolled and, taking advantage of inertia, got up right away. Her luck, no vehicles passed by.

"Help!" she screamed, desperately, running across the road.

"Mallory Jackson!" she heard him shout as she stepped onto the sidewalk on the other side.

By hearing her own name, her feet blocked as her breath. She turned toward him: arms outstretched on the car roof, he was pointing his gun on her as if he was taking aim.

She stared at him, studying the features of his face. She analyzed his voice too, looking for any indication of a past history that allowed him to know her full name.

"Get back here, Mallory. Don't force me to do this."
"Are you a cop?"
"Yes. I was assigned to protect you."

She'd asked him because this could explain how he knew her name, but his answer was bullshit.

His lie triggered her resolution.

She was the width of the road ahead of him.

Maybe he can't shoot...

He could miss her if she'd zigzag.

She turned around and started to run on the lawn toward the oak behind which she could see the Coopers' house.

She heard a gunshot, but felt no pain. Just a burst of apprehension that broke her breath. She swerved to the left. The oak was so close. She couldn't scream, tears and anguish prevented her. Another gunshot. She felt a severe pain in her shoulder. She found herself face down in the grass. It was moist and smelled good. Her breath was stuck, but she couldn't release it this time. She thought about pretending to be dead. Maybe he would leave. She saw herself with Ray, leaning on a parapet over Niagara Falls. One of Nature's masterpieces! She had seen it online and on TV, it had been her dream to visit there one day. It would be a fantastic two-week holiday, much more exciting than a new job. Yeah, if they would offer her the fuckin' job, she would reject it!

"Why don't you cheer me up now, Mallory?"

A hiss full with contempt that she felt very close, brought her back on the grass in front of Robert and Janet's house. Then a third shot, simultaneous to a sharp stab in her head.

16 – Pretzel

That bitch messed it up.

"Fuckin' cunt," he muttered, walking briskly to her car before someone was drawn by the gunshots.

He felt his face flushed with a rush of anxiety. It must be the fear of being caught, a foreign feeling to him.

Before getting in the car, he took a quick overview of the road that seemed to split a huge meadow: no one was passing by; the old people's house and the one over behind the oak looked like inanimate postcards in 3D. No people, except himself and Mallory's corpse.

He sat behind the wheel, inserted the key that he got from her, pulled the door closed and drove off.

Hope you burn in hell! he thought, while driving on Michigan Avenue.

He didn't understand what went wrong. He'd carefully conceived his plan and carried it out impeccably.

"Fuck it!" he growled, gritting his teeth. "It wasn't supposed to end like this. No. Fuck."

Rage was devouring him. He struggled to keep it away from the gas pedal.

He had created an unique recipe, barely found the rare ingredients, thoroughly made the dough, set the right temperature, baked the cake and waited, but when the moment came to taste it, it disappeared from the oven. All of the research that went into it, the cottage, flight, gun, places, stalking… Everything masterfully organized, and she died without even knowing why. If only he'd had more time to refresh her memory…

The impatience! he suddenly realized.

The treacherous bitch tamely lying in your bed, a love slave ready to submit to your cravings, but as lethal as a black widow in her obscure wefts with the thread of time: she quietly waits for your distraction in the faint light of her small flame and, once bitten your flesh, her poison starts corroding you from the inside; you feel sick, but would never think to her treason. And when you realize it, the candle is already burned out and you're delivered to gloom.

I was supposed to wait for nightfall, fuck.

Thinking back to his meeting with Mallory, comparing it to those with Emily and Nina, he noticed how his haste had affected the result. The daylight had increased his fear of witnesses, causing him to shorten his speech intended to create the psychological state of mind that would have led her to obey him.

He knew about the pitfalls of impatience. He knew them very well. Who better than him? But he got fooled anyway. Three days spent shadowing Mallory to learn her routine, until the subtle poison had begun to circulate in his system, instigating him to take the risk.

It was the only way, he thought, trying to calm down.

She slept at her man's, and there were always people on the street in that neighborhood; the old people's house, however, was in a fairly isolated area. Each day a replica of itself. Even on Sundays! No, he did well. Perhaps he hadn't scared her enough, that's why she ran away.

Or I scared her too much.

This sudden satisfaction eased his anger and addressed his focus to what he needed to do next.

Now he just had to follow his fallback plan.

He'd never needed one, and this feeling tried to ally with his lazy side; fortunately, they had educated him in the habit of x-raying any intuition to make it intelligible to the mind—a technique that proven itself effective, since he did have a fallback plan.

When he reached the stretch of road where it crossed over the Rouge River, he pulled over in the emergency lane. He got out and approached the railing, at the perpendicular point on the center of the river. The breeze was cooling his cheeks. He took a look around to make sure not to be observed and furtively grabbing the gun—he held it in his jacket pocket—he rested his elbows on the railing, dropping it with nonchalance.

Tump.

He watched it quickly sinking in the flow of the water. Then he stretched as if he were yawning and returned to the car. Five minutes later, he arrived at the crowded Fairlane Town Center parking lot. He spotted a place at the edge of the mall, away from the surveillance cameras. Pulled out a cotton cap and sunglasses from an inside pocket, he put them on. He checked his camouflage in the rearview mirror, sticking all his hair under the gray cap so that its color wouldn't be visible.

"Can work," he said, getting a grin of approval from that new himself.

He got out, "forgetting" the keys in the ignition. Pretending to check his phone, he glanced around. A group of teenagers and an African-American family walked in the area, but they were minding their own business. When he was positive that nobody was looking at him, he walked away from Mallory's car, leaving the door open a bit …

He took off his gloves and put them in his pocket. Shoulders hunched and gaze on the ground, he headed casually toward the mall.

Once inside, he sought the area with public phones.

The chaos of people and noises began to fill the silence that had amplified the harassing echo of his agitation so far. He was absorbing the normality pulsing around him. He began to feel light, as if he were just returned from a concert instead of a killing.

He walked to a phone. Rummaging in his jeans, he pulled out a few quarters; inserting them, he held the receiver between his ear and shoulder while getting out his cell phone. He scrolled through until he found the right number, then dialed it on the public phone.

"Radio Taxis. How can I help you?"

"Can you please send a cab to the Fairlane Town Center, main entrance?" he asked, putting his cell phone back into the pocket.

"It will be there in ten minutes, sir."

"Thank you, ma'am."

This matter settled, he walked to the pretzel stand he spotted when he had come in. He bought a bag of the sweet ones and a soda.

Sampling the delicious snacks, he headed toward the main entrance.

I would've enjoyed it with that dirty slut...

Compounding his regret was the inability to verify whether Mallory was as sexually transgressive as he'd assumed by observing her. The way she paraded around, her shoulders back and tits pushed out, flaunting her tight body and perky ass were all obvious symptoms of her salacious nature.

The disappointment for how it had gone bothered him but not that much, perhaps because the remains of apprehension caused by the mishap still prevented him to relax. Maybe, when he got back home, this chipped picce that distorted his precious mosaic would upset him.

Or maybe it will teach me a lesson for the next time, he thought, trying to be optimistic.

17 – Tiana

Tiana, Tiana, Tiana… Shit, why? he thought, tormented, in the dim light of his bedroom.

He was lying naked on the bed, above the sheets. It was a dreadfully hot Sunday. The air conditioner seemed to have carefully chosen this day to strike.

The sweat formed on his forehead and chest, lingering for a few breaths before slipping back through his hair and sides, while other drops already emerged to replace them.

In three weeks it would be a year. A year of torment. The bass still hammering in his brain. Damn cancer that had pushed him to the club.

The innocence shining on Tiana's face still lit up the ants' nest of his memories, dragging his sin out of the darkness where it nestled. Those features seemed dashed to inspire gentle thoughts in whoever looked at her.

How did I do such a thing?

Tears merged with sweat, mixing bitter and salty.

Perhaps the innocence didn't belong to her, though. He must have seen it because it was in his eyes, a ruthless tip from his guilt. There was something else on Tiana's face, he remembered it well. Bourbon itself couldn't have generated the horror. While they were dancing, her features had some subtle changes showing lust as she rubbed herself on him.

"*You're pretty revved up, huh?*" she'd laughed, when he held her from behind making sure she felt his hard-on.

And her flirting tone … God, she liked it!

A true innocent, one that didn't want it, would never joke about it.

Instead, she had kept rubbing her buttocks against him. His dick had gotten hard for a couple of minutes. How could he get excited from this memory?
Creep.
Conscience shouldn't be wrapped with flesh.
It was almost a year. Almost a year that these demons haunted him. A year seeking a contributory negligence.

He followed Tiana's profile in his mind, from her cheekbone to her chin, going down along her neck.
She'd left the top buttons of her blouse open.
A decent girl wouldn't show her skin where it rounds out.
But maybe she was just playing the seductress.
"Shit. Then don't complain if one puts his hands on you," he said out loud, to drown out the incessant whisper of his conscience.

He snorted and stood up, walking straight into the shower.
He moved the knob to the left and opened it. Someone had told him that a hot shower was good to stop sweating.
"Taking it cool, you refresh yourself for a while, but then you're gonna sweat worse than before."
It sounded like a contradiction, but they said so. It was about body temperatures. They compared the sweat to the fogging of the window glasses when it's warm inside and cold outside. Or something like that. Any other memory was helpful to drive Tiana's image away…
Here she is again.
Wearing a miniskirt, she was a lethal weapon. Her thighs, solid at the sight but soft to the touch… How had he wanted to put his hand in the middle as they talked on the sofa! The desire to see her

enjoying his touch. Maybe he had kept on drinking to find the courage to massage her sex.

"Stop it!" he shouted, pounding his fists against the tiles.

It's not your fault, got it? If she didn't want it, she wouldn't have stuck her tongue in your mouth. She wouldn't have moaned, as if overcome by the desire of an orgasm. She willingly went to the restroom with you, remember?

Water slid down his face, steam overwhelmed his body: water and steam, great lackeys of remorse. They were all wearing him out.

Good! That was what he hoped for. Anything to summon sleep and turn off his mind before…

If she wanted it, why the gun?

No way. There was no way to escape this fuckin' question. No matter how the sun would shine, that hellish cloud came to eclipse it soon or later. And, as always, darkness chained his heart to the admission of raping her.

18 - Tim

Natalie and Tim sat at a table at TGI Friday's.

She had wanted to meet her "cozslim"—with clothes on, her cousin looked thin enough to seem malnourished, but actually was pretty toned—since she was concerned about him after reading some controversial posts, sometimes tormented, on his Facebook profile. They began to chat via text; the conversation got deep and she suggested continuing it in person; so he invited her to get something to eat. They decided to meet up that night because it was a Sunday and they were both busy at work during the week. Waiting for the next weekend would've been like pouring water into a carafe with wine.

They had practically grown up together at Natalie's house. At the time, both Tim's parents worked for a cleaning company. His mother would leave him with her sister, whose husband ran a real estate agency allowing her to be a housewife and look after the children. After that they had taken different paths, but the bonds of childhood stood up well to Time's shoves: that's why she was very sorry to hear that he was depressed, especially due to problems that she judged as fictitious.

Tim hadn't dated anyone for almost a year, since a cheerleader whom he met at a club stood him up; brooding over the episode, he assumed that the problem was his job, because of which he was no longer feeling good enough to land a beautiful girl. He knew that the topic would pop up at some point in the conversation; and he hated inventing stories because of his habit of sincerity which precluded him the double life enjoyed by liars—in simple terms, he sucked at lying. So he better not even start: he'd bet his left nut that a girl would suddenly lose interest in him finding that, with so many professionals, employees and students around, she was wasting her time with a construction worker.

"Why, Nat, would you date me if we weren't relatives? Be honest," he asked her, while waiting for the magicians of the kitchen turning their order into food ...

"No, but not because of your job. I'd have a hard time dealing with your personality."

"My personality?" he was surprised, laughing. "But we never had a fight in our life!"

"Only because we've never had an incestuous relationship, hahaha," she joked, inspired by the cheerful atmosphere of the crowded restaurant—it was packed and it seemed that everybody was having a good time besides the busy waiters who went back and forth like ping-pong balls.

He frowned.

"Like most women, I don't like insecure men, like you. Self-confidence is everything to a woman."

"Sure. Self-confidence is the answer, nothing else!"

This time she frowned.

"I see, you belong to the race of men who think they understand women. But talking like this, you're just showing your immaturity."

"C'mon, Nat. Don't play the philosopher with me."

"I'm not, cozslim."

"The truth is that if I meet a hot chick at the club, when I tell her that I'm a bricklayer, she finds an excuse and disappears faster than light."

"Wake up, Tim. Women aspire to be financially independent nowadays. I know so many who don't give a hoot about their man's bank account."

"Where are they? I bet they're all in books."

"Look, I'm not doing a crusade in defense of the female gender," she said, realizing that he was misunderstanding. "I only want to help you knock down your mental barrier, because that's what keeps you from dating."

Tim put on a sad face and picked up a slice of bread.

"A woman looks for other things in a man," said Natalie, blowing the curl out of her face. "Kindness, protection, attention, pleasure, they all come before the job. Tim, you're a great guy. You're funny even when you're morose. Get rid of this complex if you want to leave behind these dark times. Or ..."

"Or what?"

She was about to suggest that he find another job, but given the conversation, he would certainly misinterpret her advice.

"Or keep feeling sorry in your loneliness," she explained, fixing her hair with her hand.

"But I'm not that bad in my loneliness. If I was, it wouldn't be that hard to find a girl who's just breathing."

She observed him, sensing kind of an allusion.

"Wait a minute. Are you saying that the prettier a girl is, the more she's interested in money?"

"Not in money."

"Then what?"

"Respect ... *What does your boyfriend do? / Surgeon / Wow! / And yours? / Bricklayer / Oh well, someone has to build houses, ihihih.* It's embarrassing."

"Tim, do you realize that this is old stuff? Like, really outdated."

"I know you believe in what you're saying, but it sounds like you're living in Wonderland. No beautiful chick will even consider a bricklayer. Those ones aspire to a winner. How can you deny this?"

"Maybe I live in Wonderland, but you're still trapped in the fifties, man."

"Okay, let's talk about you," Tim raised. "Your German works with computers. Tell me that you'd be with him even if he was only a bricklayer, and I'll shut up."

"First of all, he's not *my* German," she grew irritated. "I am not with him. We only went out three or four times."

"When you decide to answer my question, gimme a call."

"Of course I'd date him anyway," she retorted, resolute. "Henke is a stand-up guy. For example, he had a problem with our language. You know what he did? Instead of whining on Facebook, he confronted me in front of the whole class, blaming me for my lack of professionalism. Not that I loved that part, he was an asshole for doing that."

"So why did you date him if he's an asshole? See, you just proved yourself wrong."

"Because it showed me that he's a determined person, a type of man that doesn't give up on a problem. One you can count on, that doesn't step back, but faces things. Do you understand? Although he was unfair to me, I was fascinated by him. Also when he came to apologize, he was flawless. The fact that he's actually a computer programmer was irrelevant."

"And what are you gonna do when he's back?"

"I don't know. We just talk on Skype for now," she said, diverting her gaze to a table of young women blatantly cheerful—she didn't want to discuss her feelings for Henke with him.

"But you'd think about it if they give him a permanent job ..."

He said that with a smile, but his conclusion quite bothered her. However, she loved her cozslim and decided to change the subject.

"I think you should put aside this silly philosophy of yours about women."

"Silly? Silly cuz I say that beautiful girls like you look for the best? I don't mean that you girls are shallow. Believe me, Nat. It's fair for a girl to use her beauty to get a successful guy, or one with some potential. That's why I'll never be with a beautiful chick like you."

She shook her head.

After venting, he took the cloth napkin from under his plate and settled it on his lap. Then he filled his glass with mineral water.

She was observing him when a thought made her wince. She had sensed something strange in his invitation, but she had so many things to do that she forgot about her impression.

"Oh my God. You took me here because of that?"

He looked surprised.

"Even with your *cozslim*?" she added.

"What you're talking about?"

"Tim, I love you. I enjoy spending time with you. Who cares if we go to Fridays or Taco Bell."

"Oh ... Well, yeah ... But you came here more willingly than Burger King, didn't you?"

"You know what? If you were a woman, you'd be disgusting."

There wasn't contempt in her tone. Just sympathy. Maybe that's why he seemed to take it badly this time.

"Okay, Nat. I'm gonna listen to you. Next time I meet a hot chick who turns me on, I'll put aside my *silly philosophy* and do as you say. I'll humiliate myself just to prove to you that ... Hey, you here?"

Natalie was mentally absent because she was experiencing an awful case of *deja vu*. The news showed a brutal murder in Dearborn, the Detroit metropolitan area. She looked closely at the victim's picture, and she couldn't believe it; but eventually, she recognized her old friend Mallory.

19 – The Charges

"So, Miss Gayle. I'm listening," said Landon, from the swivel chair of his office at the police station.

The woman, an African American in her early thirties, faded jeans and orange sleeveless blouse, appeared quite tense in the chair in front of him.

"I came here to... I came here to press charges against my employer."

Her voice quivered. From how anxiety gleamed in her gaze and considering her beauty, it wasn't hard to imagine her reason. Experience had sharpened his eyes and judgment.

"All right, Miss Gayle. Um... Before moving forward, you may want to tell me what happened," he said with the utmost discretion, leaning his elbows on the desk and lacing his fingers.

"Why?" she unexpectedly flared up. "'Cause I'm black and he's white?"

"Ma'am, I have no idea who your employer is."

She looked nervous and doubtful, her right leg bouncing like a jackhammer, and her hands squeezing her purse as if it were modeling-clay. He had to reassure her.

"I only suggested that because you don't look thoroughly convinced of this step. If you prefer, we can make it official immediately. But then it would be complicated to go back."

The woman's agitation seemed to change into affliction.

"I've got two children. I need that job," she whispered passionately. "I fuckin' need it."

"Would you like some water?"

"I'd like to do my job in peace."

Landon nodded, waiting quietly for her to be ready to speak.

"I was living in Marietta, Georgia. I end up divorced 'cause my husband has always loved the bottles more than me… The kids and I came to Charleston to my friend who sublet me her apartment. I looked for a job as a waitress for a couple of weeks, till they hired me at this restaurant. After years of anguish, I thought I could finally have a normal life. But …"

A fit of despair forced her to stop.

"Miss Gayle, I'm here for you."

"Thanks, detective. The thing is, I'm exhausted. I wanna stop watching my back. I'm fine at the restaurant, you know? Pay is good. With tips, I'm able to make ends meet and my kids have everything they need. My colleagues are great and I do want to keep working there. But …" she sighed, disheartened.

"What happened?"

"Men are pigs. That's what happened."

Her sudden burst of anger led him to lower his head.

"I'm sorry, detective," she widened her eyes. "I didn't mea…"

"It's okay, Miss Gayle," he said, affably. "I understand that there's nothing personal in your outburst."

The bitter smile she displayed was an eloquent allegory of how she felt.

"By pressing charges against your employer for sexual harassment, you would be forced to find another job, which you don't wanna do. Is that it?"

She nodded.

"May I ask what the man did to you?"

"Detective, considering engagement and marriage, I've been living eight years with a fuckin' drunk. You see this?" she said, pointing to a small scar under her left cheekbone. "Once he threw a glass at me, one of those ones with a thick base, 'cause he didn't remember where he hid a bottle of whiskey, and I couldn't find it."

Anger and disdain were still so strong in her that the vibrations of her voice, associated with the thin but visible scar, gave him shivers.

"What I mean," she continued after another sigh. "Is by now I've learned to figure out what's gonna happen before it happens."

"I see, Miss Gayle. However, I need to figure out if you were verbally or physically assaulted."

Her features hardened. He felt intimidated.

"Why did I come here, I wonder," she muttered dark, standing up resolutely. "Never mind, mister detective. I'll come back once I've been raped. I should've known you guys would be a day late and a dollar short."

"Miss Gayle, please," he stood up too. "I am on your side. I understand your state of mind, and I promise you I'll do whatever I can to help you out," he added fervently. "But you must understand my necessity to have a complete picture of the situation in order for us to intervene in the most suitable way."

She changed her face pretty fast: she must be really desperate, or he'd been very persuasive. Maybe both.

"Let's sit back down, okay?" he smiled.

She did as he said, setting the purse on her lap again.

He was waiting, but she kept her eyes on a small pile of files on his desk.

Maybe she was embarrassed. Or upset. Or doubtful. So he followed his intuition.

"I assume that your employer makes you uncomfortable with glances and jokes. Therefore I'd suggest…"

"He touches my ass every time he passes behind me. Every single day. He's even got a twenty-year-old daughter, that perv."

This response deflated him.

"I try to stay away from him, but that ain't easy when you're there for eight straight hours. I pretend nothing happened, but sooner or later …"

Embarrassed, he began to roll up his shirt cuffs, a diversion to find some time to reset his mind with this new information.

"Okay, Miss Gayle. Now the situation seems clear. Unfortunately, if you pursue legal means, it would be hard, maybe impossible, to remain at that job."

"That's why I'm here. I didn't know where else to go."

He'd tried to depict the situation tactfully, but he hadn't thought that his approach would make her cry like a woman put at the corner.

This story was making him feel really bad. He understood the woman's fear and discomfort more than he could show. He kept racking his brain in search of a solution, while she wiped her eyes with a handkerchief from her purse.

"Look, Miss Gayle," he resumed, as an idea struck him. "When is your next shift?"

"Tonight."

She'd replied mechanically, looking bewildered.

"Okay. My name is Landon. My partner Devin and I will have dinner there tonight. You… What's your first name?"

"Curlene."

"Curlene. What a beautiful name."

"Thanks," she smiled, as if his compliment gave her back some hope.

"Tonight, Curlene, Devin and I will show up at the restaurant. You need to treat us as if we're your close friends. Be relaxed and joke with us, without minding our uniforms."

She frowned.

"Your boss will see that you have cops as friends, so he'll think carefully before harassing you again, and at the same time he would have no reason to be resentful towards you. It might work, what do you think?"

She brightened.

"Would you really do this for me, detective?"

"Landon," he winked, pleased by his own idea. "Tell me what restaurant it is."

With her eyes shining, she looked for something in her purse. A business card.

"I've never been here," murmured Landon, when it was in his hands.

"So, am I supposed to be casual with you?"

"Exactly. We're old friends, remember?"

She relaxed, which enhanced her beauty even more.

"I don't know what to say …"

"There's nothing to say," he comforted her, getting up and walking her to the door.

"Don't stand me up. Ok, Landon?" she said on the threshold, squeezing his hands. "I'm counting on you."

He couldn't say if, in addition to gratitude and hope, she was communicating something else through her shaking as intense as her gaze. It was certainly a pleasant sensation—he had felt something similar when, as a boy, he climbed the branches of an alder tree, staying on top to admire the countryside and breath the purer air up there.

"My partner and I will be there at seven thirty sharp. I promise."

Left alone, Landon couldn't get Curlene's lovely face out of his mind. The contrast between the green of her eyes with the brown of her complexion constantly evoked the feeling of the alder.

The thought of getting back out on the dating scene suddenly occurred to him. He was completely stranded from reality, and he didn't realize how stupid he looked with the happy smile formed on his face.

"Hey, Don Juan," Devin leaned at his door. "I guess today is your lucky day."

Landon frowned.

"Please, Miss Lunn," Devin said, turning to his left, as if speaking to someone he was about to introduce.

Landon stood up hastily, trying to compose himself—actually he had nothing to compose: he was just caught in the middle of thinking about his future.

When a magnificent blonde appeared at the door, he got Devin's joke, who had become "unbearable" since dropping twenty-five pounds.

"Detective Landon Vitman," he welcomed her, holding out his hand.

"Natalie Lunn. How do you do?"

"If you need help, you know where to find me," Devin shamelessly winked. "Nice to meet you, Natalie."

20 – Spice Girls

Landon had rarely trembled like this before a girl. Maybe never. Definitely never.

While the embarrassment caused by Devin with his smug attitude was fading, Landon let himself admire the woman in front of him. Dressed in a white fitted blouse and tight capri pants, she was slim, not too tall, with a candid face and eyes as blue as a pool.

He tried to school his expression to not let on how she suddenly affected him. As for her, she didn't seem any calmer. At least her red cheeks and body stiffness gave him that impression. She sat in the seat that had just been occupied by … what was her name?

"Miss Lunn, tell me what brings you here," he said, to shake himself more than her.

She lowered her eyes and bite her lip, then turn to the left and right as if she was looking for where she could lay her colorful nylon bag—Harlequin's wife would kill for a bag like that.

"You can place it here," he said, moving the small pile of files from the desk.

"Thanks."

More long seconds passed, he staring at her, she staring at the bag.

"Is there something wrong, Miss Lunn?"

"I'm sorry, Mr. Vitman," she said, anxiety in her voice. "Maybe I shouldn't have come."

"It's fine to have doubts. This place can be intimidating, in a way."

"I just feel so silly," she mumbled, standing up.

"Relax, Natalie," he tried to put her at ease. "We are here to help people."

"It's that … Ugh, now I understand why it took Tim two weeks to convince me to come here."

"Who's Tim?"

"My cousin."

Curiosity ousted his romantic thoughts. It was sort of a call to duty.

"Am I supposed to think that your cousin is concerned about you?"

"He is, but not …" she murmured, sitting back down. "He kept insisting that I talk to the police, and his reasons seemed to make sense. But now I'm wondering what gave me that impression."

"Let's put it this way. If there's no reason to be worried, all the better. If instead your cousin's distress has foundation, you've come to the right place."

Her smile gave him a wonderful feeling of being helpful, a feeling as essential as oxygen to him.

"I'm still here," he said, as she was quiet.

"Oh God, I don't even know where to start," she blushed more. "It seems so absurd."

He felt his patience falter, but he controlled himself.

"Have you heard about the murder of the woman in Michigan two weeks ago?" she said suddenly. "In Dearborn, close to Detroit."

"Are you talking about Mallory Jackson?" he asked, his interest piqued—even national media had picked up the case.

"Yes."

"Okay …?"

"I knew Mallory."

"Oh. I'm sorry," he said, at a loss for words.

"Four months ago ..." she hesitated, looking back as if she was distracted by voices from the hallway—the door was still open. "Four months ago, they found the body of a woman in the Colorado River. In Austin. Remember?"

Landon tried to concentrate, but it didn't ring a bell.

"Emily Wallace ...?" she insisted.

He replied by shaking his head.

"They said she was shot in the head, just like Mallory. And I knew her too."

He became pensive.

"What are you trying to tell me, Natalie?"

"I don't know," she said, moving her gaze onto the bulletin board to her right.

He studied her profile. Amid skepticism and embarrassment, he saw some fear.

"Do you think you're in danger?"

"Mr. Vitman, I..."

"Landon, please."

"Landon, I think my cousin may have gotten to me," she said, standing up again but without looking at him. "I feel ridiculous. I apologize for wasting your time."

Grabbing her bag, she walked to the door.

"May I ask how you knew the two victims?"

She stopped in the doorway and turned around. Surprise etched on her features.

He got up and approached her.

"Come on, Natalie. Take it easy," he encouraged her, closing the door.

She gave a light snort before sitting back down.

"So, tell me about the victims."

When he sat too, she began.

"I met them twelve years ago at a summer camp for girls in Maine. I bonded with Cindy from the very first moment. Later that day we made friends with Nina, Mallory and Emily. We became inseparable for the whole month," she explained, looking for something in her bag.

"Hold on. Who are Cindy and Nina?"

"The other two in the band."

"Did you guys play instruments?" he asked.

"Not really. It's that ... don't laugh ... we used to call ourselves *Spice Girls*, hahaha."

"Oh."

"You know, we were big fans and we missed them. As you undoubtedly know, the band had in fact broken up some time before ..."

"Is it already twelve years?" he played along, fascinated by her irony. "Gee, it seems like yesterday that their videos were all the rage on TV."

"Yeah. By the way, the five of us spent all this time together, because we shared a room. Look at this. I was able to find this picture from that summer."

The photo showed five beautiful teen-agers, all of them Caucasian, standing on a lawn. They all had their arms around each other like a women's basketball team posing, with a lake in the background.

"There's some color missing compared to the Spice Girls, though" he joked, to lighten the atmosphere.

"Huh? ... Oh, yeah. Hahaha. By the way, Cindy is the one in the middle. Emily and I are at her sides. Those on the outside are Mallory and Nina."

"That's Mallory," he said, recognizing her from seeing her in the news, although she was an adolescent in the photo.

"You know how it is at times like that ..." she went on. "Girls bond stronger than if they were sisters. Therefore I remember them."

"And what do Nina and Cindy think about the murders?"

"After that unforgettable summer, our paths haven't crossed again. Due to the distance, school, and life overwhelming us, we ended up only exchanging Christmas greetings for a couple of years via email. At the time, social networks weren't as popular as today, so friendships were lost. But I keep that experience among the best memories of my youth."

"Sorry, Natalie, but I didn't understand if you tried to contact them or not."

"Oh, I kept babbling. Sorry."

"That's fine."

"As I said, our paths split. I have no idea where they are or what they're doing. I searched my e-mail archive before coming here, but didn't find anything prior to 2009. I remember I'd gotten a computer virus and I had to erased everything."

"So you don't know if they were still in touch with each other ..."

"I don't think so. If they were, I guess they would have looked for me on Facebook. Or maybe not ... Actually, I didn't look for them ..."

"I presume you think there might be a connection between the murders and that summer camp?"

"It's nonsense, isn't it?" she muttered, lapsing back into the embarrassment—while recalling her memories, she was evidently distracted from the current situation.

"Frankly, I think it's more likely that it's an unfortunate coincidence."

"Yeah, I thought so. When I get home, I'm gonna strangle my cousin. Figuratively speaking."

He smiled.

He saw that shame was crushing her, so he tried to show her sympathy. Fear that a killer was after her was clearly what had led her into his office, but at this point, she would never admit it. It had happened to him too: giving credit to theories in his mind, only finding them to be utter nonsense after being discussed with others. And his pride had always come out wounded by that. So he thought to somehow sustain her theory: it wouldn't harm anyone, and she'd feel less frustrated.

"Look, Natalie. Do you remember Cindy's and Nina's last names?" he asked, pulling out a notepad from the side drawer of the desk.

"Cindy Cook and Nina Arkin. Names and surnames of our youth cannot be forgotten," she mused, while he wrote them down. "Cindy Cook, from Knoxville, Tennessee. Nina Arkin, from Springfield, Massachusetts. But if they moved elsewhere after camp, I don't know. Twelve years have passed, everything could have changed."

"Date of birth?"

"I don't remember, but summer of 2002 we all were fifteen, except Cindy who was going to eighteen. So …"

"So Cindy should be '84, while Nina '87. Like you?"

"Like me, yes."

"Okay. I'm gonna tell my colleague who takes care of this kind of thing to check them out. Maybe we'll find something that can help the Austin and Detroit Police Departments," he speculated, especially to give credibility to this attempt to comfort her.

"I don't know if Cindy and Nina were born there, though. But in 2002 they lived in Knoxville and Springfield."

"Fine. If you could leave me the picture, it would help."

"Sure, Landon."

To hear her pronounce his own name gave him a rush that reminded him of his attraction for her. Suddenly he realized that, once she would be out of his office, he may not to see her again. The fear of losing her racked his brains …

"Well," she smiled, standing up for the last time. "I guess I have nothing left but to thank you for your time and patience."

"You're very welcome, Natalie. If you can leave me your number too, I'll contact you to keep you posted."

21 – The Line

'No, it's not,' answered Dounia firmly.
'Bah! you, too, have ideals,' he muttered, looking at her almost with hatred, and smiling sarcastically. 'I ought to have considered that ... Well, that's praiseworthy, and it's better for you ... and if you reach a line you won't overstep, you will be unhappy ... and if you overstep it, maybe you will be still unhappier ... But all that's nonsense,' he added irritably, vexed at being carried away. 'I only meant to say that I beg your forgiveness, mother,' he concluded, shortly and abruptly.

Something moved, pulling his gaze away from the pages of the book. He quickly focused in that direction.

Thirty feet away from the expensive loafers he was wearing, a spot where the leafy branches of the beech didn't come between lawn and sun, a squirrel rummaged among the grass.

As he put the book down, the squirrel stopped as if someone had pressed PAUSE on its remote control. The squirrel was facing the villa, motionless as if it knew it was being watched.

Too bad I don't have a gun.

The thought of killing a squirrel had never crossed his mind in twenty-six years. This new idea intrigued him, but the only potential weapon he had was a set of keys in the pocket of his jeans. He knew the chance of hitting the squirrel with such an inadequate weapon was slim, but he enjoyed attempting the impossible.

Excited by a predators' thirst for blood, he laid the book down. He carefully drew his knees back and placed his heels on the ground, slowly pushing up as his back slid upward along the trunk he was leaning against. He had to help himself with his hands to overcome the inertia of static. The squirrel was motionless, despite the crackle of his polo against the bark.

Once standing, he slipped his hand into his pocket and grabbed his weapon of choice. He squeezed his fist to avoid the jingle that would make the little, dirty son of a bitch run away.

He pulled out the keys, as cautious as a child removing the rib in the game of Operation. When he got himself in a throwing position, the squirrel disappeared after his movement before he even had time to curse.

Disappointed, he sat back down in the shadow of the beech tree, one of the many on their huge estate.

As he re-opened the book, he went back to the last passage he had been reading. The anger it had caused him, put on hold because of the squirrel, was revived. The electricity of his wrath pushed him to get up without even realizing it.

He wasn't a happy person, despite the fact that he was the sole heir of his parents' millions and he was now healed in body and spirit—while others insinuated a sickness of the mind, he had never really believed he suffered from such a condition. The only thing that cheered him up was the awareness to continue, albeit with a few glitches, on the path which would lead him to *that line* where freedom was waiting for him. No other option had ever occurred to him before this fucking Dostoevsky came up with the bullshit that, passing that line, it would be worse.

He would abandon the book. He guessed from the first few chapters that the protagonist was too different from him.

"Fuck it," he hissed, violently throwing it against the beech.

Months of planning to build an insurmountable wall between himself and his years of torment: it was working great. It would keep working up to *that line* and beyond. There was no other option.

"No, fuck. No," he shouted, covering his hairless face with his hands, then running them among his straight, reddish blond hair.

He rejected the oppressive scenario described in those damn pages with all his being. He wished he hadn't read them. Now he could only wait for the stupid concept to evaporate from his brain.

At that very moment, he noticed that one of the maids was standing there looking at him. She had certainly heard him. Perhaps she had also seen him imitate a knife thrower with that insidious paper weapon.

"What's the matter, Erin?" he asked jovially.

The girl, fearful and petrified, standing on a sunny patch of green, remained mute. She looked at him, then down at the pages of the book scattered around the base of the beech, then back at him again.

"Arachnophobia," he said, laughing.

She frowned.

"A spider. It scared me to death. It was about to get on my neck. Brrr! I got up and threw the book at it. It's a normal reaction, I guess. You would've screamed too."

Erin's slight smile suggested that she was reassured.

He was a real genius. What a drag not to be able to share his bright ideas with anybody! Maybe one day *he* would write a book, something to pass the time in his old age.

"I'm fine now."

"I know, sir. I just came to tell you that your mother would like to talk to you."

"Okay, Erin. Thanks."

"She's waiting in the library."

"Where else?" he smiled—everybody in the house knew that library was her favorite room.

22 – Mom

He walked through his family's estate gardens for a while.

Before facing his mother, he had to silence the echoes of the discontent inspired by the Russian, and Nature guaranteed him the right support through its cathartic smells, noises and images.

He was stuck in a rut with his mother. She needed for him to be okay, otherwise she would start with her intolerable thoughtfulness, which drove him crazy. He was fine. Unhappy, but fine. Dostoevsky had presented him a problem, which would be easy enough to solve as long as it was done before his mother got involved and mucked everything up. The month of August was torn from the calendar and, within a couple of months, he would permanently bar all doors, windows and hatches on his past. He couldn't let this woman, who was unable to distinguish lower back pain from a spinal injury when it came to him, undermine his peace. The design of the last plan required extreme lucidity to identify any weak spots, especially because the only other pair of eyes he could count on were some glasses…

When he walked into the library half an hour later, she was sitting on the couch, concentrating on a book.

The only thing he had left in common with this slender and elegant fifty-year-old woman, besides a few chromosomes was a dislike of e-book readers. Those electronic slices of cheddar cheese had the power to replace a majestic room like this: they extracted and preserved the juice of a whole orchard with a click.

He had always agreed, but maybe it was time to evolve: you can't be stuck on an idea generated by an environment that no longer exists. After all, a change in habit was going to be necessary in order to cut ties with his past. And who knows, maybe some good could come from it, like more thinking before using an e-reader as a tool to kill spiders…

"Erin said you were looking for me."

"Yes, Jimmy," she said, sweet as always, inserting a bookmark among the pages and resting the book on the glass table. "Sit with me."

"I was just sitting on the grass. I don't want to dirty the sofa."

"It's just a sofa, honey. Come on."

Her love, dressed with kindness, got on his nerves but he couldn't show it.

He sluggishly patted his jeans and approached her. He sat down, leaving some space in between them.

"What are you reading?" he asked, crossing his legs and relaxing his back against the couch.

"You've been back from Florida for nearly two weeks and you haven't told us anything about your trip," she surprised him. "We were wondering how you spent your vacation, if you met someone… Things like that."

"It was a nice vacation."

"Did you stay at the resort the whole time or …"

"The beaches were amazing. White sand, water so clear you could count the shells on the bottom, and everything you could need on hand. Have you done something with your hair?"—he noticed that her usual long, brown hair had a little bit of color added to it.

"I'm glad you had fun. But have you met someone?"

"Mom, please."

"Jimmy, we're just worried about you."

"How many times do I have to tell you I'm fine?"

"Tell me!"

"I'm fine!" he laughed.

"I mean, talk to me," she replied, seriously.

Evidently she wasn't in the mood to joke or digress ...

"Remember the day you guys picked me up? What Dr. Watkins told you?"

She turned her gaze to the window.

He noticed her eyes were glistening.

"I'm trying to close that chapter in my life, and you're doing your best to keep it open. It makes all of the work over this past year meaningless."

She turned her head toward him. Yes, those were tears.

"You're right, Jimmy. Forgive me."

"By the way, you look younger with this hairstyle. If someone sees us together, they'd think you're my sister."

"Try to understand. Your father and I love you so much. We're so happy you're back home. You're the most important thing in our lives."

"I know."

"It hurts us to see you afflicted. We wa..."

"Who said I'm afflicted?" he laughed, hiding his sudden tension by scratching his nose.

"Even though you're calm and friendly, you're always on your own. You wander among the trees like a lost soul. What are we supposed to think, that you're bursting with happiness?"

"You're supposed to think that I need time to prepare myself to face Philadelphia society after what I went through. And it's not me saying that."

A reply hovered on her lips, but it didn't come out. She was struggling, so he decided to lay it on thick.

"The truth is that you guys are being selfish."

"Selfish?"

"You know what happened to me. I'm okay, now. I just need to apply what I learned to my everyday life. And that's something I have to do by myself. But you don't understand that and you get concerned. You can't bear the stress and deal with it by harassing me, when in fact I just need some peace to reorganize my life."

Now she was crying.

Maybe I finally shut her up!

But now it needed a touch of tender openness.

"I love you guys. I'm so grateful for all that you gave and are giving to me. I'm not mad at you. I understand why you did what you did. But now I have to follow my own path. I'm just asking you to show me the same understanding."

"But don't you think that starting to work at your father's office would be a good stepping stone in your new life?" she asked, wiping her eyes with the knuckle of her thumb.

Shit, he thought in a fit of anger that he hoped wasn't evident in his expression.

"All right, Mom. But not now."

"Then when, Jimmy? How long must we wait before re-embracing our son?"

"I'm here, mom. You can "embrace" me whenever you want."

"The thing is … I don't know … You seem so detached. Rational … Even when you joke … You're odd … We feel like we don't know you anymore. Talk to us. Allow us to know you."

Here we go again…

"Remember Mary Beth, Mr. Stevens's daughter? She's organizing to the party at Whisper Club next week. Mr. Stevens called me this morning and he sa…"

He cut her off with an eloquent snort. He wasn't able to control himself this time. And Mary Beth! The other cunt. Was it possible that she didn't know about Mary Beth? Maybe it was a trick to broach the topic.

"Sure I remember Mary Beth," he said, thinking that maybe he had to add her to the list, even though the fact that she lived in Philadelphia too made it dangerous. "At this time, I'm more into traveling than socializing. Period."

"But do you have an idea how worried your father and I are when you travel? We have no idea what you do, who you meet, where you stay … You just call when you arrive and when you're coming back, for God's sake."

"See? Told you. You're selfish."

What a great uppercut! He could see in her face that he had knocked her down. He thought about trying kindness again.

"Trust me, Mom. Have I always come back home safe and sound or not?"

"But…"

"Two months. Leave me alone for two more months. Then I'll stop traveling, start working with dad, go to Mary Beth's parties, and date Cinderella and Snow White. Just give me a break."

A shy ray of hope eased into her expression.

"You promise me, Jimmy? Do you promise me that after that you will let us get close to you?" she said, her eyes full of tears, caressing his cheek.

Whatever makes you stop fuckin' with me. "Okay, Mom. I promise."

23 – Hatred

His mother's talking-to was worse than a sermon from a stuttering pastor suffering from memory lapses. Before his frustration affected his behavior, he walked up to the second floor and barricaded himself in his bedroom. He needed to be alone with the visceral hatred that was burning inside of him.

At first, this hatred took possession of him and blew up in his face. But then, thanks to Dr. Watkins, he became aware of this feeling and learned how to manage it. That was necessary because the only way for him to live a normal life was to suppress his hatred. It had become the bilge of shame, humiliation, suffering, anger, frustration and helplessness caused by that damned day at the summer camp. A hatred so powerful that it changed his ideas of Good and Evil. He realized this was the case when he would commit, and enjoy, acts that in his youth he would have condemned others for. It was as if he now justified and applauded the jaguar devouring his prey instead of feeling sympathy for the 'poor helpless fawn'.

His hatred was the jaguar's hunger, but he had to keep it to himself. Is there anything more useless than explaining hunger to those who are sated?

People lived according to rules made during banquets. He wanted to sit down with them again, but his uncontrollable hunger would make him a greedy and unwanted tablemate. *To be banished in disgrace* would be his fate.

He would never accept what had happened to him. The proof was that his hatred strengthened rather than weakened by time.

Every day was a reminder of the injustice he was living. He had lost too many of them, one by one, without being able to stop the bleeding. He felt cheated by life. The mocking at school, memories of white walls, the irritated nurses and so many nutcases grazing in the recreation room around him, had all compounded his hatred. He needed to break down this fortress of pain to build a new life.

Now that I can, you bet I will! he had said to himself when they released him.

It was the only way to recover the balance to his soul that he was only pretending to maintain at this time.

Does God exist? To believe in him makes him real in any case.

This was the parachute he'd found while plummeting into the abyss of self-destruction. He had opened it and saved himself: by eliminating those who destroyed his life, he would make things right.

Believe it, and it will be real.

Yes, he just needed to believe.

Fuck Dostoevsky!

Since he had given himself this secret objective, he'd started to feel better. His first step was to create a persona capable of assuring everyone, including Dr. Watkins, that he was fine. Meanwhile he kept repeating that mantra in his mind. He did it every day, building an unshakeable foundation for his objective.

Objectives can have limitless power. A woman who dives into the ocean in Miami and tries to swim to an island in the Bahamas will drown after a couple of miles or less; but tell her that her child is alone and terrified on the island, and not even sharks will stop her. 'danger', 'reason', 'destiny', 'good' and 'evil' become groups of letters put randomly together.

To reach his objective, he first had to get out of the institute. This could only be achieved by talking to Dr. Watkins about the incident at the camp, while hiding his hatred. His parents gave credit to the doctor. It hadn't been easy, but the child's screams coming from the island amplified his fortitude and concentration. He was able to channel himself into the persona he created, and starting talking about himself as if he were a stranger. He must have done a convincing job: just a few months later Dr. Watkins guaranteed his parents that he was no longer in danger. Once at home, he dedicated himself to his great design. And it worked wonderfully: he would never have expected that his hatred would lead him to such moments of pure happiness. He did enjoy those moments. To breathe their terror when those girls realized who he was, to watch life gushing red from their heads, to hear the desperation in their last gasp while their open wide eyes were dampening, all of this took him from the freezing of unfairness they had forced him to, placing him in the warmth of justice where his heart could find peace for a while.

Peace and diligence were the supports that he built his plan upon and everything had gone perfectly. However, now he was torn. A new element was weakening the structure that he had created.

The impulse to do it quickly was becoming insistent and he didn't know whether to follow it or not. It could be the impatience of pulling up the nets to sell the day's catch and do away with the sea; or it might be an omen of a hurricane? Although there were no clouds in sight, the wrath of the waters seemed to loom closer.

He didn't watch the news or read newspapers. They would inevitably put pressure on him, causing him to make a fatal mistake. This subtle observation was a good psychological contraceptive to neutralize the human curiosity.

As far as he concerned, he'd already written his own fate if they caught him. After years as a lab monkey, he wouldn't live by hiding himself like a rat or waiting for 'Thanksgiving day' like a turkey in a cage. Now he was the jaguar, and so he would remain even in front of the hunter. Anyway, he felt safe in the savannah for now. That's why he wondered where the urgency to end it came from.

He looked for an answer in the Russian's book, but he had only found the horrible doubt that he would feel worse instead of healing in the end.

"Bullshit!"

And now his mother had started in on him as well. She was an idiot who didn't understand that he intended to end up in the very spot she wanted him to.

The son of a wealthy family, with the doors of a big and prosperous trucking company open to him, he had the world at his feet. He just had to forget his past and grab his future. This was the only way his wrath would stop fucking his regret, creating the hatred that stood between him and freedom.

These thoughts made something inside of him snap.

He got up from the bed and sat down at the computer, which was on standby. He pressed the space bar and a floral design appeared on the monitor, under which he typed the password.

Yes, man! What are you waiting for? he taunted.

He opened a folder with a hundred and twenty folders inside it, numbered consecutively. Each of which contained one-hundred Word files, which were also numbered, ranging in size between twenty and thirty KB. But he knew exactly which file contained the information he was interested in.

This information had cost him months of searching online, a nearly impossible task given that he started from a few rusty memories. But he had polished them up, and used them one by one to find out where those fuckin' Spice Girls had ended up.

Writing down Natalie Lunn's address, he got online and began looking for a flight to New Orleans, Louisiana …

24 – Cards

Natalie walked into the living room with the medicine box. She placed it on the table next to the screen door of a patio.

The intrusive sun of the late afternoon drew a frame of light—lopsided like a wooden cabin leaning on its side before collapsing—through the jambs on the beige floor; it was also trying to force its way in as a heat, but the air conditioning was a remarkable bouncer.

She had just returned from school.

"This one?" she asked her mother, showing her a tube of ointment.

"Yes. And give me a massage too."

Mrs. Lunn, carrying about two-hundred pounds of padding, badly distributed along her five foot seven inch frame, was wrapped in a dressing gown whose designs and colors evoked a tropical forest. She sat sprawled on the couch, both legs up on a stool and the gown open up to her pelvis; she suffered from rheumatism, which turned something as simple as a walk into a forced march to her.

"Where exactly does it ache?" asked Natalie, placing a chair next to the stool.

"There," she said, pointing to the side of her right shin.

Natalie sat down and covered that part of the leg with a strip of ointment. She began to spread it, wafting a strong scent of ammonia or something into the air.

"Do it upward," suggested Mrs. Lunn. "Doctor says it helps the circulation."

The movement seemed unnatural, like driving against traffic, but if the doctor said so …

"Well, what are you gonna do? Will you stay until the spineless idiot gets back?"

"I don't know if I can, mom."

"C'mon, Nat. It's just a couple of days."

"I'm sleeping here, tonight. But tomorrow, we'll see."

"Him and his freakin' jazz," grunted Mrs. Lunn.

Natalie continuing her massage couldn't help but smile at her mother's anger.

"To go and enjoy Chicago while leaving me here alone, when he knows that I'm in pain."

"He goes to the Festival every year. You know it's important to him."

"But it wasn't the right time, now. Plus we both know why he actually went there …"

"What do you mean?"

"Further down," said Mrs. Lunn, turning herself a few degrees to the left to better expose the sore area of her leg.

Natalie went along with her wishes, although she had noticed her frown.

"Why do you think he went to Chicago?"

"Who knows …"

"Why, mom?" she persisted, her curiosity spurred by the sarcasm in her mother's tone.

"'Cause it's easier for men to do it out of town."

It took her a few seconds to realize what she meant, because no one wants to picture their own parents in that scenario.

"Come on!" Natalie said, now manipulating her mother's flabby and wrinkled calf. "Dad's not that kind of man."

Mrs. Lunn didn't comment, but her grimace said it all, *Yeah, right!*

"At 65, mom? At that age you think he still ...?"

Her grimace changed a bit, *That geriatric bitch ...*

"You saw it in the cards?"

"Nat, I've known your father for 35 years. I don't need cards to read his mind."

"But you took a peek, didn't you?" Natalie winked.

"Not at all. Cards are nonsense."

"You say it's nonsense, but your friends believe in it."

"That's rubbish 'cause there's no connection between people and those cards."

"I think the connection is the person who asks for the reading."

"Nat, you wanna do the other leg too?"

She nodded, trying to mask her displeasure due to the change of subject.

"I really think I should get surgery," snorted Mrs. Lunn. "I'm only 63. Maybe I can hit 90, but I don't wanna get there with a walker."

"You know you can't have the surgery if you don't lose twenty pounds first."

"I know," she sighed, afflicted.

"Mom?"

"Yes?"

"Would you do me a favor?"

"What favor?"

"Would you read the cards for me?"

Mrs. Lunn stared at her as if she were an IRS agent. Then she stretched a corner of her mouth, giving off an inaudible grunt, and directed her eyes on her own knees.

"Come on, mom. Only once."

"Maybe I should go to a dietician."

"Mom?"

"Not a dietician. What do they call the other ones?"

"You mean a nutritionist?" Natalie comforted her, but not forgetting her own priorities.

"That's it. Vivien went to her cousin's niece who is a nutritionist. She says she's good."

"Mom?"

"You know how much she lost in the first two months?"

"You do it for everyone, for God's sake," Natalie mumbled, continuing her massage mildly. "Even for Rebecca's son. I remember. Why do you always do this when it's me who's asking?"

"Because they are friends."

"And I'm your daughter."

"Exactly. I can tell you the truth. It would be rude to them. They come 'cause they need to hear certain things, and I'm doing it as a favor. But they fool themselves 'cause reading cards is nonsense."

"You don't wanna do it 'cause you're not in the mood right now, are you?"

Mrs. Lunn shook her head no.

"Let's do this," Natalie tried again. "I'm gonna do it by myself. You just read them."

"So you dirty them with your hands."

Natalie moved her eyes down her mother's withered legs. They looked like two shrunken tree trunks with the bark peeled off. She felt really sad seeing that her mother was so indifferent to her own concerns. Her sadness was probably evident on her face …

"All right," Natalie heard her say suddenly. "Go get them. They're in the top drawer of my bedside table."

A rush of joy brightened her mood. She stood up and ran to the bathroom. As she washed her hands, she also washed away the anxiety from her heart: she hadn't spoken about that matter to anyone yet. Now it was time, because constantly mulling it over was taking its toll on her sleep and work.

She hurried into the bedroom and grabbed the stiff cardboard box that contained the mini tarot cards. It was a small deck of forty playing cards, perhaps European or Asian, not even her mother knew. They were the size of credit cards, but much thinner. Even though it was a family tradition passed down for generations from mother to daughter, Mrs. Lunn was the self-declared last link in the chain of that superstition, since her sister only had Tim. That's why she hadn't wanted to teach Natalie how to read them—actually, she would have hidden this stupid ritual she had found herself unwillingly keeper of, but Natalie caught her several times practicing it with her friends when she was a teenager.

"So?" said her mother, shuffling the cards.

Natalie sat down. She sighed and feeling her cheeks blush spoke.

"I met a man."

"Go on."

"I only talked to him once, but it was a long and intense conversation."

"What do you wanna know?" asked her mother, putting the deck face down beside herself on the couch.

"What he thinks of me."

Mrs. Lunn raised her eyebrows.

"The fact is that we met in some circumstances ... you know ... Let's say I'm afraid I didn't make a good first impression," she said in one breath, embarrassed after the latest news from Detroit.

"Cut."

Natalie did and her mother began to arrange the cards in six groups of four, symmetrical like the windows of a building. Still beside her, face down.

"What's his name?"

"Landon."

"What does he do for a living?"

"Detective."

"Detective?" her mother frowned again. "How did you meet a cop?"

"At a student's party," she down played it, since she made Tim promise to keep the secret and not upset the family—she told him the police said that there was nothing to be worried about ...

She feared more questions, but fortunately her mother focused on the cards. She turned around the groups one at a time and studied them for half a minute.

"So, mom? What does he think of me?"

"It says he doesn't think of you at all. I see another woman in his thoughts. Happy?"

"Wife? Girlfriend? Date?"

"I don't see a marriage. But I can see a bond."

The exciting fantasies she had created in those few days, especially during her lonely nights, were crushed by the steamroller of reality.

"Can you do it again?"

"I will, but I told you. It's nonsense. These pieces of paper have nothing to do with this Landon guy."

"Gotcha, but now ... will you?"

Mrs. Lunn puffed. She gathered the cards and shuffled again.

"Cut."

Natalie shut her eyes. She recalled Landon's face and, at the moment when his smile became so clear it dazzled her mind, she cut.

Mrs. Lunn put the cards as before, in two rows of three. Then she turned them around.

"What do they say?" she pressed her.

"Nat, I don't wanna lie to you. It says the same as before."

"A girlfriend?"

"Probably."

The cynicism with which her mother was maneuvering the steamroller was amazing! And if there was need for additional leveling before, it was now unnecessary. Her fantasies were officially one with the ground. However, it was better this way. To uproot illusions before they settle in the heart makes things easier. And surely, less painful.

"Don't let this nonsense put you down, kiddo."

"Two out of two. Maybe it's not nonsense."

"I'm gonna do it again."

"Wait. Can you see if he's in my future?" she asked, since she didn't want to hear her repeat that Landon had somebody else.

Mrs. Lunn got back on the hellish machine.

"Tell me, what does he look like?" she asked while shuffling.

"Tan skin and brown eyes, athletic, thick black hair pulled back, beard barely visible over his face, six feet tall, a few years older than me, I guess."

"I bet he's ugly as hell ..."

Her mother's smile softened her disappointment. Maybe it could help her live with it if the Supreme Court rejected her hope too.

"It says there is a light-skinned man for you. Or Light brown. It also says there is a journey."

"A journey?" winced Natalie, while Henke and Disney World popping up from a lost corner of her memory.

"But about a good looking brown-skinned detective, not even a shadow."

While Henke was fighting Landon in her heart, her phone ringtone brought her mind back into the living room. She looked for it in the bag hanging on her chair.

"Hello?" she said, not recognizing the number.

"Natalie?"

"Yes?"

"This is Detective Vitman. Do you remember me?"

The most unexpected and colorful fireworks exploded in the bleak sky.

"Sure. Just a second, please," she said, tense because her mother was staring at her.

She got up and looked for some privacy outside the patio.

"What can I do for you?" she asked as she closed the screen door.

"I need to talk to you."

The sudden memory of the news overwhelmed her with shame.

"Yeah, I saw it," she blushed. "They got him."

"Huh?"

"Mallory Jackson's murderer. I saw they took him in."

"Oh. No, I'm not calling you about that."

Her embarrassment vanished. He sounded like he was in a good mood, although his serious tone kept her on tenterhooks. Maybe he was just nervous.

"Then what for?" she asked, vaguely flirty.

"Um ... Could we meet up?"

"Well ... I guess ... Sure. Do you want me to come to the police station?"

"No, you don't need to. What about the Starbucks on King Street?"

It was beginning to sound like a date ...

"Okay, Landon."

"Can you make it within an hour?"

Joy was about to burst out in her voice. She had to wet the fuse to avoid ending up like Juliet caught out of the balcony.

"Um ... by six ... uh, yes. I think I can."

"Great, Natalie. See you later."

"Later."

When she returned to the living room, she hadn't even closed the screen door when ...

"You okay, Nat? Something happened?"

"You know what?"

"What?"

"I think you're right about the cards. It's nonsense."

25 – Summer Camp

Natalie got at Starbucks eight minutes early.
She had planned to join Landon at 6:10, apologizing for being late. It was a good strategy to disguise her joy, because she was afraid she wouldn't be able to feign indifference when she met him. In fact, shortness of breath due to running, embarrassment caused by her delay, and the need to explain herself were all credible reasons to justify the intensity that would surely be on her face once seeing him again. However, her plan failed because, as she got ready, as well as while she drove, she had forgotten to check the time, too busy extracting her fantasies from the asphalt...
It was 5:53. She parked at the curb in front of *Talbots*, in the shadow of one of the palm trees that lined the road. It would take a minute for her to reach the coffee shop.
A minute and a half if I walk slowly.
Then she had to leave the car at 6:09.
And the panting?
No panting if she walked slowly. She had to get out at 6:10 and run up to the shop.
And what am I supposed to do here till 6:10?
Better to go for a ride.
Yeah, she thought, with a smart grin and turning the keys. *So I won't risk* ...
A tap on the window car startled her: recognizing Landon through the glass, seeing him leaning toward her, smiling and perplexed at the same time, made her feel like she had just got caught picking food out of her teeth.

"Everything alright?"

She smiled back at him, feeling her cheeks grow hot. She nodded at him to wait, while removing the keys from the ignition and placing them, phone and lip gloss into her bag—actually she needed a few seconds to elaborate an excuse about why she'd started the engine.

"I forgot something at my mother's," she said as she got out. "Since I was early, I thought ..."

"If you need to, just go. I can wait."

His tone was polite, but a gray cloud drifted across his face. If he had thought her kind of weird, she wasn't doing much to make him change his mind.

"Don't worry. I'll go later."

Landon looked charming in a checkered shirt in different shades of blue under a black leather jacket with casual dark trousers. It seemed impossible that he hadn't been taken yet. No leash on his ring finger, though.

"Shall we go?" he said.

Once in the shop, they ordered two coffees and made their way to the table by the shop window facing the street.

"How was your day?" began Landon, when they were seated.

"Fine, even though this is one of the busiest periods at school. What about yours?"

"What are you studying?"

"Actually, I'm a teacher," she said, pleased to have shifted the center of embarrassment toward him—or so she deduced from his facial expression.

"Then, what do you teach?" he smiled.

"I teach English to foreigners who have come to the US to learn it."

"Interesting."

"Yes. Not as interesting as being a detective, but I enjoy it. You meet so many people, learn about different cultures …" she said, picking her coffee.

She sipped, keeping her eyes on him.

Landon hesitated, as if he was distracted by the convertible parked next to the trash can right before the entrance of the shop. Then he spoke again.

"You talked about Detroit on the phone."

At the memory of the news, an invincible force of gravity drew her gaze …

"I didn't understand what you meant at the moment," he continued. "Then I thought about it. I suppose you didn't hear about the latest news."

"What news?" she frowned.

"The guy they caught is just a common car thief. It seems he had just stolen Mallory's car at a mall parking lot. But they said he has nothing to do with the murder."

"Really?"

"That's what the police released to the media this morning."

She was confused and didn't know what to think. She was trying to organize her thoughts, when he continued.

"I asked you to meet me because we finished that research, as promised."

Too many thoughts. Too many emotions. She couldn't keep up in the conversation.

"Your friends, Cindy Cook and Nina Arkin. Remember?"

"Oh. Yeah, yeah. I remember. Sure."

Those names, paired with his intense expression, shocked her. She realized that the attraction to him and the embarrassment that she felt since that day at the police station had overshadowed the reason why she went to the police in the first place. Sudden and scary scribbles fell among the lines of love she had secretly been writing for several days.

"What did you find out?" she asked, apprehensive.

Landon took a sip of his coffee.

"Natalie, the news I have isn't going to be easy to hear."

"I'm listening."

"Well, Cindy worked as an escort in Nashville."

She didn't expect that her old friend ended up like that, although she wasn't too surprised.

"Ten months ago, they found her dead in the small apartment where she received her clients."

"Dead?" she shivered in a thin voice.

"Murdered."

Now she was definitely surprised.

"I'd rather not go into details. The descriptions wouldn't be pleasant," Landon said. "Let's say ... um ... The evidence makes the police think that the murderer was her last client."

"And Nina?" she asked, shaking like a flag in a storm.

"She lived in Boston since she got married two and a half years ago. Her husband reported her missing last May 7th."

She could feel the color drain from her face.

"The police are still searching, but she's missing at the moment," added Landon.

She was very sorry for her friends, but her own safety put those shattered lives on the fringe of her attention.

"Do you think I'm in danger?" she murmured, smiling nervously.

"Frankly, I don't know what to tell you."

Fear spurred her wish for protection, but seeing his doubtful expression stopped her.

"Do you feel like telling me more about your relationship with those girls?"

"Our relationship?"

"I keep thinking that it's a strange coincidence, but if it wasn't … Do you think it's possible that anyone would be mad at you girls?"

"After twelve years?"

"It sounds far-fetched, I know. But it's up to you. If you want, we can end this conversation right now and talk about something else," he smiled, then drank his coffee again.

She was under the impression that he was interested in her case. She tried to listen to her own instincts: the alarm bells still ringing.

"It was a summer camp for girls," she began, trying to dig up the past buried under tons of time. "The five of us bonded right away because we bunked together and also because we had many interests in common. Such as the Spice Girls. I remember we spent a lot of time on the archery field and canoeing on the lake. We were busy with so many activities, but the moments I remember best are the evenings, before going to bed."

"Why are those memories stronger?"

"Because we were talking about … talking about boys," she broke into a giggle.

"Oh. And can you think of anything … how can we say … creepy? Some accident that may have upset your cheerfulness? Maybe you discussed it during one of those evenings."

She inserted the film of that summer in her memory's projector, but the video quality was poor, as if shot by an amateur in the thirties.

"I don't seem to remember anything *creepy*, Landon."

"Maybe a girl with whom you all had a fight. Or an attendant who made a pass at one of you …"

"A girl?"

He frowned.

"Do you think it might be a woman?"

"If we want to try and spot a possible link, we can't leave anything out."

"Yeah, but you said that Cindy was killed by her last client."

"According to Nashville PD, she was killed by a man. No doubt. But it could have been set up by anyone, and given that there were no guys at the camp … I don't know, I'm just trying to think of something to help you remember."

"I see. Thanks, Landon."

"Maybe you guys bullied someone who hasn't forgotten. Or some girl wanted to join you and you rejected her … What's up?"

An episode had permeated the mist that separated consciousness and oblivion. Landon had stumbled upon a lode in the boundless mine of her memory leading to an ambiguous moment of that exciting summer—'ambiguous' because she had found it in the *Beautiful Memories* folder, and she couldn't understand why she had stored it in there.

"You want me to take you to the police station?"

"Huh?"

"So you can talk to a female detective."

In theory, it would be less embarrassing; in reality, it was better to find the courage to confide in him. They knew each other a little bit better by now; plus the idea of telling it all over again didn't appeal to her.

"What are you doing?" she asked when she saw him pull out his phone.

"You're blushing. I assume you remembered something delicate. Let me check if detective Peterson is available."

"No, Landon. That's not necessary. I can talk to you about it."

He put his phone and elbows on the table, ready to listen.

"My God, where do I start ... There was this boy, I don't even remember his name. He was same age as us. Perhaps a year younger, I don't know. He was the camp's owners' nephew, or a family friend, I'm not really sure. However, he was clearly an introvert," she added, with memories that were gradually resurfacing. "He often walked in the woods alone. He was at the archery section when no one was there. When you saw a lone canoe on the lake, you could bet that it was him and an instructor. He either ate in his room or in the kitchen with the cooks, because he never showed up at the dining hall."

"What happened?"

"Cindy picked on him. But it was a prank. We just wanted to have fun. You know when you're in a group ..."

"What did she do to him?"

"She was the oldest out of the five of us. She had already had some experiences. She was po..."

"Experiences like ...?"

"With guys," she said, avoiding his gaze.

"I see."

"Cindy was positive that he was a virgin. She started saying that she would make a man out of him, talking about trophies, and we encouraged her. We thought it was funny."

Digging up those moments, she felt terrible. She couldn't believe that she herself, the one who was so sensitive and respectful to the others, had been participating in such a bad joke. She looked at Landon. She got the feeling that the topic was making him as uncomfortable as she was; in addition, now that the memory was taking shape, her anxiety had begun to slow down her desire to speak ...

"So Cindy brings him into the room one afternoon. We hide in the closet and spy on them through the slats of the shutters."

The shame forced her to stop again.

"We had no malicious intentions or anything. It was just fun for us, a story to tell our friends. That's all. Now I realize that we were bitches for doing that, but it all seemed so innocent at the time."

"Of course, Natalie. I did worse things when I was fifteen," he said in a reassuring smile.

"Yeah. Thoughtlessness is normal at that age. I would never do such a thing today. Unfortunately, camping with friends, immaturity ..."

"And how did the situation evolve?"

"The boy was a schmuck. The emotion overwhelmed him and Cindy started teasing him. She knew we were watching."

"And ...?"

"And ... and nothing. Eventually he saw us and got embarrassed."

"Embarrassed enough to want revenge?"

"Maybe, but ... twelve years later?" she said, reinforcing the question mark with a skeptical face.

"Besides that episode, do you remember anything else that may have sparked someone's rage?"

"No, Landon. This is the only bad thing we did. I'm sure of it."

He sighed and pursed his lips like he was contemplating what she had said.

"So, what do you think?" she asked impatiently.

"Let's look at the facts. Three women were killed and the investigations haven't led to anything yet. A fourth woman is missing, and we don't know anything about her for four months. All four knew each other, although they hadn't hung out together in a long time. We live in a country where nearly fifteen thousand people are murdered every year, and those are just the confirmed victims."

"So?"

"Their common past makes me think. What are the chances that four victims, living in different states, know each other? And now we also have a potential suspect, although the twelve-year time gap raises doubts about the matter. In my experience, I wouldn't discard the hypothesis without first checking it out. At least until investigators find a lead."

"So you think I am in danger, don't you?"

"Do you remember that boy's name?"

She shook her head, afflicted—she didn't feel like telling him the last part of the story.

"Or where he's from, something that could help us find him …" insisted Landon.

The information she kept to herself wouldn't answer his questions anyway. Then, she had an idea.

"The camp managers might remember him."

"Great! Um … Listen, Natalie. If this guy is really involved with the murders, the case would go to the Feds, and I can't just go to them with the story you've told me. They would tell me to get lost in ten seconds. If it's 'only' about ordinary people, they will demand evidence before raising a finger. However, I have a dear friend in the FBI. I could talk about it off the record, if you agree."

"I admit I would feel better finding out that our hypothesis is far-fetched."

"Okay. There's only one problem."

"What problem?"

"You should talk to him."

"Me?"

"He's my friend, but I can tell him the story just like that, without evidence, witnesses, clues or anything concrete."

"I understand, Landon. That's fine with me."

"He works at the federal office in Columbia. You think you could go?"

"You mean ... to go there on my own?"

"Of course not," he smiled. "I'll take you there. It's just a two-hour drive."

"Okay. Let me know when, so I can get the day off at work."

26 – Duty

It was 11am and the sun shone warmly, as it did during most of the year in South Carolina. Some scattered clouds made the sky look like an endless turquoise sheet with white polka dots.

Landon was driving his dark gray Audi A4 in the middle lane on I-26. Direction, the capital city.

Natalie sat beside him.

When they left Charleston, the weather and the situation they were facing had provided good topics for conversation; but halfway there, they ran out of steam and had spent the last ten minutes in silence.

Landon was forcing himself to maintain a professional relationship with her. He made this decision the day before outside the coffee shop, the very moment he had noticed her sitting behind the wheel of her car, lost in a charming smile. The feeling was like a passer-by swept up by an unstoppable truck.

He had the tendency to mix work and his private life. He was aware of it. Actually, he did it on purpose.

It's more comfortable to hide ourselves behind the legit screen of professional ethics. Everything becomes easier.

He believed he needed to connect with the people he was supposed to help. Only in this way could he give his best, since *All are equal before the law* is not necessarily a synonym for justice. Individuals are different from each other, and so are their cases: how can it always be fair applying one-sided rule for situations with innumerable sides? But then, too many exceptions, legitimate and illegitimate, would undermine the vital order of society.

The law is an essential dog to keep the flock together, but it doesn't change the fact that each sheep has its own story was his new conviction.

His colleagues, including Devin, had a more traditional approach, avoiding any personal involvement. He understood them: in fact, that was his *modus operandi* until about a year ago. At that time he began seeing his work according to this new perspective, starting to get familiar with each of the sheep that crossed his path. And he was happy about that because the satisfaction he got was a priceless reward to him. However, he felt he didn't have to continue on this path with Natalie: this wasn't a dead-end like the others, it had a definite destination. For example, with Clarita, Carlos and Curlene—him and Devin finally went to the restaurant and now he was waiting to hear from her if the trick had worked—he was spurred by a disinterested feeling; with Natalie, instead, he felt a strong interest. And he didn't want to take advantage of his position to pursue it. Intimately speaking, the matter was different. Preventing his mind from lingering on the blonde's face as well as the thought of her from altering his heartbeat, was no different than expecting the strap of a slingshot to remain tense even after shooting the stone. But at least he could control his behavior, keeping it according with what is required of any police officer.

No interference from feelings.

During their chat at Starbucks, he had brilliantly trapped the emotions that had lived within him between the first meeting and that moment. He played his role as a detective impeccably. But between the chat and the trip to Columbia there were a couple of sleepless nights spent reliving that intense interlude, with Natalie's face becoming the catalyst of all his needs and desires.

Now it was hard to appear unaffected by the woman who had revived his heart. The only way to do that was to focus on the purpose of the trip. So he thought about a possible solution for three or four unsolved murders, the safety of a citizen asking for protection, how good it felt to help his neighbor, and also the best angle from which to present the situation to Jeff—the fear that Jeff may tease him, especially in front of Natalie, and to have come so far on the basis of questionable evidence, bothered him a lot.

Yes, he was going to Columbia just to do his duty as a policeman. He would have done it for any citizen in Natalie's situation, probably ...

"Are you worried?"

Natalie's voice sounded in the car like a flute sustaining a note, although it effected on his sensitivity like a thump of a bass drum.

"I was wondering what Jeff would say about this story," he said, forcing his heart to wear a uniform.

"Your friend in the FBI?"

"Uh-huh."

"What kind of person is he?" she was curious.

"Outspoken, I would say. If he were less blunt, he would be a really nice fellow. However, he's a good guy. Very conscientious."

"You were in the Academy together?"

"Not exactly," he said, with a grimace and a quarter of a smile.

"What do you mean?"

"We met in some circumstances ... you know," he mumbled, speeding up and leaving the wake of the truck they had been following for a while behind.

"Sorry, Landon. I didn't mean to pry."

"That's okay. You were trying to make conversation, since I'm playing the mummy."

From the way she laughed, his joke must have dispelled the discomfort that he may have caused her with the sudden overtaking or his evasive answer—he wouldn't give her a good impression of himself by telling her about Jeff.

"Have you ever been to Egypt?"

"Uh?" he said, amused. "Where did Egypt come from?"

"Well, you mentioned the mummy ..."

They were lost in subdued silence for a few seconds. Then a laugh slipped from his mouth.

"Oh my, it came to me like that," she blushed.

"Haha, your question is pertinent. I was lost in thought, that's why I didn't get it."

"Sure. I guess your mind is well trained in terms of associations because of your job," she said, relaxing.

"Yeah. Not to brag, but associations of ideas and deductions are my forte ... But no, I have never been to Egypt. Have you?"

"Nope. But I had a student from Cairo once."

Focused on taming his inner emotional chaos, he realized he knew very little about her. The thought that she might be involved with somebody gave a good squeeze to his stomach; but he wouldn't give in the temptation to 'accidentally' introduce the topic. It wouldn't be professional—or he just didn't want to know ...

"You told me that you're an English teacher."

"So you did listen when I spoke!" she retorted, benign irony in her voice.

"I know, I look distracted sometimes. Actually I scan, observe, think," he played along. "I mean, I knew you're a teacher thirty seconds after you stepped into my office."

"Well, blow me down!"

He noticed something flirtatious in her tone—or maybe he had noticed it because he wished it was really like that ...

"How did you figure it out?" she asked.

"From the polished way you express yourself. From how you cross your arms on your chest, looking patient and inquisitive at the same time. Plus from the confidence that you show when you speak, it's clear that you're used to addressing an audience."

"Really?" she said, surprised and flattered.

"Nope."

Subdued silence again.

This time, she broke it with a laugh, enticing him to do the same.

27 – Jeff

Agent Jeff Fillmore had arranged to meet Landon outside the café of Finlay Park.

Natalie didn't often go to the capital—the last time was six years earlier—plus the involvement of the FBI made her anxious; so she just followed Landon's instructions.

They crossed paths with a couple pushing a stroller down the smooth incline leading to the café. All of a sudden, a guy who was resting with his elbows on the railing—she noticed him right away because there were no other people—smiled at them and stood up.

"Is that your friend Jeff?" she whispered nervously at Landon, while the tan, thin, gray-haired gentleman in jacket and tie headed toward them.

"Don't worry. Everything will be fine."

"Hey, son," said Jeff, a couple of inches taller than Landon.

"How you doing, master?"

"I can't wait to quit and enjoy my retirement-checks," he said, hugging Landon in that masculine way that tough guys have.

"Tasteful as always," said Landon, after looking at his figure.

"One of the Feds' handicaps. I got a leather jacket like yours, but I can only wear it off duty."

"You kidding me?"

"I look ten years younger!"

Natalie watched and listened to them. They had to be very good friends, despite the clear age difference—by the slight wrinkles on his face and corners of eyes, Jeff must be older than fifty.

"Natalie, this is Jeff," said Landon. "Jeff, Natalie."

"Nice to meet my godson's new flame," Jeff said, shaking her hand.

She was so surprised by his words—as rough as his handshake—that she couldn't help but blush.

"Cut it out, Jeff," grumbled Landon, who was also turning red. "Don't listen to him, Natalie. He's like that, he thinks it's funny to embarrass people."

"Especially those who I meet for the first time," he winked.

"Pleasure to meet you, Jeff," she smiled, although the 'pleasure' was more like wearing shoes that were a couple of sizes too small …

"Let's go for a drink?" suggested Landon.

"No. I have to go back to the office because I have a matter to attend to. I'm sorry, but something came up an hour ago. You were already on your way, otherwise I would've told you not to make the trip."

"Oh, I see. Well, thanks for your time, then."

"You're welcome, son. So, tell me about this seemingly bizarre situation," said Jeff, mimicking quotation marks with his fingers as he said the last three words.

She felt like an idiot, so much so that she couldn't even get angry with Landon for the way he must have depicted her case.

Landon looked at her for a second, visibly uncomfortable, while Jeff was smirking.

They were standing by the railing. She faced them as if they were the other two angles of a small isosceles triangle, with Landon on the short side.

"These are the facts," began Landon, pulling out a notepad he had summarized them on.

"Cindy Cook, twenty-nine, murdered in Nashville last November. Emily Wallace, twenty-seven, her body was fished out of the Colorado River, near Austin, in May, but the autopsy says that she was shot in February. Mallory Jackson, twenty-seven, gunned down on the street at Dearborn, near Detroit, three weeks ago. Nina Arkin, twenty-seven, disappeared in Boston on May 7, no news about her."

"Okay. So we have ... three women, perhaps four, same age, killed in different times and places. And ...?"

"They all knew each other."

Jeff had spoken with the same uninterested expression as he had listened to Landon, but the last detail changed his face.

"Natalie was friends with all four," continued Landon. "They met twelve years ago, at a summer camp in Maine. However, their friendship lasted just that summer. Now she's the only one left of that group and we were wondering if we should be worried."

Jeff watched him, his lips and eyebrows twitching as if he was analyzing the situation.

"Tell me, Landon. How do you fit in the story?"

"Natalie recognized two of them on the news and came to the police station. She told me about the summer camp, we made some inquiries and found out that the other two are missing."

"What are you getting at, son?"

"I brought Natalie with me 'cause there's more."

Jeff looked at her for a moment before returning to Landon. She was intimidated by this man's attitude, more and more uncomfortable to her feet ...

"It was a girls only camp, but there was a boy around their age too. Cindy and her friends played a bad joke on him, so we think that ..."

"What kind of joke?"

She had feared this moment since the departure from Charleston.

"It seems that this boy was inexperienced ... and ... Cindy thought to help him ... break the ice."

"C'mon, son," Jeff snapped. "We're all adults here. Natalie knows what they've done. I guess she told you about it."

She avoided Jeff's gaze by turning to Landon, who remained looking at him and nodded.

"I don't have much time and your worries seem exaggerated. But I know you, Landon. I trust you and your instincts. If you drove all the way up here, you have your reasons. So spit it out fast."

Landon's features hardened.

"Cindy thought the guy was a virgin, and decided to have sex with him. Natalie and the other three hid in the closet to spy on them. The boy couldn't do it and Cindy began to tease him, until he realized he was being watched."

A grin formed on Jeff's face, but it was soon replaced by a grim expression.

"We were only fifteen," murmured Natalie, crushed in every way by Landon's tale and Jeff's reaction. "It was a joke. We didn't mean to hurt anybody."

"Of course, Natalie," Landon comforted her. "Nobody is judging you. We're just looking at the situation. Right, Jeff?"

"Absolutely. So, you're assuming that the boy was traumatized to the point of seeking revenge ... Is that what brought you here?"

"What do you think about that?" said Landon, uncertain. "Four out of five of those girls were taken down one after the other. That's a fact."

"Listen, I can see your concern. However, we shouldn't overlook the fact that the incident took place twelve years ago. Tell me if I'm wrong."

"You're not wrong."

"Twelve years is a long time, Landon."

"Yes it is, Jeff."

She was observing them. They were indulging her, but they looked at each other as if they were discussing something that hadn't been said. This impression tightened the grip of embarrassment and shame.

"So, Landon. What do you want me to do?"

"We just want to track down this guy. Natalie can't remember his name, but he seemed to be a nephew or an acquaintance of the camp managers. That's why they must know him," Landon added, taking the sheet of paper away from the notepad where he'd written down name and address of the place. "You know how these things work. A cop from Charleston can't just go to Maine and interrogate people. The only way we could get that information would be to tell the whole story to the local police. But I don't know what credit they would give me."

"Good point," said Jeff.

"You Feds could easily find out the boy's name and check how he's doing."

"Okay, Landon. I can do that," said Jeff, accepting the paper. "I think we'll get it within a couple of hours with a few calls."

"Thanks, Jeff. I knew I could count on you."

"We'll meet back in the same place. I'll call you later."

28 – The Past

Landon asked her to join him in the cafè to get something to eat while they waited for Jeff's call, but she preferred to take a walk because her stomach was in knots. Their meeting with Jeff had made her very uncomfortable. Moreover, the temperature was pleasant and she wanted to stay in the open air, especially since she had never visited the park before.

She understood that the situation was uncomfortable for Landon too, despite his bond with Jeff. Nevertheless, she couldn't stifle the feeling of blame toward him, even now that they were strolling in that corner of nature saved by the ravenous advance of concrete. She hoped he would give her the opportunity to vent, but, as if he felt something was off, he stood by leaving the responsibility to fill the silence to the birds' chirping and voices of other visitors who gradually passed by.

"Okay," Natalie thought out.

Landon looked dazed.

"May I ask you something?"

"Sure."

"Why did you bring me here?" she said, in the friendliest way that her mood would allow.

"What do you mean why did I bring you here?"

A smile had spiced his response. While he probably meant to relax her, she found herself irritated by it.

"My presence seemed quite pointless. Actually, you could've spoken more freely if I hadn't been in the way."

He stopped and looked at her.

She could tell he felt sorry.

He resumed walking, his hands in his jacket pockets. She rushed to get back to his side.

"Sorry, Landon. But I really don't understand."

"Hindsight, your complaint is fair," he mumbled, his head down.

"What's that supposed to mean?"

"When Jeff said he'd meet us, I thought we would've gone to his office and talked in front of his colleagues. Once I explained your situation to them, they might have had some questions that I didn't think to ask you. That's what I had assumed would happen. I brought you here because … what was I supposed to tell him if I were alone? *Hold on, let me call her and ask?* And maybe you wouldn't even pick up the phone because you were busy."

It was the first time she considered the matter from Landon's point of view: it was clear that he had only tried to help her. He was interested in her case, when most cops would have just gotten rid of her with a pseudo-reassuring *Don't worry, Miss. You'll see, it's just a coincidence. If you noticed something strange, call 911.* But he had personally escorted her to an FBI agent, 120 miles from home. And he never made her feel like she owed him. These thoughts helped her process those disturbing fifteen minutes with Jeff as an emissary of idiocy and shame.

"Natalie, I'm sorry for embarrassing you. I thought Jeff would've understood the situation and been more tactful. The glitch that put him in such a hurry must be something serious, 'cause I assure you, he's not the insensitive jerk you just met."

"How long have you known him?"

He turned toward her. He looked surprised by the friendly tone she'd spoken with.

She was walking at his side. Their arms touched one another with every step. She liked it.

"Jeff, I mean," she smiled to assure him that the storm had passed.

"Oh. It's should be … it's nine years."

"Frankly, I expected him to be younger."

"How so?" he said, copying her relaxed smile.

"I don't know. Maybe too much TV."

Despite his pensive expression, she felt the tension between them dissolve.

"I fell in with the wrong crowd when I was twenty. We lived in Baltimore."

This sudden confession surprised her. It was like being among the people on the pier waving to the cruise travelers and, a moment later, finding herself on the boat with them.

"You know, sometimes I wonder whether it's worse to grow up without any guidance or with a bad one," said Landon, meanwhile a noise, like the pounding of water, grew more intense as they walked. "My father left when I was eight. He abandoned us and we never heard from him again."

"I'm sorry," she murmured, touched by the bitterness caught in his eyes.

"Don't be sorry, Natalie. He was a bad man. I don't have any clear memories, but my mother told me a couple of things when I grew up. Him disappearing from our lives, especially hers, was a blessing."

She gave him a nod of understanding.

"A year later, a hit-run driver took my sister from us. She was only nine. If we could've afforded a specialized clinic, maybe she'd be still with us. But my mother did what she could. She was a secretary at a driving school."

He wasn't telling her about himself because he wanted her pity, she assumed; but whatever she would say at that moment, it would have been impossible not to express her sincere sorrow for him.

"Lack of money, a meaningless future, disreputable friends, eventually I found myself involved with … with some drug dealers."

At first, she was shocked by his admission. Then she began to think about it. She didn't know him well enough to say what kind of person he was, but she imagined that a police officer wouldn't go around telling questionable things of his own past. She found herself honored by such a trust. Or maybe he was doing it just to restore a balance between them, since she had confessed him about her stunt at the summer camp.

"Not that I was a drug dealer," he clarified, apprehension in his voice. "They used me and many other guys for deliveries. We were the link between an organization and some drug dealers."

Her curiosity to learn more about his redemption caused the forceful return of her attraction to him.

"One day the Feds did a blitz. Other couriers and I were in the depot of a pipelines factory in the outskirts of the city. It was the place where we gathered to pick up dope and dealers' addresses. Suddenly all hell broke loose. In the chaos, I hid in one of the big pipes stacked in a pile. I was terrified. I hadn't prayed to God since my sister's death."

"That was when you met Jeff, am I right?"

"He found me," he said, after nodding. "Later, when we spoke of that moment, he told me that he saw something in my frightened eyes. Therefore he let me go."

"He did what?"

"It went like that. I was in there, struggling to control my panting and fear so to make as little noise as possible. At one point, I saw this beanpole at the other end of the pipe. I was stuck. I couldn't escape. He noticed me. The only thing I could do was look into his eyes. We stood staring at each other for several seconds, separated only by the seven feet of that huge telescope. I've never experienced such an intense couple of seconds in my life. It was a momentary movie where I saw my past and what would be my future flash in front of me. I can't explain it any better than that."

"And what happened?"

"He told me to come out of the pipe. I obeyed, my hands up, but he came up to me and said to lower them and follow him. We walked to the exit of the depot, without looking at each other or speaking. I was kinda freakin' out."

"I do believe you!"

"Once outside, we passed the police cars crowded around the depot, still silent. Once we were clear, he said only three words, *Call me tomorrow*, and he gave me his business card. Then he turned around and headed back towards the depot, without looking back."

"And you?"

"I stood there watching him. When I realized I was alone, I looked around. My car was parked near the depot, but of course I walked in the opposite direction. When I was far enough away, I took off running faster than I ever had in my life."

The pounding of water grew louder, while the air was becoming saturated with humidity and its smell.

"What pushed you to go back to Jeff?"

"The fact is … he didn't demand any identification. He didn't even ask me my name. If I wanted, I could've disappeared and he would have never found me again."

"I suppose that's what most people would do."

"Actually, I was torn. At first, I was afraid it was a trick. That he let me go to tail me, maybe hoping that I'd lead him to some big shot. After all, he was a Fed and I didn't know him. Why should he help somebody who broke the law when he risked his life to protect it?"

"But your heart told you that Jeff wanted to give you a second chance, am I right?"

"Yeah. It all started from those few seconds, me trembling and stuck in the pipe, praying not to be found, and him staring at me from the other end. I believe a plea to get the second chance you mentioned was in my prayers. I don't want to sound too emotional by saying that someone up there heard me, pushing Jeff to grant it to me, but I'd swear that something supernatural was in the look we'd exchanged."

She was fascinated by how his eyes sparkled during this story.

"The day I met him again, we had a long talk, a father-son kind. And the best part was that he still didn't know my name. However, he concluded by demanding something from me."

"What did he want?"

"When I told him I had a clean record, he made me promise to apply to the police force, assuring me that he would be my guardian angel. And he kept his word, since I was able to become a cop. Then, when I was assigned to Charleston PD, I found two small apartments on the same block, one for me and one for my mother. I rented them both and we moved."

29 – The Fountain

Landon wondered why he'd told her those things. His mother, Devin and Jeff were the only people he had ever confessed the shadows of his past to. He only knew her for a week and, rationally speaking, it was a naive move. But he didn't regret it for a second. On the contrary, he did it out of a precise indication from his heart, the same heart that always stopped him whenever the temptation to talk about it had teased his tongue.

Yes, he was glad he opened up to her. He felt lighter.

As they continued on, walking and chatting, they came to a lake in the park with a flowing stream. It had the feel of the countryside. He wanted to sit at one of the benches, but Natalie went up the steps that lined not an actual stream but some small artificial waterfalls.

"Amazing," she said, stopping and grabbing the safety railing with both hands.

He watched her in the shade of the trees leafy branches. She stood smiling with her gaze on the spectacular flow of water among those rocks arranged as if they meant to recreate the effect of natural streams. To see her so radiant opened the windows of his heart to welcome her light and warmth.

"Let's go up there!" he suggested.

He had a taste for the pleasure of life again. Natalie seemed to release joy onto any element her eyes rested on, and he was absorbing it through his senses. Sounds and smells of nature, like the molecules of water wandering in the air and bumping against his face, were bringing peace to his soul. The peace that he was trying to find by involving himself in the stories that crossed his path at work.

On top of the little hill there was a fifteen feet high concrete fountain. Wrapping around itself in a spiral, the water coming out of it formed the falls.

"This is really like a little piece of Heaven," she sighed, leaning her elbows on the railing, in front of the fountain.

She was so beautiful. Her shining, baby-blue eyes pierced him like a ray of happiness. He wanted to move the blond lock laying on her temple, it'd be a good excuse to stroke her cheek. He didn't. A gesture like that works when both hearts are on the same frequency, but he had no idea what her thoughts were on the matter.

"Why did you choose to teach foreigners?"

She seemed surprised by the question, actually not that pertinent to the scenario—he couldn't think of anything better to resume the conversation.

"I like it. And I think I'm good at it."

"You mean you're very patient?" he smiled.

"Haha, that's another one! But I was referring to my thoroughness."

"Thoroughness?"

The more he looked at her, the more she seemed to be the human equivalent of that pure and vibrant segment of creation that was their background.

"For instance, many teachers simply correct the students who make mistakes by explaining to them the exact way of saying a certain thing."

"But you're thorough because …?"

"Because, among other things, I try to understand the reason that leads the students to make the mistake."

He wasn't sure he understood what she meant. This doubt must have shown through his expression, since she turned her body toward him, as if she was ready to explain herself.

"I have a Russian student who kept asking *How do you call...* when she wanted to know the name of a certain thing. I didn't simply explain to her that the correct question is *What do you call...* but I went to the root of the problem. Basically, Russians use the term *Kak*, which means *How*, for that type of question."

"Oh, I see. So now she thinks about your explanation before asking the question."

"Exactly. I help them to spot the source of their recurring mistakes so that ... they won't recur again, hahaha."

"And I suppose this makes you one of the most appreciated teachers."

"The most appreciated, please," she winked, with joking boastfulness, blushing right after. "Man, how boring I am with my silly stories."

In the shy look she gave him, he saw a flash of fragility. He felt his skin tingle as if there was electricity in the air between them. Maybe it was just the gentle breeze blowing, but to see her like that, he could no longer resist. He raised his hand and moved the lock of hair stirred by Nature's breath. Her expression changed suddenly. Her smile disappeared. She became serious as her gaze intensified, but she didn't back down when he began to stroke her cheek. Fresh, soft, smooth. The touch of her skin gave him the chills. The pounding of the water and the fragrance of that woodland oasis of intimacy whispered to him that if he had kissed her, he would be granting both of their wishes.

His eyes lost in hers, he bent his head to the side, moving his lips slowly toward hers, when a fat Samoan guy fell on the stage among the sensual nymphets dancing The Swan Lake—thus the effect of Landon's ringing phone.

"It's him," he said after checking the display, with an intensity that sent flames through his lungs and face.

"Je…" but he stopped because, in the agitation of the moment, the phone nearly fell from his hands.

"Jeff?"

"Landon, come to my office," he said, gravely.

"Did you find something?"

"We'll talk when you get here."

30 – FBI

Natalie had only seen an office like this on TV. Gray was the dominant color on walls and furniture (some shelves for archive and two desks) making it look like a huge tin can. The room was large, but not very high ceilings, with four square windows facing the glass wall that framed the door—adjustable blinds, also gray, secured privacy from adjoining rooms. A quarter of the office was delineated by walls—glass in the upper part, wooden in the lower—and a glass door. It served as an inner room likely for interrogations and discussions: in fact, that's where she and Landon had been led. Besides some comfortable chairs, there was only one big table, with a glassy flat surface. It was dark and she could see her own reflection, noticing she didn't look that worried. She felt intimidated because of what was happening to her, but not to the point of losing control of her emotions. Landon was with her. Now she knew she was more than an ordinary case to him.

They sat side by side, on the long side of the table. Jeff had introduced his partner to them, agent Gene Fitzgerald, and both joined them in the inner room.

"James Gerling. Does that name mean anything to you?" Jeff asked her.

She dug into her memories.

"Is he the boy from the summer camp?" said Landon, gaze bouncing between the two Feds.

"Here's his picture," said Fitzgerald, pushing it toward Natalie with his finger, like a casino dealer handing a card to the player.

By the confidence that this athletic, smooth-faced, forty-year-old man spoke with, it seemed obvious that Jeff told him everything about her situation.

If that name didn't sound familiar to her, the picture opened the curtain of her memory: it was an adult's face, but in those features she definitely recognized the boy she'd met twelve years before. The shame she'd felt by narrating the episode returned spread out enough to loosen her vocal cords. She could only nod with a sorry expression.

Jeff and Fitzgerald looked at each other as if they had bet on her confirmation.

"James belongs to the Gerlings from Philadelphia, the holders of one of the largest trucking companies in Pennsylvania," said Jeff. "The camp's owner remembers them because, in July of 2002, he contacted them needing assistance with the delivery of some equipment that was purchased from a camp that had declared bankruptcy, in the Philadelphia area. We talked to him on the phone. Among other things, he told us that he invited Mr. Gerling to discuss the contract, suggesting he bring all of his family, if he wanted. Mr. Gerling accepted, but he only showed up with his son."

"So? Do you really think that this man is involved with the murders?" said Landon, as she paled.

"Checking his background, we found out that he attempted suicide by swallowing a whole bottle of Valium, a month after the short vacation at the camp."

Fitzgerald's guttural voice and the cynicism he spoke with made the news more traumatic to her. She felt horrible. She could still see James cry in front of her and the other girls. She could hear their laughter, perhaps her own too ... Tears of remorse formed inside her eyes. Disbelief and sorrow for the consequences of that stupid joke pushed her to get a tissue from her bag.

She noticed that Landon had turned toward her, but she didn't have the guts to look at him.

"His parents found him in time to save him," Jeff continued. "Then they put him into a psychiatric clinic."

"You know something about why he did it?" said Landon. "It's not necessarily related to the accident with the girls, right?"

While she was distraught by this news, she was able to understand Landon's intention. She was touched. The sadness burning in her irises began to come down.

"It's not an official investigation, so we were vague, but ..." Jeff hesitated.

"But the suspicion that James's motivation rose from that episode is strong," Fitzgerald supported him. "We obtained this information from the clinic's archives, but we're now trying to contact the psychiatrist who followed James in his last six years there."

"Six years?" mumbled Landon, while a thud reverberated inside her.

"James only came home June of last year," explained Jeff.

"And was he in the clinic all this time?"

"Yes, Landon," Jeff confirmed. "Almost eleven years."

This further detail crushed her. She felt Landon's affectionate look on her again, but she was destroyed and couldn't face him.

"We checked the data you provided to Jeff," Fitzgerald said indifferently, as if he was mentioning the tie he wore. "Let's talk about when the murders of the three women took place. The first one was in the following November, and the other two in February and August of this year. The fourth woman has been missing since May, but at this point we believe it's only about finding the body."

She listened to them, unable to banish the image of young James in tears from her mind.

"James lives with his parents in Philadelphia now," added Jeff. "We're also trying to determine where he was during the days of the crimes, but we're almost positive we'll find traces of him in the cities of the victims."

"Miss Lunn. There's a serious chance that you're in danger," said Fitzgerald.

Natalie blanched. The materialization of her initial fear through the authoritative federal agent's voice bit her instinct of survival.

"Miss Lunn?" said Fitzgerald.

She winced.

"Is there anything else we should know? Some thorny details that you didn't feel to te…"

"Hey," flared up Landon. "This is not the right time to ask questions like that."

"Hey yourself, boy," retorted Fitzgerald. "Keep in mind where you are and who you're talking to. This guy is a potential serial killer, if you didn't get it yet."

"What's that?" stood up Landon, boldly. "You're playing the tough guy 'cause you're at home?"

"Landon, sit down," Jeff scolded at him.

The tears still dripping in the tissue didn't allow her to see Landon's face, but she could tell that Jeff's rude tone had hurt him.

"So, Miss Lunn?" Fitzgerald pressed her.

"What a piece of …" murmured Landon, after sharply looking at him. "Come on, Natalie. Let's go," he added, grabbing the back of her chair to help her get up.

"Landon, don't piss me off," Jeff stood up, blocking Natalie's motion.

"Master, what's wrong with you?" said Landon, kind of disappointed. "We came here to ask for your help, and you guys are treating her without any tact. For chrissake, have a heart! Don't you see she's upset? Give her some time ... Fuck."

"Listen, boy," Fitzgerald got up too, arrogantly moving his 150 pounds toward him. "They should've taught you that when you deal with a fede..."

"Gene, cut it out," Jeff stopped him.

Fitzgerald was speechless.

"Okay, Landon," continued Jeff. "Go and get some rest. Just don't leave the city 'cause we need to talk to her as soon as possible. I'm asking you as a personal favor. No obligation on your part, but don't forget that it is also in her best interest to understand what's going on here. Okay?"

Natalie found herself in something unimaginable. A nightmare turned into reality. The only lifeline to cling to was Landon: the vigor with which he took her side was keeping her from a nervous breakdown.

"I'll call you later," said Landon to Jeff, both ignoring a frowning Fitzgerald. "Let's go, Natalie," he added, holding out his hand.

She was the only one left sitting in the room. And also the only one who hadn't said a word during the meeting.

31 – The Song

After Natalie called school to ask for one more day of leave, Landon took her to a motel not that far from the FBI headquarters.

He took two adjoining rooms on the first floor.

It was eight in the evening. The sky just starting to give way to the moon.

With a bucket in his hand, Landon lingered near the ice machine, a couple of rooms from Natalie's ...

They hadn't planned on spending the night, and found themselves without a toothbrush or anything else they might need. So, before arriving at the motel they stopped at a discount store and, among other things, he had bought some Gatorade. This was the fifth time in an hour he was going to get some ice, a great excuse to pass in front Natalie's room in the event she'd put her nose out: in fact, he had suggested that she freshen up and get some rest, and she must have followed his advice, because once the door closed, she didn't show any signs of life. And two hours had already passed.

When someone cares about another it is natural to be selfless, although he would wonder why he acted with such selflessness when he analyzes this situation from his own selfish point of view. Landon felt this way. He was regretting his selflessness: his desire to see continued blaming his commendable behavior and his need to talk to her was undermining his selflessness by stating that it would be perfectly normal for a concerned friend to ask how she was doing; but the thought that he might wake her up or disturb her while in the bath tub kept him from knocking on her door. So his selflessness and selfishness found a compromise about the Gatorade, undrinkable at room temperature …

Returning to his room, he shamelessly slowed down at her door. This time, he even feigned some coughing and stopped to look down over the railing, admiring the dreary inside area of the motel as if it were the Grand Canyon. He couldn't see a soul. Only parked cars, with engine roars coming from the street arranging the rigmarole by an orchestra of crickets hidden somewhere around.

He turned to Natalie's window. The curtains were closed. He could only see himself frowning in the reflection of the glass. The thought of knocking unexpectedly cut all the qualms holding him until then. To do it subtly seemed like a good idea.

If she's in the tub or bed, she won't even hear me.

His knock-knock was as delicate as a fairy's tiptoeing, free from the tension that instead stiffened him up to his knuckles.

He waited thirty seconds. He went up to forty.

Nothing.

And what if she thought I told her to rest 'cause I wanna be left alone?

The fairy wore wooden clogs and knocked again.

The following minute of vain waiting discouraged him definitively.

He ruefully went back into his room. He placed the bucket of ice on the table, next to the TV, and put the bottle of Gatorade in it. Then he went to pee: the ice thrown into the toilet ten minutes before had not completely melted yet. Finally he took his phone, jumped on the bed and called Devin.

"Hey, buddy. Where are you?"

"Columbia."

"Still there?" said Devin, laughing. "Man, I meant if you were at home or in a bar, but in Charleston, hahaha."

"I'll be back tomorrow."

"Too bad. I was hoping we could double-date."

"Are you taking someone out?"

"Mya," said Devin, proudly.

"Are you kiddin' me?"

"The eye wants its share, remember?"

"Awesome, buddy. I wish we could, but Jeff and that clown of his partner seem to have found something."

"A link between Natalie and the murders?"

"Probably, but I'll tell you when I get back. I just wanted to ask you ... will you tell the boss that I got stuck here?"

"Sure."

"Thanks, buddy. I just don't wanna talk to him. He already looked at me wrong when I asked him for the authorization to escort Natalie here."

"No problem. I'll take care of the old man. So, what about the hot chick?"

"She's in quite a shock 'cause of the situation. She didn't say a word at Jeff's. She just sat there, beside me, and listened."

"Hello?! I mean did she clean your pipes?"

"Take care, buddy."

He had bonded a lot with Devin, who was the closest thing to a "best friend" he had at that time. Honest man, good heart, Devin was a funny guy, and often his jokes amused him. In this case, though, he found him annoying and to avoid a nasty response, he'd rather end the conversation.

Trying to comprehend his sudden short temper, he started to think he was falling in love with Natalie.

He'd had his fair share of women. He often happened to perceive a girl as "very special". He had been living unattached for a while and since Natalie was very sweet, beautiful and had a sexy body, it wasn't hard to confuse need or infatuation with love.

But it was different with her.

"Yeah, it's always different," he murmured, sarcastically.

He had listened to the song *This Time It's Different* enough to learn it by heart. He convinced himself that it was actually different with every single girl, a consideration that in fact removed from each one the supposed quid given by the title of the song. Then he realized that the quid was produced by the factor of Time, not by the girls: the more recent a story was, the louder the singer's voice will be, pumping up the *difference*; and since there's nothing more recent than present, the matter was solved with the fact that the current one was, is and will be always different from the others. So, to say it about Natalie made no sense, albeit she did have a new effect on him. It was like discovering a song never heard before.

He carried a darkness inside of himself. When he could, he tried to mitigate it by turning on spotlights, causing lightning and setting fires. But in the end the batteries ran out, the storms passed, the flames died, and he was a prisoner of the distressing and guilty darkness again. Natalie, however, was the sun: he no longer had to strive to create luminous phenomena to fight the darkness; he only had to think of her face and the darkness, won by light, withdrew its grim clutches from his heart.

There was something pure in her; that's why Devin got on his nerves when he talked about her as a mere toy for pleasure, although he couldn't deny feeling a side effect in his boxers when he thought of her …

Was it love? He didn't know. He only knew that a rainbow between his mind and heart sprang from her on his interior landscape devastated by storms.

Yes, *Rainbow In The Sun* was Natalie's song. A song waiting to be discovered.

32 – Associations

She had to tell Landon everything. Now she had few doubts left: "Pee-pee" was after her to get his revenge. Her guilt toward him, while devastating after what Jeff discovered, wasn't rife with the terror of ending up like Cindy and the others.

She hadn't considered it necessary to disclose the details of the episode until then, the thorny ones Fitzgerald had felt the existence of; but now danger loomed close and she feared it was unwise to continue keeping her secret. Those Feds were focusing on facts rather than on James's motive; but if they knew the rest … She needed advice and the only person she trusted was on the other side of that wall. Her issue was overcoming her shame and opening herself up to him. This had been haunting her since they left Jeff's office; therefore, at the discount store, she picked up a bottle of gin. She couldn't spill the beans without some liquid courage.

After a refreshing shower—she really needed it—she got dressed, and sat in the armchair waiting for him. Overwhelmed by tiredness, she had probably dozed off for a few minutes, but her brain didn't stop ruminating. Time was running out, she was exhausted by brooding in the wearying silence of her conscience, and he wasn't coming. So she made up her mind.

She unscrewed the stopper of her new glassy friend and looked for some courage in the first sip; then she grabbed it by its neck and, keys in her pocket, left the room. She closed her door and knocked at Landon's.

"Hey!" he said, affable but surprised.

She was pleasantly disoriented: *disoriented* because she didn't expect him to receive her by bare-chested; *pleasantly* because he had biceps, pecs and abs like a cover model.

"Am I disturbing you?"

"No, not at all," he smiled. "I was about to take a shower, that's why I ..."

"Then I did disturb you," she deduced, releasing a spontaneous and nervous giggle.

"No," he repeated, serious. "I was just explaining my lack of clothing. Please, come on in."

As he closed the door, her eye slipped on his back: toned and sculpted, it smoothly flowed down into his jeans. This vision was diverting her from her purpose. So she rested the bottle next to the ice bucket on the table against the wall, and waited for him to pay attention.

The two lamps tinged the room in amber creating an atmosphere of harmony with the quiet around them.

"Landon, I have something to tell you," she said, loading her sentence with gravity by her tone and expression.

"Okay, Natalie."

With his shirt on, he sat at the end of the bed, ready to listen. He seemed concerned about her. She needed indulgence, but she also knew she didn't deserve it. She turned instinctively toward the bottle. She had brought it for moral support, hadn't she?

She pulled the chair out from under the table and placed it in front of him. Then she approached the corner where there was a coffee maker and some glasses.

"None for me, thanks," he stopped her, resolute, when she was about to pour the gin into the second glass.

"Come on, don't make me drink alone."

"Really, Natalie. I won't let that stuff into my body."

The vehemence of his reaction stunned her.

"Okay. Sorry."

She saw him change his expression in an instant, like a traffic light changing directly from red to green. The gentle smile he had won her with erased the shadow of impoliteness.

"Forgive me, Natalie. I didn't mean to be rude."

"It's okay. I hope you don't mind if I … I let this stuff into my body."

"Absolutely."

She swigged those two fingers of gin. She shook her head and raised her other hand to her chest—she occasionally drank alcohol, but not enough to have learned to manage its sharp impact on tongue, throat and stomach.

"Fitzgerald was right," she sighed. "There's something about that damned day at the summer camp that I … You wanna know how that turned out?" she added while filling her glass again—this time, almost to the edge.

"Sure."

She sat down, without drinking. At that time, she didn't need it. She just needed to keep that comfort at hand. She pushed her chair back a bit: she'd placed it so close that any movement from either of them would cause contact between their knees. Then she began.

"The boy, James, had to be really nervous because, despite Cindy teasing him … down there, I mean … oh God, how can I explain that …?"

"James was in no condition to have sexual intercourse. So?"

It was such a relief that he got it.

"Okay. Since he couldn't, he started to cry like a baby. We watched them from the closet. He was dying of shame. In fact he begged Cindy not to tell anyone. When she gave him her word that it would remain their secret, Emily, who was next to me, started to giggle. You know how giggling can be contagious, right? So all four of us in the dark, hidden, with the heat, close to each other and not to be able to move, the sense of participation ... we found ourselves giggling without realizing it. James had to hear us, since he suddenly turned towards the closet."

It took her a shot to go on.

"I saw him head towards us through the space between the slats. He was red in the face and ... and naked. "Pee-pee, come back here," Cindy scoffed him, laughing as well. He ignored her. I was scared, but also excited. It's hard to explain."

"You explained yourself very well," he encouraged her. "And then what happened?"

"When he got to the closet, he opened the shutters."

Reliving that scene, she felt like she was drowning in her guilt; so she drowned her guilt in a big swig.

"Whoo!" she exhaled, her stomach on fire. "To see that scrawny and naked boy so close ... shocked, in tears at that point that he didn't even think to cover his genitals ... That sounds terrible, but it seemed funny at the time. His nose was dripping while he cried, and we were just silly little girls."

She moved her gaze to his: peering into his soul through his mahogany irises, she didn't feel judged by his silence. She wet her throat and continued.

"We all laughed, but Emily went crazy. So she knelt before him and promised that if he could make his dick hard she would suck it. He turned red and rushed to the chair where he'd placed his clothes. He was sobbing as he got dressed, and we couldn't stop laughing 'cause Mallory had begun to cheer him up *Go Pee-pee go, Go Pee-pee go*, clapping her hands at tempo, dragging us all in it. He ran away. I haven't seen him since then. But …"

"But?"

The thought of his suicide attempt, the psychiatric clinic and the hell that his life must have been led her to finish the glass. It was necessary to conclude her confession.

"We told the story around camp that same night. The next day, all the girls knew about Pee-pee."

The gin stalled on the finish line, when fear and shame stopped contending her heart and allied with each other against her. The tears that she'd been repressing since those terrible memories became clear in her mind began to trickle like a piece of ice in the sun.

He stood up, took the empty glass from her hands and placed it on the nightstand. After looking into her eyes, he hugged her.

Yes, she desperately needed it.

To feel the warmth of his body, the affection of his hug, the whisper of words that exonerated her, his hand caressing her head, all this helped her withstand the crushing feeling of her remorse.

"I don't remember if I laughed at him behind his back," she gasped tearfully, clinging to him harder, her cheek sheltered in the hollow of his shoulder. "I remember Cindy and Emily laughing hysterically while telling the others. Mallory and Nina took so much pleasure in describing him to everyone. Maybe I laughed too. I don't know. When you're in a group and you realize everyone thinks it's funny, you keep going without …"

"Shh. Now calm down," he whispered tenderly.

Feeling protected by his muscles, she struggled to tame her sobs.

"Breathe. Take deep breaths."

She tried to do as he said.

"Good girl."

Her emotions were coming back under control.

After a few minutes, the fear for her own safety came to be the core of her thoughts again. The need to know a certain thing became stronger than the hug-effect. Taking a step back, she staggered. Immediately she felt him grab her shoulders.

"You okay?" he asked.

She said yes, not even convincing herself.

"Natalie?"

"I feel light-headed."

"It must be that," he said, glancing at the bottle.

"Yeah, maybe I drank more than I could hold."

"Go, lie down for a moment."

She sat down on the side of the queen size bed. As she took off her shoes, Landon moved the chair beside her. Then he went to get a tissue from the table.

"Here," he handed it to her, sitting down.

She lay down. While wiping her eyes she noticed something.

"I'm sorry, I wet your shirt."

"Don't worry," he smiled, passing his hand over his shoulder. "I think you should grab a bite to eat."

"Actually, I haven't eaten anything since the donut this morning."

"I only got some snacks."

"Landon …"

"If you want something filling and you got nothing in your room, I can go dow…"

"Landon?"

"Yes?"

"I need your opinion on something."

"Sure."

He spread his thighs and, bending forward, he leaned his forearms on his knees. He entwined his fingers, his eyes locked onto hers.

"Should I tell Jeff the full story in order for them to stop James?"

"You mean … you're positive that it's him behind the murders?"

"I think so. Don't you?"

"Definitely."

"So? Am I supposed to talk to Jeff about it?"

"I think it would help."

Anxiety bit her heart.

"But … No, I don't think it's necessary," he quickly resumed. "What matters to us is that they check him out. As for me, with three dead women, one missing, the connections between you all, and the fact that he was admitted to a nuthouse for ten years … there are already enough reasons to keep him in police custody."

"You're not saying that just to reassure me, are you?"

"Natalie, I thought you were in danger even before you told me the full story. Did I drive you here or not?"

She nodded.

"Now I know I was right, and that's enough. I'll take care of it with Jeff. You don't have to worry about anything. What you told me will remain within these walls."

"Thank you, Landon," she was moved. "I appreciate it so much," she added, wiping her eyes with the tissue again.

"I'm not as callous as those two. I understand, it's embarrassing for you to talk about those things."

"It's not just about embarrassment, though."

"No?"

She turned to the other side.

"Come on, Natalie," he took her hand. "Trust me. I'm here for you."

She returned her wet eyes to him. She didn't know if it was the gentleness he was holding her hand with, the way he looked at her, or how he spoke, but she believed him.

"I'm afraid of male solidarity."

He frowned.

She felt his grip loosen. She withdrew her hand, joining it with the other holding the tissue on her stomach, moving her gaze to the ceiling.

"We were cruel, in a way. I don't know what Jeff and that other guy would think, but some men might say that Cindy and her friends deserved it."

"That's nonsense," he smiled fondly.

"I know, they wouldn't say *Those four bitches ridiculed that poor boy, they had it coming*, but they may think it."

"Natalie ..."

"Did you think that?" she pressed him all of a sudden. "When I told you about Pee-pee, you did. Am I right? Tell me the truth."

"Of course not!" he said firmly. "It's like ... I don't know ... like someone got both hands cut off by an ax for groping girls on buses. Would you think *he had it coming*?"

Putting herself in this situation, as a victim of the sneaky groper, in front of this hypothetical guy crushed by pain and with his stumps bleeding, she felt sorry. Or compassionate. Certainly not satisfied.

"You're a good person, and good people tend to be hypercritical towards their own mistakes," said Landon, getting up and going to the ice bucket. "You girls made a mistake, okay. But … c'mon! We're talking about shooting people in the head!"

Surprisingly, the weight she was carrying on her heart was no longer that oppressive. She had been locked in a cubby alone for days, and the foul air stifled her; but a draft from outside was enough to put things back in perspective. She put the drenched tissue away on the nightstand. She didn't need it anymore.

After Landon drank some Gatorade from the bottle, he approached the other side of the bed.

"I gotta tell you, your association of manhood-solidarity-revenge about men in general doesn't hold water," he said jokingly, lying on his side next to her, but with his head at the opposite end of the bed while still keeping eye contact with her. "More than insight, it sounds like a prejudice."

He was relaxed and smiling, so he could've said that to put her at ease. In fact, it was working.

He bent his arm, leaning his temple on the palm of his hand, legs bending to leave his feet off of bed. She pulled herself a little back on her elbows, crossing her legs, and challenged him …

"Tigers-Lions-Pistons."

"Huh?"

"Go ahead, Mr. Insight!"

He frowned, but only for a few seconds.

"Detroit. Man, Natalie! Are you coming to the chef's house to give cooking lessons?" he laughed. "I'm not what you'd call a sport addict, but every man knows the basics."

"Hahaha, since I was talking about animals, I thought the pistons would have misled you."

"Um, on the contrary, Detroit Pistons made me catch you."

"Okay. Score one for you."

"Moon-Trumpet-Bike," he said suddenly.

She thought for a moment. She spotted a link between the first two. But the bike? Then ...

"Armstrong!"

"Okay, I've made it really easy 'cause I'm a gentleman."

"Haha, you're hilarious."

He was so handsome, so charming that the bad thoughts were expiring like piranhas in a dried up river. He'd buttoned only a few buttons of his shirt, and she could catch a glimpse of his bronze skin. The memory of what hadn't happened at the fountain in the park because of Jeff's phone call teased her imagination ... Better do another association.

"So ... *If I can stop-Behind me dips Eternity-The only news I know.*"

"Ouch. The game is getting rough," he murmured, playfully. "Let's see ... What's that, three Spice Girls's songs?"

"What?!" she was shocked. "Well, as a teenager I was a fan of them, but I could stop talking to you for that."

"Hahaha. C'mon, I was joking. That kinds sounds like Bob Dylan's stuff."

"Cold. You just got the wrong art," she giggled.

"Are they poems?"

"Hot!"

"Okay. They are poems by ... Shakespeare?"

"Nope."
"Poe?"
"Neither."
"Whitman?"
"Still cold."
"Eliot?"
"You're not a male chauvinist, are you?"
He wrinkled his nose, as he got the clue.
"Bishop?"
"Give up?"
"Dickinson?"
"Oh! It took you a while, but you got it."
"I'm not very well versed in poetry."
When he closed his eyes to think about the next challenge, she felt free to enjoy the view. She had been only with three guys in her life (having only kissed Henke, he didn't even make the list), but no one was even close to Landon.

"*Badlands-The Promised Land-Jungleland*," he said, opening his eyes.

While she was thinking it over, she sat up and leaned her back against the headrest.

"A self-congratulatory trio, huh?" she winked, hugging her knees and placing her chin above.

"Self-what?"

"*Land*-on ..."

"Oh, I didn't notice that."

"See? Maybe I'm smarter than you are," she teased, moving her golden curl.

"For the record, it was an attempt to trick you."

"For the record, it's Bruce Springsteen."

"Wow! I'm speechless."

"You thought I was all Spice Girls, Britney Spears and Lady Gaga, am I right?"

"It never crossed my mind!" he said, with a grimace stating the contrary ...

"By the way, those aren't real association."

"Well, yes. But you started with poems."

"Fair enough. So ... just one moment."

"I'm gonna take a nap in the meantime ..."

"Got it!" she brightened. "New York-Computers-Newton."

"Um, let me think."

"Take your time, my dear. You have all night."

Given the situation, the idea of flirting with him seemed out of place; however, with the fear of James under control—at least for now—and the unexpected joy of the moment, she felt pushed by her desire to go that route.

"I think I got you this time," she said, while he scratched his head and furrowed his brow. "Weren't deductions supposed to be your forte?"

"Okay. I give up."

"Ladies and gentlemen ... Ta-Da! Apple."

He seemed to think about that. Then he admitted his defeat with a sigh.

"Don't be upset, detective. You'll do better next time."

"Don't go celebrating yet," he said. "You started. The last chance is mine."

"That's fair."

"So, here it is. Brightness-Pureness-Grace."

The three Graces came to her mind, but that couldn't be it.

"Is that about diamonds?"

"You're way off, Gorgeous."

She didn't want to lose the game, but … was coming up totally blank.

"Okay. I give up."

"Your face."

"My face what?" she frowned, feeling flushed.

"Every time you smile, I see those qualities in your face. It's bright, pure and full of grace."

What was that? Oh, just the surge of her heart.

"Exactly!" he said, sitting up and pointing his finger to her lips.

"Yeah, right …"

"I'm serious, Natalie. You're the most beautiful thing I've ever seen."

Now he looked serious. Manfully and romantically serious. As he approached, she realized she'd encouraged him even more than she meant to. But she didn't mind at all. Laying motionless, the feet between them became inches. His mouth was a breath away. In those mahogany eyes, she read she'd be his.

"Shall we try again?" he winked, with a bold look and irresistible smile.

A whirlwind of emotions sucked her heart, leaving her barely breathing for a few words.

"You need to do something first."

"What?"

"Your phone, turn it off."

33 – Act-1

It was the first time he put his foot in Charleston. His first time ever in South Carolina.

The flight was okay, except for some turbulence after take-off. But it arrived on time.

Along with dozens of other passengers huddled in the baggage claim area, he was waiting for some luggage to appear on the conveyor associated with his flight.

Sometimes, he thought that driving would be more practical than flying: by hiding one in the trunk, he would avoid the *Act-1* of the purchase, as well as those stressful waits at the airports. However, driving brought a different set of problems; therefore, Act-1 was better, also because there was the suspense. That psychological challenge made him feel more alive than hours sitting behind a steering wheel. The excitement of dealing with another human being was like visiting a big city for the first time.

The design was almost done. He only needed to sharpen the lead and draw the last segments.

At last, he thought, when some suitcases started to go around on the conveyor like cyclists at a track during their warm-up.

Spotting his black bag, he looked for a way through the crowd in order to get it in the first round.

"Excuse me," he said loudly, to make himself heard, slipping in the crack between a man in a gray suit and an Asian girl who was talking with another girl.

He grabbed his bag and joined the flow of people toward the exit.

"Taxi, sir?" asked a big man in his forties.

He shook his head no.

Following the signs for the rental car counter, he found himself sweating despite the polo shirt and shorts he was wearing.

He signed the papers, paid cash and once in the car put the destination into the navigation. Finally he started off.

Things had always worked out for him in the past. Sure, there had been some difficulties in Dearborn, but the end result had been reached without much aftermath. Now that he had revised and corrected some steps of his strategy, he just needed to stay calm. And he knew the secret to holding his nerve ...

Along the way, he was so focused on the lines of Act-1 that he almost missed the directions from the GPS. He knew he was close because, as usual, he'd checked out the place on Google Earth.

He pulled over to a brick building and checked the time on the dashboard. 6:15.

He got out of the car and walked to the trunk. Collecting his luggage, he walked to his true destination, two blocks away. It was one of his many unnecessary precautions, but since it didn't cost him anything, why shouldn't he? Plus, taking care of the details kept him focused and made him thrill with adrenaline.

There was a pleasant breeze that he found refreshing. The tile sidewalk made the screeching of the suitcase wheels quite noisy.

He had a three-minute walk down the street with little traffic from cars and passers-by. Everything was exactly like he had studied it on the laptop purchased two days earlier. Then he saw it, identical to the screen shot he'd taken.

At this point, some tension began to surface. Just like always. It couldn't be helped. But contrasting it with the memory of previous experiences—all successful—and awareness of greed inherent in the human soul, he told himself that he would get what he needed by implementing his plan with unwavering resolve.

It had been a mistake not to wear socks with his new loafers; the sides of his big toes and pinkie toes were starting to ache. He knew he was going to have blisters. Sighing, he pulled the suitcase toward the entrance of the gun shop.

Once inside, he took a look around the store. There was no one else inside except for the stocky, bespectacled guy behind the counter focused on a cell phone. As the man gave him the traditional smile with which customers are welcomed, he stepped forward.

"Mr. Oliver Leighton?" he asked, stopping in front of the long counter composed of several glass shelves containing guns.

"Yes?" frowned the middle-aged man—he had mustache too, but his had more white hair than black.

"Hi. I'm Freddy Sinclair. I contacted you via Craigslist for …"

"Oh, Freddy! I'm so sorry," he brightened. "Is it okay if I call you Freddy?" he added, reeling off the well-known friendliness of Southerners.

"That's fine, Oliver."

"Between one thing and another, I forgot you were coming today," he smiled, revealing some slightly yellowed and irregular teeth.

"Look," he lifted up his suitcase. "Straight from the airport."

Oliver nodded, before turning to the cabinet behind him and opening a drawer.

Freddy followed him with his eyes, but his mind was on the script.

"Here it is," said Oliver proudly, stretching an automatic chronograph with a gold case and leather strap on the counter. "I already adjusted it. What do you think?"

"Man! It was unbelievable in the picture, but it's an absolute gem in person."

Freddy picked it up gently and stared at it, trying to feign wonder.

"The glass is sapphire, with double anti-reflective coating. The strap is crocodile," Oliver said, as if reading from a script too.

"That's a great deal for just 600 bucks."

"You can say that again, pal," muttered Oliver, kind of melancholy. "I paid over two grand for it five years ago. As you can see, it is in excellent condition and works perfectly."

"I see. The only thing is ..." he hesitated, putting it back on the counter. "Why are you selling it at such a low price?"

"Lack of connoisseurs, I'd say. I kept it at one-thousand for a month, then dropped it down to eight hundred for the next four, but I never got a bite."

"Good for me, then."

Oliver grimaced, and continued to admire the little piece of perfection.

"I suppose you're sorry to let it go," improvised Freddy.

"Yeah, things ain't going as well as a few years ago, pal. Now it is time to make some cash, as most of the people selling on that site do."

"Um ... Listen. I don't like to take advantage of the situation. If you'd like to re-price it, that's fine with me."

Oliver stared at him in disbelief.

"Don't make that face. I'm serious. I feel like I'm swindling you … I'll tell you the truth. If I'd seen it before, I would have bought it at one thousand."

"I'm speechless, Freddy."

"So, what do you say?"

"Well, I don't know … Maybe 700?"

"I think 800 is a fair price."

"You sure? You already paid for the flight …"

Freddy winked. He reached into one of his shorts pockets and pulled out six the hundred-dollar bills that he had folded in a paper clip. Then he took his wallet and removed two more. After telling Oliver to count the money, he finally wore his new watch.

"It's all here, thank you so much," stammered Oliver.

Freddy admired the purchase on his wrist with satisfaction.

"Then, done deal?" urged Oliver.

"I'd say so."

"Thank you, Freddy. You're great," he said, pocketing the dough.

"Look, Oliver. There's something else I'd like to discuss with you."

"Sure. Tell me."

"It's a thorny matter. Could you close up for a minute?" Freddy asked, turning toward the door.

"You mean my shop?" said Oliver, perplexed.

"I don't want to be interrupted."

Oliver didn't seem willing, but he couldn't say no after their transaction.

"Don't worry, Freddy. No one ever comes by this late."

He had factored in a *No* anyway: in fact, his question aimed to figure out how far he could pull the rope now that he was about to do things seriously.

"I gotta tell you, I didn't come up to Charleston just for your watch."

"You didn't?"

"Not to drag it out, but I gotta meet some guys for a deal. I don't know them and I wanna show up to the meeting with a little friend," he said, eyeing the display case holding the guns, which they were both resting their hands on. "I would've found one back home, but I flew here, so …"

"Shit, Freddy! You scared me," Oliver relaxed into laughter. "You couldn't have come to a better place."

"The problem is that I don't have a permit for it. I never got one 'cause I thought I wouldn't need. But life sometimes forces you to sell a chronograph that you expected to take to the grave when you'd bought it."

Oliver darkened.

He felt anxiety secrete adrenaline into his system, but had to control his emotions.

"Look, Freddy. I understand your situation, but the law is strict on offenses of this type. I'm sorry, but I …"

"How much is this?" he interrupted him, pointing to a Beretta 9mm right under their nose.

"Seven-hundred bucks, but without a permit it's useless even to talk a…"

Oliver was left speechless: while he was reiterating his reasons, Freddy put his hand into another pocket and pulled out some cash rolled up in a rubber band.

"Here we have Benjamin and nineteen of his doppelgangers ... They're all yours. Right now."

"What would I do with them if they take away my license?"

The distrust in his eyes gave him an idea where that feedback came from.

"Oliver, I'm not a cop if that is what's worrying you. Wait," he said, showing his ID and plane ticket. "Check, please. I just got into town, as I said before."

People tend to believe what they want to believe; you just need to make a nice package for them. Oliver wanted that money, it was written on his face. As he eyed that roll of bills, his features contracted on the rhythm of *Come to Daddy*. He would believe any story showing a bit of plausibility. In fact, he was checking the papers. When he finished, he raised his eyes, but before he uttered a sound, Freddy spoke.

"I just need a gun to cover my ass."

"Exactly. If you make a mess, it won't take long for the cops to come here. I've already got too many problems. I don't need to add selling weapons to clients without a permit."

"I understand that. But don't tell me that you don't have one that's unregistered."

Oliver was silent.

"C'mon, pal!" insisted Freddy. "In need of cash, stolen weapons ... Someone has certainly come here to sell you one under the table."

Oliver didn't speak, but was deep in thought. At least that was what the sheen of sweat on his balding forehead suggested.

"If you sell it to me, I'll give you back your chronograph too."

"Are you kiddin' me?"

Without taking his eyes from Oliver's, Freddy took the watch off his wrist and placed it beside the two thousand dollars. Then he said: "I never met you."

Oliver was staring at him, clearly weighing the situation on the scale of *Is it worth it?*

The front boundary of Oliver's graying hair had dampened, as well as his mustache.

"Look, you're not the only gunsmith in Charleston selling stuff on Craigslist," Freddy went on. "I'm in touch with three. You won't you sell it to me, one of them gets the money. And if you gunsmiths are all honest, there are places where I can find one anyway. And much cheaper," he bluffed, having no idea where these places were or the intention to deal with some hot-headed.

Oliver's gaze faltered. He couldn't hide his interest, attracted by the green roll and chronograph like ants to sugar. He took a handkerchief from his pocket and removed his glasses. He wiped his forehead and temples.

"Oliver. I guess that 2800 bucks would help you, like you would help me by giving me something right now. I've been up since early this morning and I need some rest. So, if you ain't feelin' it, tell me 'cause I've still got time to stop by somebody else," he added, taking back the chronograph and checking the time.

"Why'd you come to me first?"

"You were selling this for 600. They have other stuff at a higher price," he explained, going with the truth but not sharing the details.

"Fine, wait here," Oliver muttered, red-faced, exhaling with a puff and leaving the counter.

He walked to the entrance with his head down and turned the *Be right back* sign. He locked the door and disappeared into the back of the warehouse.

He had done it again. He was positive he would; nevertheless, his feeling of triumph was amplified by the euphoria generated by the fear of a failure. A grin threatened to stretch across his face, but he had to maintain his composure until the end. Oliver might misinterpret it and change his mind.

He placed the watch next to the two thousand dollars and waited.

Oliver came back with a short-barreled revolver and a small box.

"This is what I got," he said, putting the gun and ammo on the counter and his glasses on his nose. "Take it or leave it."

"If you assure me that it works, I'll take it," he said, deliberately ignoring the weapon, but checking how many bullets the box contained.

"It works. Even better than the watch."

"Okay. I'm gonna test it tonight. If it's like you say, you won't see me again," he replied with a threatening tone.

"Fair enough, Freddy."

Oliver seemed intimidated. Good, because this time he wasn't bluffing.

He nodded and put his bag on the counter. He opened it and put the purchase between some jeans and a shirt.

"It was a pleasure to meet you, pal," he winked, zipping the bag.

"For me too, pal," Oliver smiled. "Farewell."

34 – The Confession

Something was tickling his nose. That was his first observation when his senses returned. He opened his eyes and found himself with his cheek resting over Natalie's head. Her tousled hair rested on his throat and under his nose. He left his arm around her shoulders, putting his other hand—after scratching his nose—between the pillow and his neck, relaxed and enjoying the rediscovered pleasure of a woman.

He was on his back and she was still hugging him. This was how he had dozed off and happily woke back up. He felt the warmth of her naked body clinging to his, in the coolness of the sheets. A pleasant contrast of temperatures. He lay in that sensual embrace with her, her breasts warming his side and her bent arm shaping a big and lopsided *V* on his chest. Her leg was against the outside of his quadriceps and the other one, arched across his lower abdomen. He realized only now that they languished in this erotic fusion of flesh, but his member already up: throbbing, pressing against the inside of her thigh like a catapult trying to throw a stone that was too heavy, with the compression swelling it to the point of bursting.

He wanted to do it again, but didn't want to disturb her blissful sleep. He wanted to motionlessly get lost in the refined composition of pleasure, but also wanted to stick it into her again. He wanted to hear her voice, but didn't want to renounce the magic of silence. He wanted to admire the candidness of her sleeping, but he also wanted to see her climax. He wanted to taste her again and again, but he also wanted to declare his surge of love.

Love?

A word that terrified him almost as much as it made him happy. Fortunately a moan distracted the poet and the animal from their dilemmas.

"Good morning, Lan," she said in a flirty tone and sleepy voice, lifting her head just enough to meet his eyes.

Disheveled and half dazed, she was fabulous.

"Good morning, Nat."

She squeezed her legs around him more, pulling her head back as if to look at him.

"What's on your mind?"

"Just thinking."

"Thinking about what?"

"About how nice last night was."

"Really?" she said, mischievously—he bet—rubbing her sex against his hip.

"Really."

"You don't have the face of somebody who's enjoying a memory."

"What face do I have?" he smiled, strongly contracting his dick against her soft flesh.

"The face of somebody who's meditating about important matters."

"Actually, I'm thinking about how I'm gonna tell my wife."

Disbelief woke her up suddenly, instantly spreading itself over her face like a sheen of oil on the ocean's surface: the raging spark in her eyes that was about ignite everything triggered his amused alarm …

"You're an ass," she said, after he'd started laughing.

"Hey, hey!" he panted, terrified, feeling the grip of her fingers around his testicles.

"Say sorry."

"Sorry, sorry, sorry."

"That's better," she was pleased, letting him go.

She was so beautiful with that angel face, the sky in her eyes and sun through her hair. The more he looked at her, the more his heart—and not only that—swelled.

"Let me check," he said, turning on his side toward her and putting his arm under the sheets.

"Check what?"

"If you want what I want," he challenged her, putting his hand between her legs. "Um! Apparently, yes."

"Wait. I'd like to talk for a moment, first."

"Talk?" he boggled, although he found it morbidly exciting the way she acquiesced to his intrusive fingers.

"Yeah, talk! Mouths serve this purpose too, am I right?"

He could no longer hold back his urge to kiss her.

She participated with passion, at north with her tongue and at south by spreading her thighs, moaning in a sinuous dance that was driving him crazy. However, she kept her eyes open with her question mark brazenly and imperturbably staring at him.

"Okay, Nat. What do you want to talk about?"

It was a delicious torture massaging her crotch and, at the same time, rubbing his member against her thigh, knowing that he had to wait. Of course, if he kept doing that he may come in the middle of the conversation, but ... whatever!

"I wasn't completely myself last night because of the incident at the summer camp. Also, I was tipsy."

Excitement and joy vanished suddenly, just as suddenly as his windpipe shut. The thought that she was going to tell him she regretted it crystallized all his being, from head to fingers …

"Hey, Lan. Don't get me wrong," she said—he must have seemed dejected. "I'm really happy it happened. Only that we practically don't know anything about each other, and I'm not the type of girl who takes this lightly."

"I don't think it's fair to imply that we are strangers," he said, hurt to the point to remove his sticky hand from her. "I told you things about myself that only a couple of people know. And you did the same."

"Sure, but I'm referring to the present time."

His disappointment subsided.

"You were joking a while ago. At least I hope so, haha. But as far as I know, you could be married for real."

He felt unfair and childish.

"You're right, Nat. I'm sorry. No, I'm not married. I'm single. No commitment. With nobody. And you?"

When a cloud obscured her enthusiastic smile that had followed his confirmation of being single, he realized he just won the prize of *Gaffe of the Year*.

"Obviously you're single too," he mumbled, as red as a strawberry. "I meant if you're dating someone."

The laughter with which she noted his embarrassment made a milkshake out of his face, then helped him regain his natural color.

"A student of mine asked me out a couple of times three months ago, but nothing serious."

"Where's he from?" he got curious, slightly apprehensive.

"Germany. He's there now, but he should be back here in about ten days."

"And how will he fit into our story?"

"He just won't," she winked, as if to reassure him. "I told you. It was only a few dates."

"So we've got a story for real, am I right?"

She nodded, but then she frowned.

"Are you making fun of me?"

"Huh?" he mumbled, trying to simulate surprise—she caught him red-handed.

"Are you mocking my *Am I right?*"

"Of course not. It's just that when you like a person, you unconsciously begin to copy them."

"Hahaha, you fuckin' shill!"

He would say bullshit over and over again in exchange for the certainty of making her laugh every time, since the outbreak of joy she caused him by laughing was the orgasm of his soul.

"Nat?"

"What?" she said, sparkles in her eyes.

"I have a confession to make."

His serious air put her on the spot.

"Do you remember when you walked into my office in Charleston?"

Her nod was very light due to the tension that turned her pale.

"That precise day, at that very exact moment, I … I fell in love with you."

She remained with her mouth half open, showing her amazement instead of issuing a reply.

His sincerity easily allowed him to hold her inquiring look.

Emotions gathered in her eyes.

"Did you just say that …?"

"I love you, Nat. Whatever that means, I do."

She frowned, then she laughed as if she'd taken a few seconds to get his joke.

He put his lips close to hers.

Joy, passion and understanding melt in the most intense kiss of their rising love.

35 – Travels

Jeff called Landon in the late morning, asking him to stop by as soon as possible. Him and Fitzgerald hadn't been sitting on their hands. They'd filled in the painting with a lot of details.

After checking out of the motel, Natalie and Landon went to see them.

As she walked into their office, she realized she had a different state of mind: Landon had made her feel protected last time, but his support felt something like duty; now she perceived his protection as totally wanted.

The scene was the same as twenty hours prior. All four of them in the inner room, sitting around that rectangular dark glassy table with its reflections still dazzling. Her across from Fitzgerald and Landon face to face with Jeff. Only difference was a couple of bottles of mineral water, one of peach tea, some paper cups, and a box with donuts. She took one with strawberry jelly—too busy in the "Biblical knowledge" with Landon to have breakfast—while the two Feds opened up their dossiers. Landon filled her glass with tea, reminding her through a confident and loving look that he was there for her.

"First of all, Miss Lunn, I want to apologize for my attitude yesterday," began Fitzgerald, lacing his fingers in a curious gesture. "I realized I showed no sensitivity towards you. It won't happen again."

"Don't worry, sir," she said, relieved by the thought that they wouldn't ask her questions about the summer camp. "The stress that you guys are exposed to with your job must be terrible. I understand."

"That's very kind of you, Miss Lunn. Everything alright between us?" he asked Landon, smiling and holding out his hand diagonally across the table.

Landon shook it, but he added a stern, perhaps wary, nod. She found it funny how the seriousness of the moment had transfigured Landon's face compared to a minute before, when he reassured her. However, she remained somber. They decided together that it was better to hide their relationship from Jeff.

"Back to us," said Jeff, getting the attention of all three. "This morning we were able to talk via videoconference with Dr. Watkins, the psychiatrist who discharged James after following him in his last six years at the clinic."

She had been living in an intense and idyllic romance for the last twelve hours, but the abrupt return to crime news shook her inside. She still had more than a half of a donut left, but placed it on the napkin. Joy and hunger must go hand in hand as well as tension and lack of appetite. She tried to appear calm, at least exteriorly, taking a handy wipe from her bag to clean her hands. In her mind she clung to Landon's statement of love.

"The conversation with Watkins lasted half an hour, so we're going to summarize the important parts," Jeff continued, peering from his file. "He cooperated, telling us whatever doctor-patient confidentiality allowed him to. Although we're the FBI, we need to be diplomatic at this stage," he addressed her specifically—she nodded. "After the suicide attempt, James's parents investigated and discovered why their son did that. However, Watkins said that they found out from "other sources", not from James. In fact, when they tried to talk about it with James, he locked himself in the bathroom. When they were able to open the door, they found him in the tub, his wrists bleeding. Needless to say, they were distraught. They realized that the subject traumatized him too much, and fearing a third attempt, they put him in the clinic. He would be safe there. During his first two years, specialists saw some improvement. James passed from silence to drawings. Naked women. He drew them on sheets of paper, pillows, tables and walls, and then he "stabbed" them with pens and pencils. When the doctors pushed him to talk, James tried to hang himself with a sheet. Then Watkins relieved them. There was a change. With him, James agreed to write kind of a diary. A therapy, he explained, which helps people get rid of their suffering by transferring it to paper. Or something like that."

The word *stabbing* took her breath away for a moment. She had first seen herself portrayed in one of those drawings, then with a real knife stuck in her flesh. She wished to grab Landon's hand, so close to hers above that cool and reflecting table, but she couldn't.

"Are you saying that James mentioned the girls in his diary?" asked Landon as she took a sip of tea to ease herself.

"No," said Fitzgerald.

"It took months to Watkins to persuade James to write this diary," Jeff clarified. "He succeeded only with the compromise to let James destroy whatever was written. They went on this way for about two years. It was Watkins who handed James a lighter and watched him burn it. Watkins wasn't that interested in the diary. His goal was to get James to talk about the camp. He knew the story because James's parents told him, but he needed to hear it from James. This was the only way for Watkins to understand if James was defeating his demons. He had to push him hard to see if the suicide idea was definitely gone."

"Of course Watkins didn't go through these details," intervened Fitzgerald. "We're just assuming, thanks to Miss Lunn's story."

"The therapy was working out," said Jeff. "James was writing less and didn't reject a dialog. Speaking with him, Watkins pushed him to find an interest. Not a hobby, but a real goal to devote himself to. This would help him get back his inner balance and give him a direction in life. There weren't many things that aroused his enthusiasm, though. The idea that took root was to see the places where, as a child, he'd fantasized about through TV."

"But in order to travel, James had to prove that his self-harming intentions had disappeared," added Fitzgerald.

Watching and listening to these two guys, her anxiety eased. They seemed to have a good understanding with each other. She wondered if they had agreed in exposing the case evenly or they were improvising, planning to offer a comprehensive and concise analysis. No doubt, they were good.

"At first, his desire to get out of there made him regress," Jeff continued. "He began with drawings and silence again, interspersed with bursts of anger against himself. But then, Watkins came up with another idea. Reading. By telling James stories of people in prison or that were bedridden who escaped within their fantasies, Watkins persuaded him that he could travel with his mind in the meantime. James's knee-jerk reactions thinned out. When he seemed to be calm and stable for over a year, Watkins thought it would be useful to let him attempt the Internet, showing him the progress of technology and the world out there waiting for him. Over the next sixteen months, among books and the Web, James improved and suddenly opened up with Watkins. Since what had happened in the beginning, it had to be him to show the intention to talk about the camp. In fact, James told him a story corresponding with the one James's parents had heard. They spoke several times, with Watkins testing him harshly. James reacted well, therefore Watkins declared him healed and his parents decided to take him back home."

"But what does Watkins say?" Landon asked. "Does he think his ex patient might have had a relapse, turning against the others instead of himself?"

She appreciated him voicing the question that had been plaguing her while the other two kept talking. Further confirmation that there was a connection between them.

"Actually ..." Fitzgerald said, but at his hesitation, Jeff interrupted.

"Not being an official investigation, we haven't mentioned the real reason for our interest in James."

"We prompted it by hinting about an experimental procedure about patients discharged after a hospitalization longer than a decade," explained Fitzgerald.

"Experimental procedure ... Okay, everyone has his own ways," murmured Landon, bothered. "But now?"

She was surprised by his tone. She didn't understand why he was being unpleasant and this agitated her, also because Jeff and Fitzgerald exchanged an odd look.

"We checked all of James's air travel since his return home in June last year," Jeff replied. "His first trip was to New York City in September, after he got his drivers license."

"He probably didn't feel ready for the highway yet," Fitzgerald grinned, his eyes on his own dossier. "The guy traveled a lot. New York, as we said. Then St. Louis, Missouri. Charlotte, North Carolina. Dallas, Texas. Las Vegas, Nevada. Denver, Colorado. Little Rock ... What the fuck would he do in Arkansas? There's nothing there hahaha ... Sorry," he flushed, she didn't get whether it was due the f-word or because he was the only one laughing.

"Going on ... Baltimore, Maryland. Cleveland, Ohio. Seattle, Washington. Memphis, Tennessee. Tampa, Florida. New Orleans, Louisiana. Slowly, he's going to baptize all the states. He's lucky he can afford that."

"Anyway," Jeff interrupted him. "On the dates of the crimes, James was elsewhere. Cindy Cook, killed November 16th in Nashville. James flew to Charlotte on the 7th, flying back to Philadelphia on the 23rd. He hadn't taken any other flights during his stay in Charlotte. Needless to say, we checked out his bank withdrawals, charges on his credit cards, and the hotel where he stayed, including his checking in and out. Everything confirms that James was in North Carolina, not Tennessee."

This news was a blow that wiped out the puzzle painfully assembled last night during the dramatic confession to Landon. And he had to feel the same way from how he paled.

"Autopsy report shows that Emily Wallace died between the 21st and 24th of February," continued Jeff. "The murder took place in Austin, Texas. James was in Vegas from the 11th to the 28th of February, not only from his round trip flights to and from Philadelphia, but also from his financial operations and hotel registration."

"Same goes for Mallory Jackson," added Fitzgerald. "Her murder is dated August 18th, in Dearborn, Michigan, but James was living it up at a resort in Tampa, from August 10th to 23rd. Once again, everything matches."

Now the puzzle pieces were thrown out of the window. She was completely lost. What seemed to be a solid marble statue a few hours earlier was now liquefying like a snowman in the tropics. She had sparked such an uproar for nothing.

"What about the other one?" said Landon, giving her a start—embarrassment had annihilated her. "The missing woman."

"James arrived in Cleveland on April 27th, left on May 12th," said Fitzgerald. "The report for Nina Arkin Walsh's disappearance dates back to May 7th, stating her absence since almost 48 hours prior."

"But this case is less complicated," Jeff pointed out. "While the police have no clues about the three murders, here they have a suspect. It's true that the report was filed by Mr. Walsh, her husband, but he's also the main suspect in the investigation of Boston PD."

"It seems that she wasn't exactly a Suzy homemaker," said Fitzgerald, in a gossipy tone. "The lady had an ongoing affair, and he moved from unaware to aware …"

The carrot was the only thing left of the snowman. She was fighting her need to cry. She had taken part in ruining James's life and now that he had recovered, she was putting the FBI after him.

"So, Jeff. What are you gonna do?" Landon frowned.

"James is currently in New Orleans. Natalie's story presents some aspects that we have no intention of underestimating. In other words, since money isn't an issue for him, he could have hired a professional killer."

"Possibly even more than one, whereas the victims were killed with different weapons," Fitzgerald speculated. "Maybe he travels with the aim of getting some alibis. We noticed that the crimes were always committed while he was on a vacation, although it could be a coincidence given the frequency of his trips."

Her brain and heart were bursting. She didn't know what to think or how to feel.

"We're now checking out his cell phone and other accounts, social networks, e-mail, and whatever he's got. Meanwhile, we arranged a security detail for Natalie," explained Jeff and, speaking to her with a paternal smile, "Honey, you have nothing to fear."

"Thank you, Jeff," she said, although the emotional part of her wanted to apologize to everyone—to the two Feds for turning them away from real cases, to Landon for harassing him with her silly obsession, and even to James who was minding his own business.

"So you're not even going to interrogate James?"

"Take it easy, Landon," said Jeff, quietly. "Two of ours are leaving for New Orleans today. They'll be watching him."

"Watching?!"

"Landon ..."

"Shit, but he drew naked women and stabbed them. You know what happened at that camp. He went nuts for ten years. Four out of five girls are dead. What else is supposed to happen to take him into fuckin' custody, tell me that."

Perhaps, she was really in danger if Landon blew up like that and the Feds were giving her some body guards. They certainly knew more about crimes than she did. Maybe it wasn't snow, but real marble.

"What you say is true, Landon" said Jeff, surprisingly submissive. "Unfortunately, there's nothing substantial that links James to the murders. Only our inferences. That's why it would be a mistake to waste the advantage we got on him, if he's really the murderer."

"James doesn't know he's being investigated," said Fitzgerald, looking at her as if he had realized that she didn't understand what the advantage was. "The only people aware of the links between the victims, are in this room."

"James doesn't seem to be here..."

"C'mon, Landon. He's saying that the media dealt with the crimes individually, just because they were news at the time," Jeff paraphrased. "So James has no reason to think that we're breathing down his neck."

She was confused. She stared at those three guys, Jeff looking confident, Landon looking very upset, and Fitzgerald with a touch of mockery in his expression.

"We will continue to run-through James's past in search of evidence," said Jeff. "But for now it's imperative that he feels free to move. If he's clean, we won't embarrass ourselves and look like the bad guys who persecute a poor tormented boy. If he's involved, we're going to arrest him. Notwithstanding that Natalie is getting our protection until we cleared this up, in one way or another."

"Which means you can sleep tight," said Fitzgerald, addressing her with a reassuring smile under Landon's perplexed expression.

36 – The Worm...

Landon was driving on I-26. Natalie sat beside him, restless. They were heading home.

She was confused, not because of the discussion that took place at Jeff's office, but because of Landon's subsequent attitude. Leaving the FBI headquarters, she had been a storm of questions, all tampered down by uninterrupted sunshine of *Don't worry, everything will be fine* from him, although a big cloud had stayed on his tanned face. Once in the car, he focused on driving through the traffic of the capital city up to the highway. In a huff, she zipped her lips too, waiting for him to start talking. They had a two-hour drive and he couldn't stay quiet the whole time—and if that was his intention, once in Charleston, she wouldn't leave his Audi until he explained himself.

"I was thinking..."

The silence—embarrassing in the beginning, then draining—had lasted for a half an hour, and his voice startled her like a phone ringing in the middle of the night. The cloud had spread into his voice, making it low and husky. Almost a murmur. But that didn't lighten her bad mood: she was graced by his attention after long minutes of nothing, so she couldn't help to sharpen her tone.

"That's amazing!"

He looked at her briefly. He seemed surprised by her reaction.

"And what you're thinking about?"

"You should move in with me."

An outburst of laughter overcame her, as if the actor unintentionally farted at the peak of Hamlet's despair during *To be or not to be*.

"What's so funny?" he asked, as if offended.

"You're joking, aren't you?"

Steering wheel in his hands and his eyes on the road, his features didn't change one bit.

"Wait a minute. Maybe I didn't get it. Did you just ask me to come and live with you?"

"Let's try. Doesn't work, you move back home."

"But ..."

"What?"

"Oh c'mon, Lan. You can't be serious," she laughed again.

"Why not? I love you. You made love to me last night. And you did it again this morning. So, unless you're a one-night stand kind of girl ..."

Surprise and hilarity were swept away by the shock wave of her indignation. She felt Herculean strength in her hands, and the will to use it on him was out of control. Almost.

"You should thank God you're driving, otherwise ..."

He stamped his foot on the gas pedal causing the engine to roar. The speed gauge marked 95 miles per hour.

He seemed to be mad ... Him?

Their lane was empty, but speeding past other vehicles so easily turned her anger into anxiety.

"Landon!" she yelled. "Slow down, dammit!"

He did. His compliance toned down her rage, but just enough to hold back her desire to punch him.

"If you thought that I was a one-night stand girl, even for a moment, you didn't understand anything at all about me."

"Nat, please!"

"Or are you trying to keep me in your bed, maybe until you're sick of me?" she pressed him with a trembling voice, destroyed by this terrible and suddenly likely thought. "That's how you deal with women, isn't it? I should've expected it from a guy like you. Kind, caring, sweet, everything to pull off my pa…"

"Cut it out, Nat! Don't be a hysterical little girl like in those ridiculous romantic movies. You're better than that."

She stared at him like he stared at the road. Nobody ever threw a bucket of ice on her, but she imagined it would feel something like this.

She didn't reply. She'd rather look at the road too.

On the echo of Landon's few lines, she was thinking. More than the sense of his words, his firm and pragmatic tone was what froze her. He'd never thought of her as an easy girl. It was a provocation, as strong as it was stupid, to persuade her to accept. So the right question to ask herself was: why had he proposed such a thing?

She crossed her arms on her chest and turned to look out of the window in search of an answer.

Perhaps he really believed that she was the love of his life, and being a determined man, he didn't want to waste time with rituals.

Yeah, rituals to him.

Sure she had fallen for him, but she also loved her life. If she moved in with him, that abrupt change would upset her world. No, she wasn't ready for that. She loved to manage her life how she wanted. She always did. But when you're with somebody, sacrifices are inevitable. And she wanted to be with Landon. She had had three boyfriends, but *all with their own place* with all three. It certainly wasn't in her plans to change her policy because of

Landon. "Certainly" in the sense of "not yet". Emily, Mallory, fear, Cindy, James, the journey, the FBI, danger … everything was too confusing in order for that possibility to come to her mind. Furthermore, a week earlier, she didn't even know Landon. Nevertheless, he was now the North to the compass of her heart. Maybe she wanted to live with him too: she was just scared. Maybe she needed some time to become familiar with the idea. Maybe she was alone for too long: used to playing an Amazon, she had forgotten how nice it was to hug a knight and let him control the steed. Or she could control it and feel the knight's hug. The point wasn't who held the reins, but that they both stayed on the horse.

The turn into a service area brought her attention back into the car. It had been ten minutes of silence. Maybe he needed some fresh air, that's why he stopped.

"Nat, listen," he said, as he turned off the engine. "Forgive me. I got pissed off 'cause you laughed in my face, so I said some shit I didn't mean. Ask your heart, it knows I never thought those things about you."

Before replying, she stared at him carefully. She sought the source of his unusual behavior in his eyes, but the waters of his irises were dark. She could only see that while she was reflecting, he was tormenting himself for the way he'd treated her. This made his apology acceptable.

"What's the purpose of the police?" he asked suddenly, before she could comfort him.

"Come again?"

"What's the purpose of the police?"

"What are you talking about?"

"The police, what are they supposed to do?"

The puzzling change of subject paired with his insistence, reawakened her rage.

"The police, what are they supposed to do?" repeated Landon, while her blood was bubbling like lava in a crater.

"To protect citizens. But what the hell does this ha..."

"*To protect*, what does it mean?"

"It means go buy a fuckin' dictionary," the volcano erupted.

She opened the door and jumped out of the car. The indulgence that she intended to show him was already prehistory.

"Nat!" he shouted, getting out too. "Wait."

She was too irritated to understand whether she was angry with him due to his ravings or with herself because she couldn't go back into a normal conversation. She walked quickly along the path lined with lawn, overtaking other vehicles parked; passing by a pick-up, she ran into the gaze of a lady sitting on the passenger side with a baby in her arms: from her face, she realized she must look out of her mind.

"Don't you get it?" she heard him say loud. "They wanna use you."

She stopped, as if she'd slammed against an invisible wall. She turned around. He stood by the car, leaning over the roof, facing her. They were twenty yards apart, but she could see the anguish in his expression. Bewildered and sluggish, she returned to him. While the breeze caressed her cheeks, moved her curl, and brought high quality oxygen to her, she analyzed the sentence with which he had harpooned her. At the same time, she also was studying him. Not a trace of hard feelings was in his face. Only so much distress standing out against the blue sky that was his background.

When only his Audi was left between them, she crossed her forearms on the roof too, her chin on the back of her hand and her eyes straight into his. She was ready to listen.

"Police protect citizens by arresting criminals," he began. "But a criminal doesn't become such until there is evidence that he broke the law. Evidence, do you understand?"

Now she noticed some cities on the surrealistic map that he was trying to sketch for her, but the roads connecting each other weren't drawn yet.

"Jeff has no evidence to arrest James," he continued, resolute. "James's family is rich. They would hire the best criminal lawyer and James would be cleared, even before he was taken in, if the Feds intervened now. And they won't because their intervention would open loopholes for James, like the possibility of contaminating the evidence, or destroying it, or fleeing abroad. And be sure he'll take advantage of them to avoid the death penalty, 'cause that is what's gonna happen to him."

This was the Landon that she had lost her head over. To hear him so positive that James was the murderer—wonderful reflection of his concern for her—made her feel like he was an extension of herself.

"You heard what they said," he insisted. "Their only advantage is that James doesn't know he's being investigated. This means that he won't destroy evidence or attempt to escape 'cause … because he's focused on you, Nat. And what better chance, to arrest him, than catching him in the act?"

She had listened to him with a pulsing mixture of apprehension and joy, but the last assumption made her shiver. He had to feel the vibration of her heart, so much so that he promptly joined his hands with hers over the roof.

"They will protect you, but their goal will be to find a way to incriminate James. If one of the two candies is poisoned, I'd take both from you and throw them away. Period. Instead, they need to know which the bad one is. They make you eat one, hoping that you pick the good one. Otherwise, they got a medical team ready for you and cross their fingers ... Nat, they won't stop James at the airport to ask him why he came to Charleston. They're gonna tail him, waiting for him to approach you and try to ..."

His voice failed. A violent contraction of her stomach made her swallow. She shook his hands as hard as she could, seeking refuge in his passionate look.

"Forensics and coroners in Nashville, Austin and Detroit PDs, have collected the evidence on the crime scenes and victims' bodies. If they found any trace of James, everything would end there. But let's say that he was clever enough not to leave any, which we'll only discover after the DNA tests and all the other tests that are impossible to carry out without probably cause ... If he didn't leave any evidence, you're the only chance to connect him to the murders of your friends. I know Jeff. He won't run the risk of continuing without evidence or illegally gathering any, given that it can't be used in the process. So the Feds will put all their time and energy only in your direction ... Why do you think him and his partner were so tolerant to my intemperance and kind with you? They don't want James to stop, Nat. The escort is 49% to protect you, but 51% to catch him."

Only now she realized that the popsicle they offered her at Jeff's office was actually just the tip of the ice-berg. That flow of information with which he was overwhelming her made her throat rusty. She didn't know much about the law, but she'd seen on TV about cases of injustice where criminals were released for lack of evidence. Landon was a detective and what he said made a great deal of sense. In addition, he loved her. She had to leave him the reins and only worry about one thing: holding onto him for dear life.

"I was an idiot to ask you to come and stay with me like that," he continued, heartfelt. "I'm so sorry, Nat. I didn't want to scare you with the truth, but the stress made me act like an asshole."

Since this story had begun, she had been living with the dear of danger on different levels. Now, after Landon's forthright statement of the facts, while her rescuers were planning to use her as a worm on a hook, she saw the danger looming like THE END screenshot to the movie of her life.

"Come with me, Nat. Allow me to be closer to you than the escort will," he said, his voice and gaze steadfast in his love.

Love … Love was speaking through his mouth.

Fear and happiness melted in the crucible of her soul, producing bittersweet tears that slid down to moisten her lips.

"Tomorrow is Friday. I'm not working," he said. "I'll help you get your things. We're gonna do this together. Okay?"

"Okay, Lan," she whispered, trembling.

He walked around the car and hugged her.

In his arms, she lost herself. It was the safest place in the world.

"Nat … I found you by chance, but I'm not gonna lose you for any reason."

37 – At last!

He couldn't wait to see Natalie's expression when she found herself face to face with him. Certainly, she would be surprised. An interesting way to start her week …

It was six in the evening. She should've been back an hour ago, according to her routine. She lived in a residential area a few miles away from downtown, in one of the two-story condos lined on both sides of the wide street. Some units had stairways separating one condo from another, and between them and the street there were some wide strips of grass, intersected by walkways leading to the front door.

His desire had unfairly slowed down the clock, forcing him into an endless waiting game. It was wearing him out, although it added excitement to the upcoming moment.

After seeing that she wasn't at home, he had parked the rental car on the opposite side of the street about thirty yards away, camouflaging it among those parked by the tenants who apparently didn't have indoor garages. She wouldn't notice him.

Every vehicle entering his hearing range elicited a gasp, followed by the immediate disappointment when it passed to the visual range, and he could see that it wasn't her Toyota.

His heart seemed to be a hot title in a Wall Street hectic day.

She must have had a mishap, he thought, impatient behind the wheel.

While he wondered, again, if the approach he'd planned to meet her was appropriate, a red car came from the opposite direction. When he saw the blinker flashing and it slowing down at Natalie's house, adrenaline gave him a rush shaking his stomach. His hand darted onto the handle.

It was her Toyota. She parked right there.

He didn't have much time. The distance between them was more than double the length of her walkway.

Before she got out of the car, he opened the door, slipped out and crouched. After closing it quietly, so as not to attract her attention, he furtively peeked over the front hood. Natalie was already out of the car: seeing her unleashed a tsunami inside him. She slammed the door, set the alarm, and headed toward the walkway.

She had her back to him.

Carpe Diem.

Due to her wedge sandals, Natalie walked with the sluggish pace of someone coming home after a long work day, while he rushed, crossing the street on the balls of his feet. He took three or four steps for each of hers. The distance between them was decreasing second by second. In white jeans, bag on her shoulder, with the gold of her hair fraying on the fuchsia of her blouse, she was extremely sexy. He prayed so much that she wouldn't turn around. His eyes on her round and teasing backside, he moved faster, pushed by his excitement. He started down the walkway too. Now she was a few yards from the door, some less than what remained to him for reaching her. A grin stretched his lips. He passed from running to walking, but lengthening his stride that his rubber shoes kept silent. He intended to grab her when she inserted the key in the lock.

When he was a few steps from her ...

"Don't move!" he heard behind him. "Hands up!"

He turned around instinctively. Two men, one white, one African American, were at the beginning of the walkway. They approached him, determined and threatening with their guns raised, wearing jackets with FBI printed on one side of the chest.

A wave of terror crossed him inside from his bowel to throat.

"No! Don't shoot! Don't shoot," he cried out, his hands up and eyes wide.

"Miss Lunn, step aside," said the African American, holding him at gunpoint.

"Hands behind your head," ordered him the white guy.

"Henke?" he heard from Natalie, while carrying out the order.

"I did nothing. Please, don't shoot. I have my green card," he gasped, his legs trembling under the rumble in his chest.

He couldn't see anything. Fear to be killed must have shut his eyes. He heard only his own gasping. And Natalie's voice …

"What are you doing here?"

He opened his eyes.

The two agents, now no more than five yards away, seemed doubtful, remaining in firing position. The one who had spoken to Natalie addressed her again.

"You know him?"

"He's my friend, agent Clancy. He's okay."

He couldn't see her because he was stuck on those terrifying guys, but she sounded as shaken as he was.

"Yes, I'm her friend. I have my papers."

The two looked at each other, even though their guns still threatened him.

"His name is Henke. He's one of my students. He's German," she added, placing her hand on his shoulder.

"All right, Miss Lunn" said agent Clancy, holstering his weapon.

"Sir," said the white one, imitating him. "You shouldn't approach people like that on the street. You could find yourself in trouble."

"I'm sorry, Officer," stammered Henke, anything but reassured. "I came to visit her. She wasn't here, so I waited, thinking to surprise her."

He explained the situation with friendly intentions, but he felt even more intimidated by how they stared at him.

"Thank you, agent Clancy," said Natalie. "I very much appreciate your diligence."

"It's our job, Miss Lunn," said Clancy, in a serious tone. "Good night."

"You too."

When the two were far enough away, he turned to Natalie.

"You can put them down now," she said, more amused than tense.

He realized he still had his hands behind his head.

"What the fuck is going on here?" he said, still trembling in his body and voice.

"Come inside. I guess you need something to drink."

He entered the house with her, looking back at the street to make sure that those fanatics were really gone. And even before he closed the door, he took another look. He followed her to the island surrounded by the stove, sink, shelves and cupboards, in that large room with no dividing walls serving as a kitchen and living room.

"What are FBI doing at your house?" he asked, still upset.

"Is gin okay?"

"Yes, thanks."

She looked distracted. While watching her prepare the drink, he remembered that he hadn't set the car alarm—he didn't want to make noise …

"Wait, I'll be right back," he said, hurrying to the door. *All we need now is someone stealing it.*

As he put his nose outside, he looked for the agents with his gaze.

There were several cars parked along the roadsides. Despite a meticulous scanning, he wasn't able to locate them. He picked up the remote control and then, hands in plain sight, he started down the walkway. He went toward the car, continuing to press the button until the headlights confirmed it was locked.

I looked like a chicken shit, he flushed, angry with himself.

On the other hand, it was the first time in his life that he saw a gun pointed at him.

He went back into the house.

His fright gradually receding, he joined Natalie in the sitting area. He flopped on the couch, placing the keys next to a ceramic ashtray on the small table in front of him.

"Here you go," she said, handing him the glass.

He thanked her with a nod and took a sip.

Fear and shame were almost completely absorbed. Because of those feelings, he noticed his progress only now: when they were dating, he picked up and took her home, but she had never invited him in.

"This is amazing. You've got a wonderful house."

"I wish it were mine."

"Yes, you told me that you're renting it. I meant that it's well furnished and big."

"Oh. But it's not only me. There's a family living in the apartment upstairs."

While he wondered why she was still standing …

"I didn't know you were back."

Her tone had changed. He watched her carefully. He got the impression that the anxiety he'd felt in her voice reflected into her expression too.

"I got here this morning. I meant to surprise you," he said, placing the glass in the ashtray to avoid staining the table. "But apparently, when it comes to surprises I'm an amateur compared to you."

She smiled feebly. She kept standing with the bottle in her hand and a veil of sadness on her face.

"What's up, Nat?"

"Henke, something important happened in the last week."

She spoke gravely, diverting her gaze to the glass.

He frowned.

She poured another drop of liquor into the glass. Then she rested the bottle on the table.

He could feel her tension. Analyzing the scene on the walkway with a cool head and seeing her so afraid, he thought she may be in some trouble. He got up to comfort her: she must need it.

"Come here, Nat."

He hugged her. This warm contact unpredictably shook him in his senses. The selfless intention was driven away by a greedy selfish instinct. The excitement reminded him that he had been waiting for this moment since he left three months ago. He pulled back to look at her face.

"I missed you," he whispered tenderly, drowning in the mountain lake of her irises.

He brought his lips to hers, but she looked down and turned her head away in one motion.

Baffled by her reaction, he looked for her eyes again, but she denied them to him.

"Nat?"

"person met week I last another," she said, as quick as downing a shot.

He stared at her, wondering what the hell she just said …

Then, when those words wandering in his head found their place in a meaningful sentence, he felt embarrassment warm his cheeks. He couldn't put two words together.

"I found myself in a very dangerous situation," she continued, going back to look at him. "He's helping me get out of it."

The connection between that phrase and the agents outside was immediate and left him speechless.

"I'm sorry, Henke. They said I can't talk about it."

She looked pretty scared.

"Is there anything I can do?"

"Henke. It's hard and embarrassing for me. I remember what we said on Skype, but this situation fell on me just like that, totally unexpected."

This response scorched his heart. He cared for her, and she was annoyed by it? His feelings began to burn. In all senses.

"And this man, who is he?"

"I came here to get some things becau…"

"Will you stop evading my questions?" he got mad, barely holding back the urge to grab her arm. "I asked you who this man is."

"Henke, I can't talk."

"Is he another student?"

"Of course not."

"And what the hell is this *I can't talk* supposed to mean?"

"It means that I've been living at his house since Friday. Happy now?"

"Huh?"

She stood stern, as if to confirm what she said.

"Oh ... Wow! I mean ... Wow!" he laughed, agitated, putting his hands on his hips while disappointment was beating his pride.

"It's more complicated than you may think."

"Actually, I'm not thinking at all. I just can't right now ... I mean, you were flirting with me on Skype just ten days ago, for God's sake. You couldn't wait for me to be back, we talked about Disney World, New York, Vegas ... And now you're telling me that three days ago you moved in with a man you just met?"

"There's more to it than that, Henke," she retorted, flushing and her eyes flickering.

In that very instant, his parents flashed in his brain. He was dumbfounded. He realized he was doing exactly what he despised in others: to indulge in fits of anger, jealousy or any feeling apart from a civilized behavior. As a child, he had witnessed too many scenes, and when his parents finally separated, he promised himself that he would never go down to their level.

Demeanor, Henke! he imposed himself, convening the strict standards he was following since he was thirteen. *It's over anyway. She moved onto this guy.*

"Well, Nat," he said, putting himself in front of her. "I guess you have your reasons to take a step like that."

She frowned as if surprised. Then her features squeezed of with sadness.

"I'm really sorry, Henke."

Be a sport. Think of Brigitte. You were dating her.

"I hope you can forgive me if I hurt you."

If you'd fallen for Brigitte as she did for this guy, maybe you would've stayed in Stuttgart.

"That's true, I said that we would keep dating on Skype ..."

Or, if Brigitte were an American and Nat were a German ...

"...and I meant it at the time."

... I bet you wanted to be with Brigitte.

"But these last few days were unimaginable."

No, Henke. It's your American dream putting Nat on the pedestal.

"As I said, I can't talk about it. But you'll be the first to know the whole story as soon as it's over."

Now you got a job. You don't need her to be here. She's nothing. There are plenty more fish in the sea.

"I haven't been on Skype, but I thought to call you tomorrow and clarify, since I believed you were coming back Sunday."

Tell her something, or she'll think you're upset.

"It's all right, Nat. You were clear. I think I understand what happened. In a sense, at least. Anyway, I passed by to tell you that they hired me. I got a two-year contract. That's why I came back early."

"Really? That's great," she beamed, her eyes wide with enthusiasm. "I'm happy for you. You deserve it."

Bitch. "Thank you, Nat."

That fit of rage made him think. He wondered why people that break your heart don't understand that they only crush the pieces left by sincerely rejoicing for your success.

She invited him in by spreading her arms.

He accepted.

Hugging her again, feeling her body against his, it was clear beyond any doubt why he thought *people who break your heart* ...

"Now your dream to settle down here has become true."

"It seems so," he replied, struggling to prevent his hurt from marring his tone. "Even though I guess I have to change my plan."

"I know that I was part of it ..." she said, patting his shoulder.

Shit! he got mad at himself—his hurt fooled him by making him sound like a loser.

"... and I was happy to be. Believe me. Unfortunately, a mess happened. It was like being caught in an avalanche."

"You don't have to explain anything, Natalie," he stopped her, fearing she was about to voice the joy that this other man gave to her.

"Natalie?" she frowned.

"Okay, Nat."

It was wonderful to feel so close to her, but he recognized the sensation: melancholy was preparing the final assault to the castle of his dignity.

"Henke, is everything all right?"

"Yup. I only ask you one favor."

"Sure."

"Walk me to the car. Those two hippies could shoot me for real this time."

He knew that this joke would cost him some tears once he was alone; however, he just wanted to save face at this time.

"Are you serious?" she laughed, stepping back and looking at him.

"Just kidding," he winked, masking his sadness. "I'd better go, now."

"Okay, Henke," she smiled, holding out her hand. "See you at school?"

My ass. "You bet," he said, shaking it coldly.

"You know, now I have a level 2 group. But I'll surely see you around."

Fuck you. "Surely."

"Maybe sometimes we could have lunch together, if you like."

"See you, Natalie," he said, picking up the keys from the table. "Take care."

38 – And You Are ...?

The idea of making dinner for Landon stayed with Natalie throughout her day at school. The previous night, he enjoyed her fried rice with vegetables—from her Filipino student's recipe—and now she intended to delight him with her mom's scallops in white wine; but Henke's unexpected visit had taken a couple of stars away from her top mood.

Dumping him in person rather than on video drained a lot of energy from her. She hadn't had the opportunity to call him on Skype: upset by the whole thing with James and physically busy trying to organize her life at Landon's apartment in that weekend, she was drunk on a cocktail of love and sex, and hadn't worried about it. Especially because she had a week of time.

Impeccable but deceitful reasoning. She realized it now.

It was a matter of honor and cowardice. She just hadn't had the courage to tell Henke that she'd fell for another man while he was in Germany. This was the main reason why she hadn't spoken with him sooner.

It was good that Landon's figure was inseparable from the FBI's secret operation. This had provided her strong pretext to avoid the labyrinth of explanations where she would have stumbled into blame, anger, and resentment. So, why should she go through it? However, she had to tell Henke something to ease his burden. She was sorry for hurting him like she did, also because it painted her in a bad light; but it is better for everybody to put a horse out of its misery rather than let it suffer in agony.

The worst part was to see the concern for her on his face, while she was cynically loading the shotgun, although not yet sure of using it. But when he tried to kiss her, the thought of Landon pulled the trigger.

Henke was a handsome guy. Smart, determined and nice. She felt something for him, even though it had remained in the embryo stage. There were two reasons why she hadn't let him get any closer than her clothes ... The first one was the nature of her attraction to him, more rational than instinctive; the second one was that he came from another country, so who could assure her that he would be back in the States?

She thought she could make his forced departure productive by testing their relationship through the arduous distances of space and time. Skype would allow her to look deeply inside herself and, at the same time, ponder the seriousness of Henke's intentions. The test gave a positive result. When they talked about visiting Orlando together, she was excited: that's why he had taken her seriously, because she **was** serious. But things change. People change. A new, lightning-fast, impetuous sentiment had reset her heart. To use some blue on the palette to paint the sky is fine; but if that blue is blended with yellow, you have to change the subject. A green sky doesn't exist. It would be a stretch, as well as to stubbornly claim the pure blue, a color that is no longer on the palette. The Natalie who dated Henke, the one who chatted with him online, was trapped in the ether forever. Her fault? No. That little tube of yellow acrylic had been shot into her heart. Nobody could be blamed for that. It just happened.

The root of her torment was the fear of doing the wrong thing. She got it while driving to Landon's home. So, what was the right thing? If she no longer felt any interest toward Henke, what was she supposed to do? To go to Las Vegas with him as she would buy an ice-cream to a child to make him happy? Landon had come into her life by chance or fate, just like Henke did six months before. The difference was that while kissing Henke she wondered if she should take the next step, while kissing Landon she wanted nothing else but to take the next step.

She solved the problem with her conscience by referring to the law that balances loving relationships: in order for someone to rejoice, someone else needs to suffer. She had no responsibility if it was like that, so her guilt wasn't justified. She just had to go with the flow and enjoy the sea on Landon's sailboat.

Once she decided to give up on cooking, she turned to junk food. He confessed he was a chicken nuggets addict, especially if he could dip them in blue cheese dressing. He said it was good for the body every now and then: she didn't know from what source he got this information, maybe he made it up, but to fight him on this subject was the last thing she cared about. She just wanted his strong arms to hold her as soon as possible, to warm her and take away some of the coldness left by Henke—as he said good-bye, she got the feeling that he meant it.

The nuggets were ready for the microwave. The table, already set with candlelight, cutlery, napkins, glasses, mineral water and, of course, blue cheese, was just waiting for the two lovebirds.

She was making her corn salad when the doorbell startled her.

A sudden discomfort replaced her impatience to see Landon. She had been living in his first floor apartment in a building downtown for three days, but to have a visitor when she was alone hadn't happened yet. She was anxious because they rang at the door instead of intercom. In addition to the embarrassment of explaining her presence to someone who might know Landon better than she did, the problem was that she didn't know how to handle the situation.

Should I invite them to come in? she wondered, wiping her hands on a dish towel.

Another ring canceled her hope that they were gone.

She looked at the clock on the wall. Landon wouldn't be home from at least a half hour, too long for entertaining a stranger who Landon himself may not let in.

While going to get her phone, just in case she needed to call him, they knocked again.

Maybe it's the agents?

She tiptoed to the door and peered through the peephole. It was a girl.

She felt inclined to open the door. And she did.

It was a pretty brunette with straight hair reaching her breasts and cheekbones that accentuated her jaw. She was wearing stonewashed jeans and a thin white jacket, she had minimal makeup on and a baby in her arms.

"Good evening."

"Isn't this Landon Vitman's house? The cop," the girl began, frowning, her eyes onto the door plate.

She must be close to her age. Perhaps a few years younger.

"Yes, it is."

"Are you his wife?" urged the girl, surprised or aggressive, it wasn't clear.

She had an attitude like she was chewing nails and spitting tacks, although the only thing in her mouth was some dazzling white teeth. This girl's intrusiveness roused her awareness that she was on the side of the threshold authorizing questions.

"I'm a friend. And you are…?"

"I'm a friend too."

Perhaps it was the way the girl stared at her with her big dark eyes, or the fact that she seemed so relaxed, but Natalie had to admit she was feeling intimidated ... But no, there was nothing to be worried about. Although it might seem like it, it was impossible for the girl to be a rival. Landon loved her. Plus he assured her he didn't have any commitments with anyone. And he wasn't a liar. It had to be something related to his work. Maybe a girl in trouble whom he was helping, since she introduced herself as a friend and not as his cousin or whatever.

"Listen. Landon isn't here right now," she said, friendly. "Do you want to leave him a message?"

"What time will he be back?"

"In about thirty minutes."

The girl pursed her lips, thinking. She continued to gently cradle the baby, wrapped in a purple shawl, who slept with his chubby cheek resting on her shoulder.

The awkwardness of the moment was taking over. The girl was standing in front of her, now avoiding her gaze; however, since she didn't give any indication of speaking or leaving, Natalie took a step forward on the landing to see the baby.

"So gorgeous. What's his name?"

"April. It's a she."

She was about to ask her how old the baby was, but she realized that her kindness wasn't appreciated. The girl's face said she'd rather hit her finger with a hammer than have a conversation.

"Never mind," murmured the girl. "I'll come back later."

The girl turned around, without looking at her or waiting for her reply, and walked to the stairs at a slow pace, as if not to disturb her daughter's sleep.

Bewildered, Natalie went back inside and closed the door.

She collapsed into a chair to think about what just happened.

39 – No Problema

Landon spent all afternoon at his office. As usual, when he didn't patrol Charleston's streets with Devin, the time moved like a waltz instead of samba; but maybe the slowness of the metronome hinged on his impatience to embrace his girlfriend again.

My girlfriend!

To think of Natalie like that turned him to mush. The smile blossoming on his face was a symptom of his welcome inner peace.

He was driving on the way home when the phone rang. He answered, putting it on speakerphone.

"Hello?"

"Landon? It's Carlos."

"Hey, dude. What's up? How you doin' at the store?" he asked, putting the window up—the noise from the street nearly covering his voice.

"I'm doing good, man. Nitya, Mr. Stone's wife, gave birth to a girl three weeks ago. Everybody's fine now."

"I'm glad. Give 'em my best."

"You know, Mr. Stone wants Nitya to take some time for herself and the baby. This means he's gonna keep me for another four or five months."

"Really?"

"Fuck yeah."

"What great news, Carlos. I knew you'd prove to Stone that you're a good boy," he said, happy and proud. "And what about school?"

"I'm not the first in my class, but I'm doing fine. Listen …"

"Yes?"

"I called you 'cause it's mom's birthday the day after tomorrow. Will you come over for dinner?"

"The day after tomorrow, Wednesday ... I can do it."

"Awesome!"

"Is it okay if I bring my girlfriend?"

"*No problema*. It's important for mom to have you with us on her special day 'cause she considers you like family. If it wasn't for you, we ..."

"Clarita once told me that she was the greatest cook in all Puerto Rico," he swerved, to keep the conversation light.

"She's not bad."

"Not bad? Hahaha. Man, I'm gonna tell her how you talk about her culinary genius."

Carlos was laughing.

"Ungrateful child!"

"Then we'll see you tomorrow at seven?"

"Let's do seven-thirty."

"Okay."

"Say hi to Clarita for me."

"Oh, by the way. I forgot."

"What?"

"*Clarita* said that if you dare bring dessert, wine or any gift, she's gonna kick you out. And she means it."

"Hahaha. Okay, dude. We'll only bring ourselves."

He had risked his career for Carlos, and that he was winning the bet made him feel incredibly good. It was like Jeff told him the day he became a detective: the greatest satisfaction is seeing someone that you believed in succeed.

When he arrived at his neighborhood, he parked in the closest free space to his building, about ten yards away from the front door. Then he got out.

The sun was still strong. The shops were about to close. Some passers-by were ahead of him on the sidewalk, some coming in his direction, and a few more walked on the sidewalk across the street. The traffic in the street was flowing. He was walking and looking around. His pulse quickened when he noticed Natalie's Toyota, although it wasn't the one he was trying to spot. He studied the parked cars in the area, when the high beams of one on the opposite side of the road drew his attention by flashing. When he saw the Feds, he felt better. He gave them a nod and pulled out the keys from his pocket.

"Pssst!" he heard as he was about to open the front door.

He turned in the direction the sound had come from, the other side from where he left his Audi. An elegant lady in a suit was coming toward him, but she was too far away to be calling him as if he were a cat; maybe the man who had just passed by, but in this case he was calling to someone else, since he was going on his way. Then he noticed a waving arm in a white sleeve out the window of a car stopped along his sidewalk. It was no more than six yards away. It was curiously parked in a different direction compared to the other cars, with the hood angled toward him.

The hand seemed to wave at him to approach. He looked around again. There was nobody else in the area. They must mean him.

Frowning, he went to check.

By the pink nails, the insistent hand belonged to a woman. When he reached a point from which he could see her face through the windshield, he stopped thunderstruck. He felt his heart and stomach clench in alarm. He couldn't move.

What he had convinced himself was a bad dream—it took months—was now ambushing him in reality.

"Get in the car," she seemed to say.

She leaned out of the open car window on the passenger side which looked out on the sidewalk. While she spoke in a low voice, her expression and tone were very clear in their animosity.

There was some fear in what he felt; in fact his lips were trembling.

She leant out again. The anger that he read in her face was the *lasso* she caught him with.

With a swirl of memories and feelings crowding his throat, making it hard to breathe, he started toward her. He stopped right away as he stepped on something. He looked down. It was his house keys. He picked them up and, still in disbelief, headed toward the car, which was in catastrophic condition—dents on door and fender, it looked like it hadn't gone through a car wash for years.

He opened the door, but hesitated. He felt like once he entered this contraption, things would never be the same. He turned to the front door and looked up at his window. The light was on: he used it as a flash for the last photo of the world that he built before it collapsed on him.

He sighed and sat down beside her.

"Keep quiet," she ordered him when he was about to close the door.

There was a strange smell of vomit in there, despite the open windows. Probably his sickness about the situation was fooling his sense of smell.

"From the way you paled, you must remember me even though it's been twelve months and you were drunk," she welcomed him, tartly, putting the windows up.

"How are you, Tiana?" he stammered, his fists clenched and eyes lost on his knees, lacking the courage to look at her.

"Wow. You even remember my name! I'm impressed."

His head turned to her as if against his will.

He remembered her with a short ponytail, while her hair had grown out past her breasts now. She was more beautiful than the image of her that he kept in his mind. Maybe it depended on the sadness that shone under the veil of sarcasm she spoke to him with. Or it was his guilt that distorted all of his perceptions.

"What the fuck," she hissed on a few honks from traffic, turning to the unaware driver.

His eye uncontrollably slid to her breast, more endowed than he remembered.

Why the fuck are you looking at her boobs? he cursed himself, even though he did without malice—he'd just noticed a difference.

As she looked at him again, his gaze went hastily back to her face.

Dozens of times he was tempted to find her and answer for his crime; but then, he always bumped into a *Why* which was more solid than his conscience. It had happened by now. To manage his remorse had frightened him less than to watch his life fall apart.

"Have you seen her?" she said suddenly.

Every time her voice passed through his ears, it was an internal upheaval.

She must have seen that her question wasn't clear to him, since she pointed to the back seat with a slight and resolute movement of her head. Her long hair moved as driven by the wind.

He turned to the back seat and realized that there was a child seat with a baby inside right behind him. A fit of surprise pushed his eyes on Tiana again.

"She's yours, asshole."

"Mine?!"

"Yours, fuck."

"Yeah, right."

She was impassive.

His laughter died. He looked back at the baby.

"We'll do the DNA testing and all the shit you want, who cares. She's yours. You were the only bastard coming inside me at the time."

Tiana was frightfully serious. The words she uttered bounced between the walls of his mind like balls in a squash court. A hellish din. He swallowed. Thousands of thoughts were emerging from his brain and each slimly twisted into his heart like a tentacle: his mother, the damned night at the club, the gun, his guilt, his shame, the process, Jeff, his career, Natalie, the baby … His life would never be the same again.

"I didn't want to come to you. But fuck, man!" Tiana whispered, furious. "My mother is right. The priest said it too. I despise you. I didn't want to see you again, but it's unfair that April pays for your callousness while you keep enjo…"

"April?" he drawled.

"I tried to find a fuckin' job before giving birth. I tried, shit. But they didn't hire me. And things are gonna be worse now, 'cause the son of bitch don't hire single mothers."

As she spoke, he thought of how tough her life was after the conception…

No, man. Rape!

...pregnancy, loneliness, childbirth, trauma and economic troubles. He tried, but he couldn't comprehend even a bit of what she faced because of him. To realize that he wasn't any better than the criminals he arrested destroyed him. He decided to turn himself in.

"We've been struggling for three months," Tiana roared, fierce. "My parents are helping us, but they've already got their own shit and ... and April is so small."

He listened. He also wanted to look at her, but he couldn't take his eyes off the ... his daughter? Her round little face, dark complexion, brown hair standing upon her head as she had some gel, her chubby little hands, she slept hugging a plush doll, giving some sudden sucking to the pacifier in her mouth. That little angel was the allegory of innocence. He could even hear her funny feeble snore.

"Have you enjoyed fucking me?" she continued, brutal. "And here she is. We can't make it by ourselves. You see how you wanna deal with it, but take your fuckin' responsibility. Don't force me to go to a lawyer. I really don't feel like telling him how it started."

He was paralyzed. Maybe she wouldn't press charges. Among the thousand maimed thoughts, rambling ideas, and chaotic frames of memory stunning him in that moment, only one intent was clear: to find a bond, establish a contact between himself and the tender creature napping in the seat. He didn't know how, but his temptation to touch her was stronger than anything. He slowly reached out his hand to her feet that were covered by white socks. He felt them with his fingers. They were so small and soft. He could feel their delicacy through the cotton. A rush of chills creased his skin and numbed his back.

He realized he was smiling. Despite the tragedy, he was smiling? Shit, his life was going to the dogs and he …

A sudden, sharp pain at his ribs cut short his thoughts. He turned to Tiana: she had just hit him with her elbow.

He was angry, but immediately the intense gaze of her big dark eyes disarmed him. They were tremendously bright. He felt that the harshness with which she was legitimately treating him was about to melt into tears of emotion.

The bullet that had exploded twelve months ago went astray in a curve of Time and only now found its target.

"This is my number. Call me within a week … Now … Now get out of my fuckin' car," she said quickly, her voice broken from a tension that evidently she could no longer hold.

He accepted the card she was handing him, his eyes stuck in hers. An odd anger sparkled on the beauty streaked by her tears.

Now he understood why she hit him: by making contact with April's feet, he'd moved her. A torture to her, maybe worse than the rape.

40 – Just...

He lived on the first floor, but it took fifteen minutes to climb the stairs. The only thing that he understood during this time was that it required longer to recover from the Tiana-earthquake: it wasn't enough to accept the idea of being a father or to decide how to handle the situation. Now he could just take care of Natalie, the only person in the world—including himself—that still meant something to him.

He'd been tormenting himself about how to approach the truth for months. He had denied, ignored, hidden, altered, disguised, fooled, shifted, fought and rejected it. A complete fiasco. Tiana just taught him that no truth can be faced if you don't accept it in the first place. He wouldn't repeat the same mistake with Natalie. No excuses. No tricks. No filtering information. Just the facts. Nitty-gritty.

Yeah. This is how it must be, he thought, opening the door.

His blonde sat at the table, charming in a fuchsia blouse. She looked deep in thought, but, as she saw him, the sun came up on her lips. This dawn lasted for a moment though, obscured by a sudden cloud of concern.

"Lan?" she said thoughtful, heading toward him. "You okay?"

"Why?"

"You're so pale. Something happened?"

"Yes."

He didn't see curiosity in her face. Or, if it was there, the apprehension had put it beneath her curl.

"Nat, we need to talk."

He took off his leather jacket. While he was hanging it on the hat hanger next to the door …

"A girl came by for you a while ago."

Boom. The anxiety that was threatening him just exploded in his stomach.

"What girl?"

"She didn't say her name. Only that she's your friend. She was a brunette, long hair, mid-twenties. She was carrying her baby. A few months old, I guess."

The echo of the explosion increased.

"She came here?"

"An hour ago, more or less."

The terror that Tiana had anticipated him …

No, it can't be.

Natalie would never have welcomed him so lovingly if she knew.

"But I didn't let her in. I said you weren't here and you'd be back later. She walked away without leaving a message."

She sounded like she was trying to justify herself for doing something wrong. He felt like shit. Everything he did hurt others. He needed to get rid of his burden as soon as possible.

"What's the matter, Lan?"

Now she seemed frightened.

"Nat. I do love you. I'm not gonna hide anything from you."

He remembered something about the trip from Columbia. Albeit he had good intentions, he didn't tell her right away the real reason he wanted her to move to him. Result: their first fight.

"It's about the girl, am I right?"

Whatever she was assuming, the absence of indignation in her expression showed that she was not even close to the truth.

He cleared his throat.

"I didn't mention it 'cause I thought she was out of my life. But now she reappears, so I have to ... I want to tell the whole story."

She frowned. Her lips furrowed approaching the corners of her mouth. She was on the defensive. At least that was his impression.

He grabbed her hand and led her to the table, but seeing it set for dinner, he swerved toward the sofa.

"Will you?"

She sat on edge of the pillow, half-turned to the left. He sat next to her on that side.

"This is hard for me, Nat. I always kept this secret locked in here," he added, pointing to his head. "It's the first time I let it out."

Her beauty was lifeless in body and features. For a moment, he felt like he was in the showcase of a boutique talking to a mannequin. Then a sigh slightly swelled her cheeks.

"As I told you in Columbia, in the park, my father left when I was six. So my relationship with my mother was strengthened a lot. It was me and her against the world. There was my sister too, but she passed away soon after being hit by a car while playing in front of our house. I barely remember her. Before meeting Jeff, my mother was the only person who ever did anything for me. No one had ever cared about me. Only her. I loved her so much."

He expected a question about his mother or an objection about why he'd started from his childhood to explain a current event. Nothing like that. She was there stiff and sullen, looking at him with her blue and shiny eyes. However, thinking about that, he was wrong to expect it. He noticed that she tended to be quiet and listen when she was worried.

"My mother was sick. She had been struggling with diabetes since she was twenty. Three years ago, she fell down the stairs and broke her femur. No longer able to go to work, the rent became a problem. My pay was what it was and she needed two more years until she could retire. The only solution was to bring her here. I took care of her. Can you imagine what the inability to walk means to a sixty-year old lady with an ancient modesty, diabetic, suffering from osteoporosis? It was a problem even to go to the bathroom ... However, after almost two years of suffering, when she's finally able to go out by herself again, she starts to have severe abdominal pain. I take her to the hospital for a checkup and they find out she has cancer. One of the worst. In her pancreas. It was at an advanced stage and not even chemo could do anything. They told me it was better to keep her at home and take care of her, since she would live two months at most."

He took a break to get a glass of water, making sure to give her his back. He didn't want her to see him emotional. To tell his mother's story always resurrected pain, regret and anger that buried his joy of living. It was like putting a flame to an endless stream of gas: the pain flared up, burning his heart and making a lot of smoke to moisten his eyes ...

After drinking, he furtively ran his fingers on his eyelids and went back to sit. She was still unflappable in her composure of a delightful mannequin in fuchsia and white.

"When I was done with the doctor, I took her back here before returning to the police station. I went work, but my head wasn't in the game. My mother has always worked, since she was eleven. She had a hard childhood, in a family where there was never enough money. Nobody looked after her 'cause she was the youngest out of eight siblings. Today it would be different, but parents had a different mentality back then. When her diabetes appeared, she had to handle it on her own. Needless to say how this disease affects the life of those who have it. Then she got married, hoping to find support not only moral but material too. Instead, my father was a loser who got angry with her every time he got fired from a job. You know when you're too tired to keep carrying your baggage and you meet an apparently kind fellow? You think he's gonna give you a hand, but he burdens you with his too. That was my father. Luckily he left, although my sister's death ruined my mother's relief to be rid of him. The loss of a child marks a mother forever. It's like an infection that doesn't kill you but leaves you hanging on in agony till the end. However, she still had me. I was seven. She raised me by herself. She did what she could, poor thing, until Jeff put me back on track. Then I had some problems with a couple of corrupt cops at Baltimore PD, so I asked Jeff if he would help me move. He was in Columbia and made arrangements to send me to Charleston. And he also recommended my mother to a driving school here. Things got better, they were finally looking up for us and those up there must have been afraid that she would steal a little peace. I'm not talking about happiness. Just peace. So *they* arranged for her to break her leg. But she was a fighter. She was recovering well from this too. Therefore, since she didn't give up and also began to get her retirement check, *they* decided to settle their accounts, sentencing her to a painful death through an inoperable cancer. She suffered like a dog. Excruciating pain that made her beg for death to take her and me to give her some morphine in the meantime while she waited to die. It was like that at every hour of the day. Okay. Destiny is destiny. Fine. And fuck destiny. But at least give her some peace, man. If she hadn't stumbled on that fuckin' last step bringing down the trash, she wouldn't have broken her leg and she would've lived decently for a couple of years. Instead she suffered all the way down, from when she was born until she passed away. No break. Nat, she didn't deserve any of the pains she'd suffered."

He realized that his voice gradually started to vibrate as well as his eyes to water, but he didn't stop because the same traces of emotion had appeared in her face.

"The day they told me about the cancer, these thoughts were tearing me apart. She didn't know yet. Once I was done with my shift, I immediately went back to her. We spent the evening together watching DVDs. She was crazy for The King of Queens. She'd bought all nine seasons. She thought Doug, Carrie and Arthur were funny as hell. When she fell asleep, I had to get out because those thoughts were driving me crazy. I laughed with her for two hours, but I felt like hell inside. I drove to a club. I don't know. Maybe I was hoping that the deafening music would break through my brain, so I'd stop thinking. I didn't want to think about how life sucks. You see people worthy of reaching Heaven in a carriage drawn by winged horses suffer so badly, while criminals who fuck up their neighbors, even enjoying it, end up with health, money and happiness ... So, once at the bar, I asked for a bourbon. And another. And then again. The music was numbing me. Great! That was the plan. At one point this girl comes up to me and says 'Would you buy one for me too?'. You know, I was alone, sad, with a rage in my body that I could uproot a tree with just my teeth. And then this top model ... you saw she looks like a top model ... she comes to me with her miniskirt, smiling, simpering, eager to play. What's your name, a drink, what do you do, another drink, and the next moment we are on the dance floor. We share looks and touches with each other, the bass rumbles, she flirts with me, she rubs on me while dancing, the bourbon starts affecting me ... I still felt my anger inside, but my senses were distracted ... I don't know how, we end up in the restroom ... kissing ..."

He kept his eyes down. He was sick of hearing his own voice. He wanted to hear hers. He wanted to know what she was thinking. He raised his gaze that he had dropped when his story moved from that same apartment to the club ...

Here we are.

She'd darkened. When he had been speaking of his mother, she had the face of those who cry for a departed relative; now she looked as if her best friend didn't invite her to her own wedding. She must have sensed something. Certainly not everything. How could he confess that too? Maybe he'd better skip that part.

"Are you telling me that the child is yours?"

It was a shock to hear her speak. He instantly regretted he wished it.

"Tiana says yes, but I don't kn..."

"Tiana?"

"Her name is Tiana. That's the only thing I know about her. I don't know her, Nat. Counting tonight, I've seen her twice in my life. I know nothing about this wo..."

"Tonight?" she interrupted him, confused.

"She was in her car in front of the building when I came back... Tonight and a year ago. I've only met her twice. I swear."

"So, should I assume that you did her in the restroom of the club?"

He stood still in front her, as if no one had spoken.

She pulled back her curl and nodded, embittered.

The cowardly impulse to end the story right there acquired authority. Now she knew about April, who would come into his life anyway. Why add the rest? He would financially help Tiana, and she had no intention of going to a lawyer. Maybe it was better to leave the dead buried and rebuild on the grave.

While he was considering this opportunity, she stood up.

"Where are you going?"

She answered with facts, heading toward the bedroom.

He followed her.

She walked up to the closet and pulled out her suitcase.

"Nat?"

She ignored him, opening it on the bed.

"Please."

In response, she went into the bathroom and came out a minute later with her things, throwing them all in the suitcase.

"Okay. I'm gonna stand aside if that's what you want."

"I don't know what I want, Landon."

He felt his dream of love vanishing through his fingers.

She opened the drawer of the dresser that he made available for her and took out her linen.

He would do anything to stop her from filling that damned suitcase.

"Can I finish the story before you leave?"

She paused, giving him a look of disappointment instead of hate.

"Shit, Lan. You told me you had no commitments to anyone, and now I find out that you have a daughter?"

"But I only found that out half an hour ago! I swear, Nat. When I told you I was free, I was 100% positive."

The best thing about the truth is that you can support your voice and gaze forever and ever without worrying that they might betray you. In fact, she calmed down. She seemed disoriented.

"If you met her only that time at the club and had sex with her there, can you tell me how she knew your address?"

"I have no idea, Nat. I guess I told her I'm a cop. By knowing my name, it's not that hard to find out where I live. Plus you just need to look on the Internet."

"And what does she want from you?"

Her voice trembled this time.

"Nat, I'm not gonna hide anything from you 'cause I love you."

"Why the hell do you keep saying that?"

"Because … because there's more. Okay?"

He realized he had shouted. She looked petrified.

He couldn't look at her. He just couldn't while revealing his sin. Yes, he must tell her. If she found it out later, he would lose the last thing left too: his credibility.

He leaned his back against the door and lowered his head. In his peripheral vision, he could see her sandals' wedges. She didn't move from beside the bed.

"While we were kissing in the restroom, I remember that I wanted her … She was taking part in the game, but when … when I put my hands under her clothes, she said no. I was drunk and excited … and her attitude roused all the rage for my mother."

He expected a gush of blame, but nothing arrived at all. His need to know how his confession affected her made him lift his head.

Her expression was the same as before. Disoriented. Maybe he was too cryptic. Maybe she didn't get it because she didn't think he was capable of that. Or simply, she couldn't believe it.

"I was drunk, Nat. Can't remember ... I think I forced her to ... My memory is so shaky ..."

Her eyes quickly filled with tears. Her half-open mouth silently screamed her dismay. Now she understood. He got the urge to cry too. He went with it. He couldn't use his remaining energy to fight it. He needed it all to be able to reveal her the worst part.

Nitty-gritty truth. Fuck everything else.

Yes, but that was hard. The fuck if it was.

"When I try to remember ... it's all confused. I think ... I think I forced her to it ... I forced her, yes. I forced her, Nat. I'm sorry ... I'm fuckin' sorry ... I think I threatened her ... She didn't wanna be still ... That night I think ... That night I think I was carrying my gun on me ... and she ... she was crying ..."

To live the moment in his memory had always been a torment, but to hear it from his own voice sounded like an abomination.

God, what have I done?

She had started to sob, putting her hands through her hair. To see her like that, to hear her gasps, turned him into a torrent of pain.

The finishing blow was when he mentioned the gun. Until then she must have thought only about the physical violence and that was shocking. The idea of the psychological violence killed her.

"The bourbon, Tiana flirting with me and then denying it, my rage due to my mother's fate ... I'm not justifying, Nat. I'm a monster, I got that. I've already decided I will face all the consequences. Just ..."

"Just what?" she interrupted him, weeping bitterly, broken by anger and disappointment, panting as if they held her head under water and counted up to hundred. "Just what, Lan? You raped that poor girl. You did that with the gun they gave you to protect people. And you got her pregnant too. *Just* what?"

Just nothing. She was totally right. There was nothing he could say or do. He just wished he'd never been born. He could only take the shame and indignation in silence. That's why he stayed motionless when she passed beside him like a train, leaving the room in tears and with her suitcase.

41 – The Premonition

Sitting in her car, Natalie was at a cross road. The traffic lights had stopped her and a few other vehicles. It was dark by now, the only thing that her blurred sight could discern. She pulled out a tissue from her bag lying on the passenger seat and took advantage of the moment to wipe her eyes.

She was half-way between Landon's house and her own, and wondered how the hell she gotten that far. She'd been driving with the flow of the traffic, evidently moving from Broad Street to Meeting Street, slowing down not to rear-end anybody and respecting the signs; and yet, not a memory of the distance driven came to her. It was as if, once in her car, an autopilot somewhere inside her had taken the wheel, forgetting to record his shift. Upset, she rummaged through her memory, but the only recollection she found of the last ten minutes were thoughts and feelings hanging on Landon's voice like bats under the vault of a cave. Her last visual memory was of her suitcase, when she'd thrown it into the back seat. She turned back to check. It was there.

Landon's confession left her wandering through a desert. Wherever she looked at, she could see only dunes, with the wind howling *Over here!* but she unable to figure out where the voice came from.

She just wished to stop loving Landon for a day.

When we love someone, it's impossible to know if we are judging them objectively. We tend toward indulgence, we "adjust"—more or less unconsciously—the scale of the facts, we use a magnifying glass to evaluate their motives, justifying ourselves that our sight might not be as reliable as before. But we also run the opposite risk of exceeding in severity: aware of being dragged down by indulgence, we desperately row against the current to prove to the others—and ourselves—that our wisdom is strong, immune to the fallout of love.

The best place to judge is from a calm body of water, without even the smallest wave disturbing our concentration. Not a great place to live, but good for a day … Even there, though, a doubt would remain. To put yourself in the felon's shoes in order to grasp the shades of his act and then analyze it better? Or not to get too close to him so these shades don't divert your intent of identifying the basic color?

Landon's actions were inexcusable, from whatever angle she looked at it. Would this actually turn him into a monster, as he himself said? He didn't go to the club to please his lowest instincts, but to escape his unbearable and ruthless pain.

She couldn't believe she was driving again. When had she started moving? She didn't recall seeing the light change to green. Perhaps she'd better focus on the road, picking up her train of thought at the station of her bed. But how could she ignore her soul's cries? They were sharp enough to pierce her eardrums. Landon loved her, just as much as she loved him. She blindly believed that. The child, however, opened up a new scenario. He grew up with a lousy father for half of his childhood and without a father for the other half. To live the most delicate years without the protection and guidance of a respectable male presence will mark a life. He experienced it. He wouldn't let his own daughter suffer that fate. And because of himself! The Landon she knew would never allow it, and she certainly wouldn't be the one who dissuaded him from his noble intention. Plus, he liked Tiana. He said she looked like a model, fuck him. How could she ignore the classic family picture? She herself would be a rose among Van Gogh's sunflowers. If it were only Tiana, she would fight for Landon; but the feelings of the three of them paled when a baby was involved.

She still could see him before her, ashen complexion, absent in his gaze, stiff in his movements, a slave of his shame. He kept repeating that he loved her, as those who are about to dump somebody do …

A thought struck her.

What a bastard! He'd already made up his mind.

He just tried to make the separation less dramatic for both of them. That's why he confessed his wickedness: he hoped that she would be disgusted enough to leave voluntarily. He opened the door to her and said *Go* in such a subtle way that she had not realized. And she bought it. In fact, she left the apartment on her initiative and he didn't even try to stop her. He had invited her to stay at his place and, after only three days, *You gotta leave 'cause Tiana and my daughter are coming* … He must not have had the guts to do it up front. She was positive that he didn't plan their living together this way. No doubt. That unforeseen event had destroyed him for real. But nothing changed for her: the fox doesn't care if it's an organized hunt or a solitary hunter.

The autopilot told her she had made it home. She pulled over and turned off the engine. When it was time, instead of getting out, she relaxed her forehead on the steering wheel. The rope binding her lungs was loosening. She could feel the tension draining from her body and weep freely, not like while driving, when she was unconsciously tense.

It's true that the most acute mind isn't as good as an ordinary heart in terms of insights, she thought, with a smile as bitter as the tears she was tasting.

Before Landon returned, she'd tried to figure out who Tiana could be. She formulated a dozen hypothesis, all plausible rationally speaking, and all acceptable because they didn't threaten her position as "Landon's girl." But the premonition had knocked. She'd heard that shy rat-tat-tat, even though she didn't open. Pessimism or superstition, she didn't remember how she branded it, supported by the other logical hypothesis' solidity. Instead … her fuckin' curl was getting on her nerves! It tickled. She really needed to make up her mind and cut it.

She fixed her hair. As she wiped her eyes, an idea started whispering to her … The thought that he wanted to dump her knocked—very loudly—against the feeling produced by the image of him talking about Tiana. He nervously passed his hands through his hair, he struggled against sobs that seemed to want to censor him, tears flowed from his eyes as blood from a broken nose. She saw him destroyed by remorse. She could feel his pain. That was not a man who was conspiring to drop his girlfriend; it was a lonely and unarmed man who had given up under the blows of an injustice that hadn't hit him, but the person most dear to him.

She was missing something …

His mother!

She didn't ask him anything about her. Now she felt horrified by her own insensitivity. At first she was moved by her story; but then she thought he was using her to justify the rape. Impeccable deduction. Yes, that was consistent with Landon's style: she noticed how he liked to give the back story when he wanted to explain something, like on the return from Columbia.

Her feeling, however, shot down this reasoning.

She didn't trust her premonition when she spoke with Tiana, and she was wrong. Her heart! Premonitions and feelings are the heart's ways to communicate. So, what was the message?

Landon wants you, not Tiana.

It wasn't just optimism. Her heart meant so. She could feel it now.

She had been too hasty. He didn't want to dump her. He was only looking for a way to remedy his mistake without losing her.

No, she couldn't have thought of it as a *mistake*. Violence is never a mistake. It can't be. But maybe, *mistake* wasn't referring to the act of violence. The mistake was getting drunk, although after helplessly watching his mother's unjust conviction, he had every right to let himself go.

But the gun, no.

There was no excuse for that.

Suddenly another thought took shape, like when you notice that a plant you considered dead had begun to sprout.

What if the baby wasn't his?

Landon believed Tiana. But this Tiana, why didn't she show up after the rape? Or when she realized she was pregnant? Or when the child was born? Why did she only look for him now? He admitted his crime and was ready to answer for it; but perhaps there was a chance for them to work through this together. She knew too little of the story to give up the most beautiful thing that had ever happened to her. Now she regretted that she had spit on Landon's honesty just because the core of the truth was unacceptable. Maybe there was another solution. She had to go back to him. They needed to analyze the situ…

The door on the passenger side opened, startling her.

"Excuse me," a mustachioed, curly black-haired man smiled at her.

She didn't have even time to scream *Hey!* before his friendly expression became diabolic. She saw him pull out a gun and quickly sit next to her, throwing her purse into the back seat.

"Start the car," he ordered her, slamming the door and pressing the weapon against her side.

42 – The Theorem

No account remains open. Sooner or later, one way or another, for better or worse, they all will be closed. Always.

Landon had started thinking this way after meeting Jeff the very first time. Some proof came later, when he saw this 'Theorem of pending accounts' repeatedly applied to reality.

A friend in Baltimore who had been lonely for years, suddenly found Love. The one with the capital L.

A gangster who lived as a kingpin off of bloody money was viciously consumed by the HIV virus that no retaliation was able to thwart.

An old neighbor who had nothing left but to feed pigeons and strays, won half a million dollars in the lottery.

A woman left her husband, an honest worker, for a brilliant businessman who was arrested the following month.

His mother was the unfortunate exception and Tiana was the ruthless confirmation that life was ruled by this theorem.

He knew that his sin was shadowing him. He had always felt it lurking behind him, although nothing was visible when he looked back. So, with the passing of the time, the idea that it wasn't real, that he was being influenced by his guilt became stronger. But he also thought that this was a trap and he warned himself …

Don't get caught off guard. Remember the Theorem!

If you expect it, even a heavyweight's punch causes less damage. Therefore he didn't want to be caught off guard by his sin.

But the shock he had felt when he recognized Tiana through the windshield proved that he was foolishly watching the ring girl parade when the punch hit him. And now that he was down, he could see the unrelenting power of Time.

Through its flowing, Time expands your thoughts, dilutes your feelings, distracts you with some news and fades out your memory. Our reason isn't able to fight Time and its tricks: she tries, obstinately repeating to us that they're all special effects intended to mislead us in an attempt to catch us off guard; but her voice gradually acquires the typical accent of a court jester or a nut because nothing happens in the reality.

Be careful, man. This is just a mind game with which Time is trying to make you lower your guard.

So he kept his guard up, but then the exhausting and endless silence had him muddled. At some point, he believed he'd heard the bell, so he relaxed; but the round was still going on and the inevitably KO came.

Fear of wasting—with a distressing and vain wait—the miserable gray grain given to him from the grand hourglass and desire to dye this grain with bright colors of joy, these two feelings had slowly defeated him, sanctioning the hegemony of Time.

His wrongdoing was more atrocious than he'd ever thought. He realized that by measuring it with the fear of losing Natalie. And according to the Theorem, he would lose her.

She, the woman of his dreams.

When she had become real, a hope for happiness blossomed among his fear of the Theorem. The canceled Tiana-debt and the cashed Natalie-credit were suggesting that the Theorem could be just his delirium. Life, however, does not tolerate imbalances. She shows up suddenly like a debt collector or a benefactor, ready to cash in or pay, according to the nature of the pending account.

She's neither cynical nor generous: regardless of when and how, situations and people, she only minds to balance things.

While he was racking his brain amid the restless fog of doubt, an idea came to him.

What if Tiana was bluffing?

She sounded sincere, but people know how to pretend. Actors do it for a living. Wretches can do it out of necessity. Maybe she was struggling and decided to roll the dice on the chance that he might pay out.

He could elaborate dozens of hypothesis, though. The only concrete thing tying him to Tiana was his guilt. As for the rest, he didn't know anything about her. Sure she had probably told him about herself at the club, but he was drunk. He couldn't remember.

He tried to focus.

First of all, he needed to find out whether he was really April's father. Atonement could wait.

He got out of the bed and rushed to the hat rack. Frantically rummaging through his jacket pockets, he found Tiana's note. He pulled out his cell phone, which was in another pocket. With the apprehension of hearing her spiteful voice again devouring his heart, he began to dial the number, when the doorbell rang.

He opened it.

He frowned seeing Ramirez, one of Natalie's security detail.

"Are you okay, Vitman?" he asked. "You look troubled."

"What are you doin' here?"

"Miss Lunn's car isn't downstairs. We looked around the whole block and wonde…"

"She left about twenty minutes ago."

A shadow of worry, which likely reflected his own, fell on Ramirez's face.

"What's up?"

"Vitman, Johnson and I just got here to relieve Clancy for the night."

"Okay. Then call him," he perked up. "They must have followed her."

"I've already called," he murmured, his Mexican features twitching, making his complexion pale and revealing his discomfort. "When they left, Miss Lunn's Toyota was still here."

"What does *When they left* suppose to mean?"

"Clancy didn't wait for us."

It took him a few seconds to read between the lines.

"How the fuck do you guys relieve each other?" he hissed, putting Tiana's note in his pocket and looking for *Nat* on his phone.

"C'mon, Vitman. Don't play the model cop."

He called her.

"It's reasonable that they made one mistake," played down Ramirez. "Beside Friday and today, when she went to school, she never left this apartment without you."

"Dickheads," he murmured, staring into space with the phone on his ear. "Yet Clancy seemed a good one."

"You were already home, she was with you, we were on our way, and they were tired … It's understandable."

Come on, babe. Answer! he thought, irritated by each ring.

"We've been sticking to her like glue for three days, and nothing happened, apart from the incident with the German. So they thou…"

"What incident?" he jumped, also because he got disconnected.

"Didn't she tell you?"

"No, she didn't."

"One of her students came to see her and Clancy laid into him thinking he was the killer …"

While Ramirez spoke, he remembered the German she was dating before they found each other.

"Let's focus on finding Miss Lunn, shall we? So, Vitman. Is there anything we should know?"

"Huh?" he frowned, calling her again.

"Who was that girl? Has she something to do with the case?"

"What girl?"

"The one you entertained before getting home."

Now Natalie was not available. She must have turned off her phone, determined not to talk to him. His worries piled up … Natalie's disappointment and being without security, the fear of losing her, the German popping up, Tiana's return, fatherhood, his future, what to do next… He'd lost control and found himself imprisoned in a suffocating tangle of thoughts. But telling Ramirez about Tiana was out of question.

"They saw her prowling around with a child in her arms at the front door of this building," Ramirez continued, as Landon tried to contact Natalie again. "Clancy told me about the episode. He said that, when a neighbor came out, she snuck inside. He followed her to see where she was going. He climbed the stairs when he saw her in front of your door. Miss Lunn opened up and spoke to her. He listened to them, uncertain whether to intervene, but she left right away. He went back to his car without being noticed. They've been watching her, as she turned the car around and sat there waiting. Then you came along."

"She has nothing to do with the case," he cut short, eager to close the subject. "The phone rang a moment ago. Now it's off, so she's fine. She must be at home. Don't waste any more time. Go there and let me know if you find her. Otherwise, I'll alert my guys."

Ramirez nodded and dashed down the stairs as if he received the order from his superior, probably spurred on by the awareness that his colleagues were at fault.

It would take ten, maybe fifteen, minutes to get to Natalie's house. It was useless for him to go too. Maybe she was coming back, that's why she turned off the phone. It would be better for him not to leave the apartment, just in case. Meanwhile, he couldn't do anything but call Jeff to see how the investigation proceeded.

"Landon!"

"Jeff, listen to me."

"Wait. I got big news."

"Your guys lost Natalie," he said, realizing what Jeff told him only after speaking.

"They what?"

"They lost her. What news?"

"Holy shit!" Jeff shouted. "Call Clancy and Ramirez right now," he heard him yell, perhaps addressing Fitzgerald. "Tell 'em if they don't immediately find the witness, I'm gonna personally hang 'em."

"What the fuck is going on, Jeff?"

"Landon, James Gerling is our man," he stated it with seriousness and conviction. "I submitted the case to headquarters' attention. We got top priority."

Good on one side, but on the other hand his apprehension swelled as if it were about to burst in his chest.

"We found out how he does it," continued Jeff. "The motherfucker is acting on his own."

"How?"

"Our guys in New Orleans tried to shadow him. But guess what? They never saw him put foot outside the motel where he's supposed to stay right now."

"What the fuck are you telling me, Jeff?"

"They talked to the front desk employee. James Gerling checked in a week ago Friday. She noticed him having breakfast, coming and going till last Wednesday. So my guys asked the maids. They say that his room is in perfect order since Wednesday, as if nobody is in there. Today is Monday. Considering that his check-out is scheduled to be this Sunday and that the last flight taken by James Gerling is still the Philadelphia-New Orleans of that Friday ten days ago, the only alternative is that he got false papers. With all his money, it must have been easy to arrange."

"Hold on. Are you telling me that he could be in Charleston … right now?"

"Landon, we're reviewing the passenger lists of all airlines. We'll find him."

"Fuck, Jeff," he growled, stopping himself at the last moment from throwing the phone against the wall.

"We will narrow it down. We're checking out the passengers' names on the flights from Charlotte-Nashville and Tampa-Detroit in the days before Cindy Cook's and Mallory Jackson's murders. James was supposed to be in Charlotte and Tampa, but he was actually in Nashville and Detroit under a false identity. Think about it. How many passengers can we find on both routes, flying back within some days after the crimes? We'll be able to count them on one hand. We know what James looks like, and it will be easy to catch his disguise. We will check his movements under the false name, and you can bet we'll find he was in Boston, Austin and, now, Charleston."

"Good plan! In the meantime he's here, and Natalie is on her own ..."

"Landon ..."

"I knew I shouldn't trust Feds."

"Don't worry, son. Everything is gonna be fine."

"And what if he isn't traveling by plane? If he got different identities for each murder? Have you thought about that?"

Jeff was quiet for a moment.

"Listen, Landon. Given the distances, he must have been flying. It's all about identifying the false name he's using. The switchboard is at our disposal. We've already passed them the list of all hotels and B&Bs in Charleston with their phone numbers. Each operator is gonna check three of them once we got the name. We'll settle all this in five minutes. Also, we've already arranged to fly to Charleston. Take it easy."

He didn't comment, since he should have asked him why he didn't say anything about the possibility that James had more than one fake identity ... Anyway, the main problem was that Natalie was alone. He would solve this.

"Jeff, I'm gonna tell the Commissioner the whole story and we'll getting moving."

"Wait until Ramirez gets to Natalie's place. Gene just spoke to him. They're almost there. If she's home, it's all under control. If she's not, then you do whatever you feel is right. Okay?"

"Nothing is okay, Jeff. I'm gonna call him right now. I won't waste one more second. I just wanted to let you know before I do."

He heard a sigh. Then, Jeff's soothing voice.

"All right, son."

43 – The Temple

Something was wrong. The quirks of this mission kept piling up.

The other bitches had frozen like fish in ice when they saw the gun; instead, this one, while submissive and in tears, maintained her human alertness and color. To make the others obey him, he had to play the "icy killer" role created while making plans for his revenge. But with her, he had only had to say it once. And that she didn't appear frightened added an annoying twist on the straight path that, at this point, he expected to run.

Maybe he was paranoid due to the half nervous breakdown he experienced that terrible weekend living in ghost-Natalie's shadow. Or maybe it depended on the different approach he'd used this time, in the sense that the icy killer scared more. But he got burned in Dearborn. He needed to change his strategy. Apart from the mysterious Natalie's routine didn't give him the chance to act that way, he doubted that his nerves would withstand another change of plan in the middle of the situation. Plan B worked well as a lifeboat, not as a travel option. Moreover, with Mallory, he didn't sexually enjoy his revenge. Now, on the last one, he didn't want to risk the same end. The last one? There was still Mary Beth, if his thirst for revenge wasn't extinguished.

However, maybe the inconvenience in Dearborn was a sign. He should stop.

Stop? he thought while she was driving, silent but with her eyes bouncing between road and the rearview mirror.

He'd chased away this thought the same day that he booked the flight to New Orleans. A thought that had the nerve to show up again during his endless and exhausting stalking of Natalie's house; but he ignored it. And now it was returning again, like an insatiable mosquito.

Stop?

How could he? Those five cunts ruined his existence. Without any reason. Their wickedness had stolen his best years, and no one could return them to him. He could have had a normal life, enjoying his luck of being born healthy into a wealthy family. Instead … That's why they had to pay. All five of them. That those fuckin' Spice Girls had a good time while he was living in a nuthouse because of them was an unacceptable injusti…

The ringing of a cell phone cut off his thoughts. He would let it play, but those old-fashioned rings amplified his anxiety. Holding the gun on her, he grabbed her bag with his other hand and placed it on his lap. While she continuously turned toward him, he followed the ringing and found the devise in a small inner pocket. He turned it off and threw the bag on the backseat.

"You're James Gerling, am I right?"

Those words petrified him. No, she couldn't have really spoken them. He felt his blood boil in his cheeks. He swallowed the saliva accumulated in those twenty surreal seconds.

"James Gerling, from Philadelphia."

What the fuck …? She had only looked at him once! Compared to twelve years ago, he looked completely different with a wig and fake mustache. He went to fuck Cindy twice before taking her out, and he had to tell her who he was! This one, instead … Plus his voice was that of a man's, not the teenager's that she had heard. Provided that she could still remember it.

"I don't know what the fuck you're talking about. You better shut up and keep driving," he said, pushing the revolver against her side.

She pursed her lips.

With the rumble of the engine in the background, he contemplated on his own reaction. He didn't like it. His outburst showed nervousness and insecurity. But how could he not to be nervous and insecure? It was impossible she'd recognized him, and yet ...

"Take the next right," he ordered, firmly, as they passed the shopping center that he used as a landmark for the past few days.

Much better this time, although his tone lacked the composure that shows emotional detachment. Nevertheless, he had to admit that something unexpected was coming between him and his goal. He had to know what it was. It was necessary to get around the obstacle.

"Who's James Gerling?"

Before answering, she hesitated, turning to look at him again.

"The police are after him," she said hesitantly. "They know he's hunting me. I was also assigned an FBI escort, which is following me."

A shiver made the skin on his arms and back tingle. His heart was pounding. He peered through the rear window.

Only darkness.

Furious, he rested the barrel of the revolver on her blond hair, at her temple.

"Fuck with me again, and you're done."

"No shit, James," she whimpered, her voice now trembling. "I'm being watched becau..."

"Stop calling me James! My goddamn name is Freddy."

The pressure of the revolver silenced her. Not that long, though …

"James is in New Orleans. And my security team is here."

Another blow. If she kept going on like this, she would give him a heart attack.

She was breathing nervously. Holding her at gunpoint, he turned back again. He checked more carefully. If someone was following them, the darkness would reveal the headlights. Instead, there were no other lights along the secondary road leading to the cabin. But there must be some truth to what she was saying.

"How do you know about New Orleans? Spill the beans, or I'll blow a hole in your skull."

"While I'm driving?"

Her answer surprised him. Maybe this was why she wasn't scared. Or maybe because she did have a security… He pricked up his ears, looking up to the sky through the window first, then the windshield, since she had mentioned the FBI.

Nothing.

"Listen, James," she resumed, surprising him with sudden tears. "I'm really sorry for what we did to you at the summer camp. We were bitches. You have every reason to be mad at us. But that's the past. Think about the future. If you kill me too, the police will have the evidence they need to prove that you're behind Emily's, Nina's, Cindy's and Mallory's deaths. That's why they're keeping an eye on me. They're using me as bait because they have no evidence against you. If anything happens to me, they will get you at Philadelphia and send you straight to the gas chamber."

Too many details in her story. Too much spontaneity in her voice, even though it was broken by sobs.

The temple patiently built for the goddess Vendetta at a hermitage impossible to spot, was mined at its foundations, and a hidden blaster watching him, for who knows how long, was ready to tear it down.

Five minutes ago, he was looking forward to enjoying the sacrificial ceremony. Now, it seemed as though he would have to prepare himself for the destruction of the myth.

He felt his strength abandon him. He couldn't even reiterate that his name was Freddy. He could barely hold on to the revolver.

"James?"

He winced.

"Why don't you get out of the car and go back home?" she continued, with the empathy of an accomplice. "They have nothing against you at this time. Only speculation. That's why they've been using me. They were just waiting for you to get close."

If she meant to scare him, fuck, she was succeeding.

"I won't tell anyone about this meeting. I'll say I left my escort behind 'cause I needed to be alone after fighting my boyfriend. My boyfriend is a cop. He will confirm my story. Meanwhile you go back to Philadelphia and they'll still have nothing on you."

"Yeah, right. So when you're safe you can fuck me over."

"I won't say anything. You have my word. I don't care whether you go to jail or not. I just want to go home."

A sudden violent surge of anger revived his hatred.

"The word of you bitches is shit," he thundered fiercely, feeling his strength come back, vigorous like his determination. "Now I don't wanna hear one more word. Just drive."

These unforeseen developments forced him to make the change he was dreading. And it was even worse because he would have to implement a nonexistent Plan C.

Her story was believable. But her FBI escort? There was no real evidence that proved it. Maybe she came up with it by mixing memories, fear and fantasy.

Trying to understand how much truth was in her words and then figure out his next moves, he schematically analyzed the stressful adventure in Charleston from this new perspective ...

He spent all day Thursday organizing himself in the cabin that he had rented online for eight days (testing the gun that he bought from Oliver, checking out his plan, exploring the place inside and outside, resupplying, et cetera). Friday morning he got up at six, eager to personally see the residential area where Natalie Lunn lived. He would recognize her easily, having also seen her on her Facebook.

At ten, she hadn't come out yet.

The hours passed, slowly and stressfully. He started to wonder if he was at the right address. But no, that website for finding people was reliable and up to date.

Maybe she was sick. Or maybe out of town, as it had happened with Nina, which had unexpectedly caused him to go back to Boston a second time.

Now, however, he was there and could only wait.

At about six thirty, when he was almost out of sandwiches and water, a gray car stopped at the walkway of the house he was watching. A man in black leather jacket and a slender, pretty blonde got out. There she was. They each carried a seemingly empty box.

After half an hour, they came back out with full boxes and a suitcase, loading them into the backseat and trunk. They drove away together. He wanted to follow them, but the car that came with them started up too. He thought they were friends of theirs, and he didn't want to be noticed.

He stood there, since she would return to her house anyway. Hopefully alone.

It was around nine when he started to feel the pressure of bodily needs. He thought that it was enough for that day, with it being Friday night who knows what time she would be back.

He returned to the cabin.

He spent the night dozing and thinking.

The next day, at seven, he was back in front of her home, across the street. The gray car wasn't there.

He waited all day in vain, taking a couple of breaks at a shopping center nearby. At ten, he returned to the cabin, physically and mentally exhausted.

Sunday, the same thing. He almost died of boredom sitting in the car. Those seemingly endless hours were like watching paint dry, so much so that he took five trips to the shopping center.

She probably spent the weekend out of town, that assumption reinforced by the memory of her with boxes and a suitcase.

He should see her again Monday. Instead, there was no sign of her for the whole morning.

By now he had become a regular at that shopping center.

Due to his constant back and forth there, he started thinking that she may have come back home when he wasn't there.

He realized that it wasn't the case at five thirty, when a blond man probably in his early thirties came to her door. The guy knocked and waited for a while, before going back where he had come from.

Natalie wasn't at home. Tired, he started the car and went back to the shopping center.

At seven thirty, too early to go to sleep, he thought to check one more time. And it was a good idea he did because a car showed up about one hour later.

It was red, not gray, but it parked exactly in front of her walkway. He saw only one person inside, but couldn't tell if it was her.

Remembering how he spent the last three days, he couldn't miss the opportunity. Utilizing the adrenaline rushing through him, he psyched himself up and decided to go check.

He took his gloves from the glove compartment and put them on. Then he grabbed the revolver, putting it in the pocket of the jacket he wore. He got out of the car, locked it and walked briskly toward the passenger side of what was a red Toyota.

44 – The Showdown

Natalie had been sitting in the middle of an upstairs bedroom in the cabin, for an hour. Maybe two. The light was on. She was alone, with a wide strip of tape covering her mouth. The rope binding her wrists behind her back was even tighter than the one that he forced her to tie, securing her ankles to the legs of the chair. She tried to break free a couple of times, but her thrashing was about to make her lose balance: the fear of falling and crushing her hands, banging her head or making James mad convinced her to stop.

Exhausted, she was crying. Every now and then her despair was distracted by loneliness and accentuated by helplessness, but it rose again when the concept of "being in danger" formed in the image of the gun, most likely loaded, pointed toward her. While she was driving, the thought of the FBI escort and then the dialogue with that loon, placed themselves before the realization that only the trigger on which he kept his finger remained between her and Death. Now that she was alone, she remembered what it would mean *to die*. Or more accurately, she was discovering more branches of it than she wanted: never seeing her parents again, not being able to embrace Landon anymore, to leave the job she loved, saying goodbye to the pleasure of reading and listening to music as well as the flavor of food, to abandon her dream to travel before she ever even got the chance to, to give up the joy of the simply breathing among nature. It was like checking the contents of a trunk kept in the attic for years, now that the time had come to throw it away.

The sound of footsteps walking up the stairs tensed her muscles. She stared at the closed door as if it were the jaws of a shark coming to her. Anxiety shook her when she heard those steps on the floor. She lost control of her body and began to tremble. Only one thing remained clear in her mind: survival. She would do anything to get out of there alive.

It was just about the two of them. One against the other.

The door opened. A clean shaven young man with reddish blond hair, dressed in T-shirt with a gun in his hand, appeared. He looked angry but lucid.

She didn't think about an accomplice. Her guts tangled and the thudding of her heart dampened her eyes.

At the mercy of two criminals, she would never make it.

Fitzgerald said that, she despaired, remembering his hypothesis that James hired a professional killer.

Associating this memory to the appearance of this man who was staring at her now, another detail came to her mind. The photo that Fitzgerald had showed her.

This is James!

So Freddy was the one who carried out the kidnappings.

She looked at the sky through the French window of the balcony. She saw the moon and a few stars. She implored them to watch over her.

James's movement stopped her prayer. He was approaching. She yelled not to harm her, that she would do anything he wanted, but the tape let only pass some terrified barking.

"I analyzed the situation," he began calmly. "I need some answers. And you're gonna give them to me."

It was a shock for her to hear his voice. It was identical to Freddy's.

"You understand me?"

She nodded with conviction.

Up close, she realized that his straight hair was damp, as if he had just taken a shower.

"Open your ears and pay attention. You say I shouldn't kill you. You may be right. But mind what you do, 'cause I shouldn't let you go either. And I can be right too."

As he spoke, she noticed that his pants were the same ones that Freddy had been wearing. Even his body was similar ...

Of course!

The black hair and mustache were only a disguise.

"You got me?" he pressed her.

She nodded again, more convinced than before.

"I say, you do. I ask, you answer."

Relieved by the fact that it was still a battle between the two of them, although uneven, she repeated the nod, the only gesture that seemed to give her some hope.

Seeing him extend his fingers toward the tape, she closed her eyes.

A burning like she had never experienced in her life made her teeth clench so hard that they seemed to crack. While she got used to the pain, with a trickle of tears becoming a stream, he moved behind her.

She couldn't see him. An agoraphobia anxiety attacked her. She could hear his breathing and the sounds he caused—he seemed to have placed the weapon on the wood flooring. She felt like the space around her became exterminated.

She froze when she felt him touch her hands. Then she realized he was liberating her.

"Untie your feet," he said, walking back in front of her.

She had to flex her wrists and shake her arms to regain feeling in them, before she could undo the knots that she herself was forced to make strong—she'd tried to tie them loosely in the beginning, but he noticed that and pressed the gun to her head, ordering her to tighten them up.

She ran her hand over her mouth. It pinched all around. The signs of the rope on her wrists scared her. As she wiped her eyes ...

"Get up."

Her stiff knees were shaking, but she was able to stand up.

"Take off your clothes," he said, his gaze as resolute as his tone.

Her desire to see the sun one more time pushed her to unbutton her blouse. Before removing it, she bent down to unbuckle the straps of her sandals. A sense of perdition affected her heartbeat. She kept her eyes down as she lowered her white jeans: she didn't want to see his lustful face.

"Everything," he said.

The memory of how nice it was to walk along the cold Atlantic's fingernails scratching the shoreline overwhelmed her shame.

She unhooked her bra and slid it down her arms, dropping it on her jeans. Then she pulled her panties down to her ankles, using her feet to step out of them.

"So you're one of those that don't like the bush ..."

She overcame her instinct to cover herself by clenching her fists and sticking her arms to her hips.

"Lie down on the bed."

He didn't seem equipped with cigarettes, blades or other sadistic tools. She didn't even see any on the bedside tables next to the bed. She knew what was about to happen, but at least he didn't plan to torture her.

She reached the side of the bed facing the door, careful not to give her back to him. The bed faced the balcony with the back leaning against a wall; at the end of this wall, there was another door, presumably the bathroom.

"Move."

She was looking around for a way out, and his voice startled her. The line between the gun and herself was still direct. She sat. Then she lay on her back.

"Pull yourself higher."

She pulled herself back with her elbows, keeping her thighs closed, until she found herself parallel to the pillows. She rested her head down on the bed, joining her hands on her sex, unable to control her embarrassment this time.

"Good girl. Now close your eyes."

Lost in the dark, she could hear him fumble. She swallowed. She was cold, but it might have a little to do with the temperature. Her only concern was to stay alive, no matter what he did to her.

She opened her eyes as he touched her feet. He was naked, with a lecherous grin, his gun and dick aimed at her.

"No no no," he crooned, sardonic. "Close your eyes, stretch your hands above your head, and spread your legs."

In that condition, what else could she do?

She felt him climb up the bed, in the space that she had been forced to make for him. Helpless prey, crashed by shame, she felt his palm on a side, a mixture of flesh and metal on the other side, get under her knee joints.

She thought about kicking, but that he could turn her off forever with a quick movement of his index finger advised her to be meek.

"You're too tense," he said, while she felt a light and devastating pressure on her clitoris. "Easy."

She had to strain to satisfy his order.

He went back with both of his hands underneath her thighs and lifted them up, pushing her knees toward her chest.

A slight coolness stroked the folds of her sex. He had arched her looking for an angle that favored his penetration. Glimpses of thoughts pricked her mind.

God. I'm sorry. I deserve this. Do I? It was just a joke. Ow, his nails are sharp. Bastard. Please. No! AIDS. Help. Ouch. You make me sick. You will pay for this. Landon. Tiana ... I want to live. Jesus. Mom. Give me the stre...

"We can talk, now. Look at me."

She saw the muzzle of the gun in the foreground, a few inches from her. Behind it, him. Blurred. She felt her own tears trace lines of despair on her temples while he was moving inside her.

"So," he continued, pausing his sinuous motion but staying inside of her like the most unpleasant guest. "You say that the FBI is after me. Now explain to me how they found me."

That black hole where it was hiding the bullet that could separate her soul from her body sucked all other thoughts out of her head. Her wish to save herself outweighed the repugnance of being one with her tormentor and activated her brain.

"Facebook."

"Go ahead. But don't shit me ..." and he put the muzzle on her forehead. "Is that clear?"

"Clear. But ... Can you please take it away from my face? I can't talk like that."

He stared at her with those two gray pieces of ice chipped with hatred. Then he appeased her, giving her some blows of virility as if to remind her who was boss.

"I don't know much," she began, uneasily on all fronts. "I can tell you what they told me. There is a special section inside the FBI dealing ... dealing with social networks," she hesitated, when he grabbed her breast with the other hand. "During the investigation on Emily's murder, they noticed there was a girl killed among her Facebook friends. Cindy. When ..." now he was titillating her nipple with his thumb and index finger, although he seemed focused on what she was saying. "When Mallory was killed, they started investigating her life and noticed that there were two girls killed among her Facebook friends. Emily and Cindy. From their posts or searching through their friends, I don't know, the FBI found out that they met at a summer camp twelve years ago, and they were part of a group with two other girls. Nina and I. Nina was missing, so they came to me."

"And how the fuck did they connect me to you, huh?" he thundered, in an unthinkable outburst of rage, pressing the gun between her breasts. "You told them, didn't you?"

"No," she cried in a breath, since the terror had struck down her voice before it reached her mouth. Then she shook her head no.

The cold metal on her chest, his angry tone, his deranged person face, the fear that her features would betray her ... she thought he would shoot her within a few seconds.

"No, James. I swear," she was able to mumble through her tears, trying to come up with something.

"Then how? How?" he shouted, giving her more pelvic blows.

"Please ... put it away ... please ... please," she sobbed, her eyes on the weapon, not daring to move anything but her lips.

He snorted.

"Okay. But tell me the goddamn truth," he threatened her, using the gun as a warning finger.

"I'll tell you everything I know."

It seemed he was taking back the control of his nerves. She sighed and began again.

"The camp's owner remembered you. He told them about your suicide attempt that summer, after you ..." she stopped because of the metal that she now felt on her stomach, while a grimace of hatred transfigured him, "after you were back in Philadelphia. They did some research and tracked down a doctor who told them about your years in the clinic."

"Dr. Kincaid?" his eyes opened wide.

Her fear to die forged lies and truth in one shield. She couldn't distinguish them anymore, but she was positive she'd never heard that name either from Jeff or Fitzgerald.

"No. I think it was Dr. Willams ... Wilson ... Wait ... Wilkins! Yes, Wilkins."

"There was no Wilkins."

"Yes, there was. They talked to him on a videoconference."

"Maybe Watkins?" he got pale.

"Yes, Watkins," she immediately corrected herself, noticing by chance a scar on the inner part of his wrist. "Watkins."

His face became red-hot like an iron beaten by a blacksmith. His eyes soaked with tears.

"Fuckin' bitches! It's all your fault," he roared, his voice thick with despair. "Pee-pee, huh? Pee-pee," and she saw him raise his other hand as to load a backhand, sensing a severe ache on her whole face a moment later. "Now I'll show you Pee-pee."

He bent down over her. A strong smell of cologne burned her sense of smell. He began to push like hell.

"Open your mouth," he ordered, putting the gun to her head.

Overwhelmed by grief and panic, she shut her eyelids and obeyed. He licked and sucked her tongue with depraved insistence. As she let it out through her nose, she was disgusted by a nauseating taste of acid.

As he broke the repellent unilateral kiss, he began slamming in and out of her hard.

While he was taking her, she opened her wet eyes, turning her head toward the balcony. She saw the stars laughing at her. She could feel the pressure of the gun against the back of her head. His groans were needles piercing her soul, even worse than his drops of sweat dirtying her aching cheekbone.

She wanted to beg him not to hurt her anymore, but yelping, not words, came out from her.

"You know that there was a girl from Philadelphia who knew me at that camp?" he stopped suddenly. Now she felt the metal of the weapon close to her fingers. "Of course you don't know. And you don't know that she blurted out the story at school," he added angrily. He grabbed her throat with his other hand. "Because of you, I became a laughingstock." He held his grip, but she could still breathe. "Do you have an idea what it means to feel a shame at any goddamn second?" he shouted in her ear, crying. An unexpected taste of blood revealed a cut on her cheekbone or that some small vein of her nose was broken. "It's like breathing with a strip of shit as your mustache. And it's not that by holding on, you can get rid of the stink any time soon." He was washing her cheek with his saliva and tears. She didn't have the courage to look at him. "Because the shit is still under your nose. You can only kill yourself to escape that," he continued with a pain in his voice that projected an image into her mind—he as a boy hanging from a sheet rolled up as a rope around his neck. Despite what he was doing to her, she felt sorry for him. "Wherever I went, I saw them look at me and laugh. Everyone laughed at me ... *Pee-pee*, they grinned ... Why did you do that to me? Why?" Now she could breathe. He removed his hand from her throat, grabbing her chin to force her to look at him. "I was minding my own fuckin' business, bitch! Cindy called me."

There was so much suffering on his face. She could see some traces of his dramatic past in his shocked gaze.

"I'm so sorry, James," she mumbled, in tears, helpless under the weight of his body and her own guilt.

"I'm so sorry, James," he mocked at her, sticking then his tongue into her mouth again. This time she was tempted to snap her jaws and goodnight. Contempt and pity were playing a cruel hide and seek with her soul. She couldn't stand this any longer. Instead, he took his lips away and began banging her, so violently that he hurt her groin. "You're sorry now, huh? ... The others ... were ... sorry ... too ... But ... you all ... were not ... sorry ... when ... you laughed ... at me ... aaahhh!"

A sudden whipping inside her and the following heat announced that the abuse was over.

He collapsed on her, exhausted. He was panting, even though the intervals between the inhale and the exhale were increasing.

His head was over her shoulder. His hair tickled her ear. She turned her head to see if he'd dropped the gun. The grip was under his relaxed hand. His finger, however, wasn't inserted into the trigger guard.

Now his breathing was almost normal, as if he was recovering from the big effort.

She swallowed. She pursed her lips. It was her chance to disarm him, but she needed to be cautious. So far she must have lived the same experience of the other four. She knew how it was ended for them. But for her, it wasn't over yet.

She had to take advantage of the softness of the blanket and inch her hand closer until she could grab the grip from below. His reaction would give her the courage to pull the trigger. Unfortunately, she wasn't left-handed. If she could use her right hand, she would try with greater confidence.

"Have you ever hated someone?" he asked, sudden like a saber cutting through her abdomen. "Rationally, I mean." His cold, surgical tone was a transfusion of death to her. "It's a very powerful feeling. It's not the flame of an angry moment that burns you. It's a planned fire that razes everything." While he was babbling, she studied how to steal the gun. "I had no purpose in my life. My future was in that nuthouse. I was saved by the idea of making you cunts pay for that. I grabbed it with all my strength," he continued, as if in a trance. "I was self-destroying with that hatred. I couldn't get rid of it. So I turned it against you all." She held her breath, slowly moving her left arm to get closer to the gun. "I wrote and rewrote what I suffered. And your names were always on those pages, as well as your faces before my eyes and your laughter in my ears." She moved her forearm to align her hand with the grip of the weapon. "Revenge won't heal you if you don't feed it with a pulsing hatred. The memory of the hatred is not enough. You need to feel it." Now she just needed to slide the back of her hand on the blanket and grab the gun. "This pulsing hatred allowed me to reach you all. It's my pass to a new life." She only had one chance. She couldn't miss it. "I am full of hatred now. I hate all of you more than I love myself. I enjoy the idea that you suffer." *Come on, Nat. You can do it.* "But I'm tired of hating. When you're all dead, I…"

He stopped, stiffening. He sat up above her. He must have heard that unexpected noise too.

It sounded like a helicopter.

They both looked toward the balcony.

The noise quickly became louder and louder as the lights flashed in the air.

"James Gerling, alias Alfred Sinclair," said an amplified voice. "This is the FBI. We know you are there with the girl. Let her go and come out with your hands up. The house is surrounded. You have no chance to escape."

With disbelief and terror changing James into the humiliated and afraid boy he was, she hit the gun with her hand, and it ended up on the ground, to the other side of the bed.

"Bitch," he growled, returning to look like the murdering rapist he had become, slapping her harder than before.

He followed the gun, jumping over her. She took the opportunity and even though she was in pain and panting, with her sight blurred, desperation gave her the strength she needed. The door was open in front of her: it would take five steps to go out, then there were stairs on the right.

She rushed toward freedom.

When they'd found the name Alfred Sinclair on the passengers lists, it was easy to discover that he was in Charleston at that time.

The FBI had found his credit card: he'd been using it only to make a few online purchases, the last of which was booking a cabin just out of town for the week that was going ...

Once the local police and Feds had silently surrounded the cabin, Jeff communicated to the pilot of the helicopter that he could approach. He needed Fitzgerald and Devin's help to physically restrain Landon, since he wanted to burst into the place as soon as he saw her Toyota. Then Jeff spoke to the megaphone.

Since Jeff ran the military operation, he was also on a radio connection with the sniper in the helicopter. This one described what he saw through the scope to the balcony French window. When he said that the target was clear and was behaving in a threatening way to the girl, Jeff gave the order right away.

They heard two gunshots, almost simultaneous. The French window was shattered.

Landon, who was eating his heart out listening to the sniper's descriptions, freed himself as if he were struck by lightning, and rushed to the cabin.

"Wait!" Jeff tried to stop him, in vain.

"Target down," Landon heard over the radio on his leather jacket.

The door was locked from the inside. Devastated by anguish, he didn't think twice to blow the lock with his Beretta. He opened it with a kick. The light was on and he immediately spotted the stairs. When he was at the top, he stopped.

"No!" he shivered, his heart stopping.

He saw Natalie's upper body on the wooden floor, just over the threshold of a room.

He recovered and hastened to her.

She was lying naked and motionless, face down, with a hole in the middle of her back that was dripping blood.

45 – Hope

The news of what happened to Natalie quickly spread through the school where she worked, although the circumstances remained a mystery. It was only said that she had been the victim of an accidentally shooting. Like all her colleagues and students, her former student Henke also came by to pay his respect with some flowers.

It had been six days since that terrible night at the cabin.

The bullet shot by James broke her rib, stopping half an inch from her pericardium; the stump of bone penetrated the pleura, tearing the lung tissue. If it wasn't for the ambulance that had followed the police to the cabin, there would've been nothing they could do for her; instead, immediate help—Landon was decisive in gaining those few vital minutes—allowed her to reach the hospital alive. Once the bullet was removed, she got a surgical pleurodesis to eliminate the accumulation of air in the pleural cavity procured by the tearing.

After five days in intensive care due to some emerging complications, doctors were able to announce to her family that the surgery was successful.

Thanks to the helicopter sniper who had struck James—if he did just a second before, it would have been perfect—Natalie was alive. Now she just needed to rest, waiting to recover.

That morning she was alone in her room full of flowers. Her mother—despite her difficulty walking—and father were there with her in the hospital since the night of the accident. They left now because there was a special visit for her, detective Vitman. They were grateful to this policeman for saving their only child's life, also because, thanks to him, the jackals of the media had not spotted the carcass of the Gerling case yet. Moreover, when he'd introduced himself, her mother immediately remembered 'Landon the detective' in whose mind she had nosed around through the tarot-cards on Natalie's request: that's why she told her husband to take her to get some breakfast …

Natalie was very weak, but at least now she could rest in a supine position. The upper part of the bed was raised to about thirty degrees, so that the weight of her body wouldn't place a burden on the wound. By the colors and fragrance around her, she seemed to be in a garden. Her gaze was languishing on the most inexhaustible sources of reflection: from the big window of her room, she could admire a blue surplus of sky, with some wispy and white cotton balls sitting idly due to the absence of wind.

"Hey."

The sound aroused her. She turned toward the voice.

Landon was in the doorway.

She looked at him like she was reminiscing through a photo album of memories.

They hadn't seen each other since she left his apartment.

"May I?"

Natalie nodded.

Landon walked in. He approached the chair that was next to the bed, on the opposite side to where the support of the drip-feed stood as sentinel. He sat like he usually did when he was tense: legs bent and wide, his forearms resting on his thighs.

Natalie had a bruise on her left jaw and a small dressing at her cheekbone on the same side. She was laying on top of the sheets, barefoot and wearing a light blue hospital robe. The bedspread was folded at the foot of the bed.

Landon kept his eyes on the needle of the drip that she had in her arm. He had many things to say, but none wanted to be the first. They were hiding behind each other, like unprepared students on the day of an oral exam.

Only their breath was audible in the clean and fragrant room.

When Landon looked up, Natalie was watching him.

The emotion was much more visible on Landon's face. Natalie still appeared suffering, despite her *The worst is over* smile.

Landon's eyes filled with sadness.

"I'm so sorry, Nat. It's my ... my fault. I shouldn't have let you go."

His voice had failed in the characteristic gasp of those who strive to sound calm when they're not.

Natalie told him not to worry with an affectionate smile.

"My job was to protect you. And I failed. We have to thank the good fortune if ..."

Some tears of guilt slid down his cheeks when she looked for his hand. He sweetly grabbed it with his own.

"I don't know if you can forgive me," he whispered, heartfelt, dropping to touch her hand with his lips. "I made so many mistakes. I just want to say I love you more than my own life."

"What was your mother's name?"

Landon's eyes, vibrating with emotion, held hers. The look they exchanged meant all the explanations in the world.

"Hope. Her name was Hope."

"Hope. She had a special name."

He nodded with a nostalgic smile.

"I'm sorry I couldn't meet her. She must have been an extraordinary woman."

"She was."

The dearest person to him had just played the most sensitive chord of his soul.

They stayed like that for a while, her hand in his, in a sweet and melancholy silence.

"Doctors say that you will be okay soon," sighed Landon, after wiping his face.

She smiled.

"I never doubted you would make it. Therefore, while you've been in here fighting, I tried to resolve the situation with Tiana."

Natalie's features twitched, erasing her smile.

"If you think this isn't the right time to talk about it, just te…"

"Have you met her?" she asked in a faint voice.

"We did the DNA test to ascertain my fatherhood," he announced, distressed.

It was pointless to ask him the result. She could read it in his face. However, she remained impassive. Inside and out.

After what she had been through with James, the feeling of being violated still vivid inside her as much as the pain in her back, surgery and intensive care, this news was like receiving whip number 51 on her mangled skin. At that very moment, she realized that James had accomplished his revenge. First with rape, then with the gunshot, he had killed her. He had taken away her soul, leaving her only a body where a new soul was wandering now. An insensitive soul. Maybe not insensitive, but different. A new feeling that she would have to explore. She remembered all of her life, but her memories didn't generate the same emotion like before. For example, she remembered how she feared that Landon could be April's father, and now that she was walking on that bridge that terrified her because she imagined it was shaky, she felt calm like she was passing through a solid corridor leading her to an unknown place. And she wasn't afraid of what she would find.

An irreparable rift happened in her, perhaps the same one that her friends and she caused to James years ago.

"I made my decision," continued Landon, resolute. "I'm gonna ask for custody of my daughter. I know that the truth of the story will come out, but I don't care. I'm ready to pay for my crime."

Natalie closed her eyes.

He didn't expect such a reaction. He hesitated for several seconds. He didn't understand whether she needed to rest or if she didn't agree with his plan.

"Okay. Maybe I'd better go. I may return ano…"

"No judge would take a three-month old baby away from her mother to give her to the father."

This response relieved him. Indeed, it excited him.

"I thought about that. So I wanted to ask you …" and he left the rest of the proposal to the white little box that pulled out from his leather jacket pocket.

She stared at it. She had no doubt about the content. She closed her eyes. The darkness helped her explore her new sensitivity.

"Lan …"

"Will you marry me, Nat?" he asked, opening the case for her.

A diamond ring sparkled like his eyes.

She heard the echo of a feeling that she knew once. Joy. But, as said, it was just an echo. Joy was singing on the opposite edge of the ravine of bitterness that James had dug between her and her heart. It was too far away. It couldn't even reach a corner of her face.

"Lan, you know that this isn't the way to go about it."

Analyzing her answer and the way he had presented the situation to her, an awful doubt shook him.

"Wait, Nat. It's not how it seems. I'm not trying to use you to have a better chance of getting custody of April."

Natalie frowned.

"I'm asking you to marry me because I love you, because I want to spend the rest of my life with you. That's the only reason."

"I know, Lan. I would never think you planned to use me."

She spoke looking into his eyes. He believed her. Continuing to stare at her though, a light suddenly illuminated a whole valley never reported on his map…

He snorted, ashamed of himself. He closed the case and put it back in his pocket.

"I'm a fool," he said bitterly. "You are in this condition, you just went through a delicate surgery, and here I come asking you to accept the daughter I have with another woman, without even wondering if you want this change in your life."

"Hey," she said affectionately.

"It's that I'm fuckin' afraid to lose you, Nat. I don't want a life without you. I really don't."

"Lan, I'd be happy to marry you, to try to be a mother to your daughter. And maybe give her a little brother or sister," she added, finding the strength to lengthen her sentences in her wish of reassuring him. "I love you too, and I can't imagine my life without you either."

A simple *I accept your apology* would've been more than enough for him; instead she surprised him with some wonderful words that he never imagined hearing. However, her expression clashed with her statement of love. He felt like he got the most luxurious room in Count Dracula's castle.

"You know, Nat, Tiana doesn't have a job. She's unable to take care of April properly. I am the biological father and if you'll be my wife ... You and I both have a job ... You'll see that the judge will give her to us ... Please, don't shake your head at me."

"Lan, what you're saying is not right."

"What do you mean *it's not right?*"

"I mean you can't take the baby away from her mother."

"But she doesn't have a jo..."

"Landon! You got her pregnant against her will. And in spite of that, she kept April. You have no right even to think of taking the baby away from her."

The determination with which she had spoken pulverized the strategy that he devised—with the help of a lawyer friend—in three seconds flat. Those words were an unappealable verdict. No objection could dent that truth. He mentally placed himself in front of Tiana. He saw himself as Natalie was seeing him at that moment. Petty and mean.

"Fine, Nat. You're right," he sighed, broken. "I hadn't considered it from that point of view ... I won't do anything of what I had in mind ... I'm gonna give Tiana all the financial and moral support she will need."

Natalie closed her eyes and shook her head again.

"What?" he frowned.

"You won't let your daughter grow up without her father. You yourself experienced what that means. If you did such a thing, you'd never forgive yourself."

"But ..."

"Have you thought about how I would feel if that innocent child grew up without her dad because of me? Have you thought about how you will feel when another man steps in to raise your daughter? You couldn't live with it ... Tiana is young and pretty. It's unthinkable that she will remain alone for long."

"But what do you know?" Landon got mad, while keeping his voice low. "You sound like you know everything, fuck ... I'm sorry. But, fuck! What do you know? How do you know that she doesn't have a man?"

"If she did, she wouldn't look for her daughter's father."

After speaking, Natalie added more meaning with her eyes.

"Wait a second," Landon dumbfounded. "What are you saying? Do you think she's intentionally single because she hopes to come live with me?"

In response, Natalie left her grim expression unchanged.

"This is crazy," he laughed nervously. "I've raped her, for God's sake! I raped her pointing a fuckin' gun to her head!" he whispered angrily, looking back at the door. "She hates me. I'm just a checkbook to her."

"Lan, you were drunk and desperate because of your mother, but you're not a drunkard or a criminal. You are a good person. And she knows it. I don't know how, but she knows."

He looked at her as if she were raving, but he was upset in his heart. In fact, although Tiana was dismissive and aggressive all three times they met, he had felt something strange and intense in her attitude. He'd bypassed it, archiving it among those fleeting and abstruse impressions that sometimes knock at our door, vanishing before we open. But now, Natalie's interpretation of the situation seemed to have opened the door on time...

"I know how Tiana felt that night at the club. I know," she repeated, steady gaze. "If she looked for you despite what you've done ... You know, I might be in the very same situation a year from now. James is dead, but if he were alive, I wouldn't look for him even if I lived under a bridge and he was the richest man in America."

Natalie had spoken coldly.

"You're dumping me, Nat?" he asked, suddenly icy.

"No, Lan. I'm not. I'm just saying that it's not your call. It's up to Tiana. She could have had an abortion. She would have had every reason to. But she decided to face the situation that you put her in. She did out of respect for the child she was carrying inside. She earned your respect. And you owe her. I owe her too. Because, frankly I don't know if I'd have her courage in the event that …"

Landon's imperturbability dissolved as quickly as it formed.

"Maybe it was fate that our lives crossed each other only for a few days," murmured Natalie, bitter.

"Don't say that," blanched Landon.

"Maybe it was meant for you to end up with Tiana."

She turned to the other side. She didn't want to cry right now. It would happen if she had looked at him for a few more seconds. Her eyes rested on the note accompanying the roses sent to her by Henke.

Landon was watching her. She was silent, but her words were spinning like a record on the turntable of his mind. It was associating them to her afflicted air that he realized how much she was suffering. It had cost her heart to speak that way. She was trying to do what he felt was right too. She was trying because she understood that he didn't have the strength to do it. And her, raped, wounded and weakened was facing this too. Alone against all, because he not only wasn't helping her, but he was making it even harder.

He felt like an immature worm.

Lashed in his pride, he summoned Destiny and looked into its eyes.

"You're right, Nat. It's up to Tiana. We'll do what she decides."

Natalie turned to him. She was a mask of sorrow.

"But I want to promise you one thing," continued Landon, pulling the box out of his pocket again and squeezing it in his fist with passion. "You and I will end up together. I don't know when, I don't know how, but I swear to my mother that one day we will be you and me. Together."

"How can you promise me something like that, Lan?" she said, eventually letting her tears and sobs go, after stoically holding them until then.

"Because we're doing the right thing. And Life will reward us for that, just like It punished us for our mistakes."

INDICE

Bibliography: English...3
Bibliography: Italian..4
1 – The Memory..7
2 – Emily...9
3 – Excuse Me..13
4 – Colorado River...17
5 – The Request...19
6 – Landon...25
7 – The Fasting..29
8 – The Robbery..31
9 – Carlos...35
10 – The Chance..41
11 – Natalie..45
12 – Confrontation...49
13 – Starbucks..53
14 – Mallory...59
15 – The Mishap..63
16 – Pretzel..66
17 – Tiana...71
18 – Tim...75
19 – The Charges...81
20 – Spice Girls...87
21 – The Line...94
22 – Mom...98
23 – Hatred..103

24 – Cards 108
25 – Summer Camp 117
26 – Duty 127
27 – Jeff 132
28 – The Past 137
29 – The Fountain 143
30 – FBI 147
31 – The Song 152
32 – Associations 157
33 – Act-1 170
34 – The Confession 179
35 – Travels 185
36 – The Worm… 194
37 – At last! 202
38 – And You Are …? 213
39 – No Problema 219
40 – Just… 227
41 – The Premonition 239
42 – The Theorem 245
43 – The Temple 255
44 – The Showdown 263
45 – Hope 277

Finito di stampare nel mese di Marzo 2016
per conto di Youcanprint *Self-Publishing*